THE
SUGAR
MEN

ALSO BY RAY KINGFISHER

HOLOCAUST ECHOES
Rosa's Gold

Tales of Loss and Guilt
Matchbox Memories
Slow Burning Lies
Easy Money
Bad and Badder
E.T. the Extra Tortilla

THE
SUGAR
MEN

Holocaust Echoes

RAY KINGFISHER

LAKE UNION
PUBLISHING

Text copyright © 2016 Ray Kingfisher

Published by Lake Union Publishing, Seattle

www.apub.com

Amazon, the Amazon logo, and Lake Union Publishing are trademarks of Amazon.com, Inc., or its affiliates.

ISBN-13: 9781503936591
ISBN-10: 1503936597

Cover design by Debbie Clement

Printed in the United States of America

FOREWORD

Although this is a work of fiction, many of the places and events depicted are real. As befitting the subject matter I have tried as far as possible to create a story that could, realistically, have happened, and included many events that actually did. I hope my writing does justice to such an important subject, but if the story contains historical inaccuracies or I have taken liberties with some events, then I apologize beforehand.

PART ONE
Weeks Not Hours

CHAPTER ONE

She feels a sense of the passive, calming her and soothing her worries.

There is no concept of near and far; they are one and the same.

The experience is familiar – like revisiting a half-forgotten childhood haunt.

She does not merely see, but feels part of.

There is no colour, yet the scene is bathed in light of every hue. She feels water, cool, pure and refreshing, lapping around her ankles like a milky balm.

Then the figures slowly appear from the clear light – figures so bright they *are* the light – approaching her effortlessly as if riding a celestial wave. She has known them a long time, but they are beyond reach, and also beyond the world of pain and suffering. Her heart aches at being near them, and feelings of love are elevated to an intensity she finds exhilarating.

They wear white robes that are plain in design yet shimmer in the immaculate brightness. The light refracting along the edges of their garments creates a spectrum like no other – hazy and ethereal but somehow also vibrant and scintillating.

She hears them all mention her name and they smile astral smiles.

And then they ask her.

She wills them to come closer – to where they belong – and as they approach she sees each one has skin as flawless as a sea of sand, and silky hair that flows like a lion's mane.

She has experienced this before, but now something is different: a sense of immediacy. Sometimes there are four or five of them; this time there are only three – the three tied by blood.

Blood – a pinprick appears on the clean white robe of one of them, and his smile falters as he looks down. The pinprick quickly grows, as if engorging itself, the deep red streak soon trailing down to the bottom of the robe. Below is now only dusty earth, which scatters as drops fall onto it. One of the other figures looks down and sees that her robe too is now drenched in the blood of abandonment. She throws her head back, displaying a mouth lined with dark decaying teeth, and lets out a scream that drowns out all other noise. Then the third figure screams too, his robe now also soaked red, his skin dirty and pallid, his eyes grey and hollow above cheekbones jutting towards the sky.

The sky.

The sky has now turned from a white heavenly fog to a bluish-grey mist, and then it changes further to a murky black all-encompassing cloud fractured with crimson shards of lightning.

All three figures come closer still, asking her again, and although she wants to speak to them a presence grabs her around her neck and locks her throat.

The first figure, his face now filthy and purulent, pulls apart the top of his robe to expose a torso that barely has substance – flesh that has been eaten away from the inside, and sallow skin, ravaged by scabs and rashes, pulled taut over bones.

She tells them 'No!' but still they come, reaching out their

4

gnarled and scarred hands, the bones whitening the skin, the nails deformed, filthy and twisted.

As they reach out and touch her she inhales and tries to force out a scream, but the presence holding her neck tightens further and there is sound only in her head.

And at the very moment she feels the deathly touch of their clammy flesh, she wakes.

❦

She sat up in bed for a few moments, then slowly slid her legs to the side and eased herself onto her feet. She held her head in her hands for a moment, then wiped the perspiration from her brow and went to get a glass of milk.

'Happy Birthday?' she asked herself as she left the bedroom and headed for the stairs.

CHAPTER TWO

For a terrifying moment Judy thought the doctor had said 'hours not weeks'.

Her face must have blanched slightly at the idea, because the doctor repeated his prognosis, which was actually the reverse. As his words registered Judy let her fright go with a sigh of relief, knowing full well the relief was going to prove temporary.

'However,' the doctor added as if reading her thoughts, 'they aren't going to be pleasant weeks – for Susannah or you or David.'

Judy forgave him calling her mother 'Susannah' instead of 'Mrs Morgan' – he'd known her almost as long as she had and his eyes spoke of sympathy.

As they stepped over to the door together he continued, 'I take it you were at the hospital with her when they went through the options for pain relief and palliative treatment.'

Not only had Judy been there, but the memory of that day at Wilmington General was etched in her mind like words scraped on stone with the point of a dagger. The truth was that she'd seemed more upset by the news than her mother had.

So, yes, she was acutely aware of the options available and nodded to the doctor. He drew breath, then took a glance up the stairs and lowered his voice. 'I'm only warning you, Judy. You know I'll do all I can but it might not be pretty.'

'No.'

'As I say, we'll make her as comfortable as possible.'

Judy went to say something like 'Of course you will' out of politeness, but only a swallow came. The doctor stood at the door and more words tumbled out of his mouth. She didn't hear them; all she heard was her mind screaming for him to get out, take her mother's cancer with him and never come back. But she thanked him, gave him one of those closed-eye nods her mother always said were a speciality of hers, and opened the door. No more words were exchanged. The doctor just pursed his lips, returned her polite, reverential nod and left.

Judy closed the door and held her hands flat on it for a few minutes, trying to halt the trembling, trying to still the storm that was whirling around inside her head.

So it was final.

There was to be no miracle.

Visits from esteemed professors and media hordes eager to learn about a recovery that had defied the odds and astounded medical science were not going to happen. Her mother's luck had finally run out.

As she turned, David appeared at the top of the stairs and started loping down towards her.

'Well?' he said.

She just shrugged. What did he expect her to say? To his credit, he'd tried to take his half share in looking after their mother, but inevitably they'd grown apart sometime between their teenage years and middle age, resulting in a certain awkwardness between them when it came to discussing all things emotional. Judy desperately wanted to tell him how she felt about their mother, how the words and images in her mind got washed away with the rain whenever she tried to think what life would be like without her, but she didn't think he would understand. Sure, she was a woman of the world and a mother herself, but at that moment she wanted him to be the big brother she'd felt so protected by when they were kids, to ask her how she felt, to reassure her that she wouldn't fall apart without the piece of her that would disappear along with their mother.

And then, right on cue, his phone rang.

His first words into it were 'I can't be disturbed now.'

A few seconds later he cursed, and said, 'You know, Gary, difficult though it might be for you to understand, I just don't care about the monthly sales figures right now. I'm at my mother's.'

Another pause, then: 'I know it's important, and I know you don't normally compile the reports, but I'm busy. I'll leave my phone on, but only call me if you come across any problems, okay?'

'Couldn't you switch that off?' Judy said when he'd closed the call and put his phone away.

He drew his head back and a hint of a scowl flashed on his face. 'Life goes on,' he said. 'I still have a business to run, a family to feed, and a government to give truckloads of tax to.'

Like Mother had always said, David was about as sensitive as a Sherman tank with its throttle jammed open. But Mother knew just as well as she did that it was little more than a front. As with all people you're close to, they have one face for you and one face for everyone else. It was just that Judy hadn't seen David's face-for-Judy for some time.

'So what did he say?' He nodded to the door the doctor had just left by.

'A few weeks.'

'Oh.'

But never mind that, Judy felt like asking, *what about your sales figures?*

'I don't think we should tell her,' he said.

Judy tried a frown that said, *Why the heck not?*

He evidently got it and said, 'At least, not for . . .'

'A few weeks?' she suggested.

He rolled the palms of both hands over his head and they came to rest on the back of his neck. 'I just . . . don't want to upset her – not just yet, not tonight.'

'What if she asks? She's sure to ask what he said.'

'We can just say he wasn't specific.'

'Mmm . . . okay.' Judy nodded unconvincingly. 'But I think one of us should stay overnight with her.'

'I thought you could do that,' David said as he headed for the kitchen door.

And that was just like him, leaving the scene when she wanted to call him every name under the sun for being presumptuous and selfish and unfeeling. But he turned at the last moment and her face must have said it for her.

'Oh, don't be like that, Judy. Just for tonight, I promise. It's bad timing, I know, but it's a critical period for the business. I should really check on it.'

'And are you going now?'

'No-*o*,' he said, pushing his head forward as if he was speaking to a three-year-old. 'I'm going to get a drink of water *now*.'

'Well, make it quick. I'll see you upstairs.'

CHAPTER THREE

S o what did old penguin face have to say?' Susannah said as Judy entered the bedroom a minute later.

She was sitting up in bed with a bolster cushion behind the small of her back, her frame sagging a little at the neck. Judy didn't answer – or at least her hesitation spoke for her.

'Tell me,' Susannah said. 'How long have I got?'

At that moment Judy could almost feel her face go rigid with fear – not a fear of her mother, but of telling her a truth that would upset her. All three of them had known for months that the cancer was inoperable. It had a hold on her liver and wasn't letting go, but how long it would take for that hold to turn to a squeeze that would extinguish her life was anyone's guess – at least, anyone but 'old penguin face'.

'He was talking about palliative treatment,' Judy said, fully expecting her mother to pull her up for sidestepping her question.

Susannah screwed up her face, her wrinkles concertinaing for a few seconds. 'It's that time, huh?' she said in a tone that answered its own question.

'He didn't really say much about timescales,' Judy said. 'But it's probably worth upping the dosage of pain relief.'

Just then, David's washed-out figure entered the bedroom.

'So are *you* going to tell me?' Susannah said to him.

He gave an unconvincing smile and she flapped the lapels of her pure-white cotton nightdress and glanced to the window.

Judy immediately stood up and hooked her hand towards the window. 'Do you want that open, Mom? Are you too hot?'

'I'm as fine as I can be,' she replied, showing Judy a softer voice than she had David. Her face cracked into a fleeting grimace as she turned back to him. 'So am I going to have to beat it out of you?' she said.

This time David's eyes smiled along with his mouth. 'God, Mom,' he muttered under his breath. He sat down next to the bed on the opposite side to Judy. He crossed his legs, then uncrossed them and leaned forward, joining the palms of his hands together in front of his mouth, as if praying.

'That bad, huh?' Susannah said.

'I think we should tell her,' Judy said over the bed to her brother. 'She can take it. She deserves to know the truth.'

'You bet your sweet ass I do,' Susannah said. 'And I'll thank you not to speak about me like I'm not here. You'll have plenty of time for that when I'm not here for real.'

That hit Judy as surely as if her mother had given her a sharp poke with one of her knitting needles. She leaned over and laid a hand on her arm – its thin leather bruised and dotted from recent blood tests. 'Please, Mom,' she said. 'Don't say things like that.'

Susannah held her arms out and Judy leaned further in for a brief embrace. 'I'm sorry, my dear,' Susannah whispered. 'It's just my way of dealing with it. You do understand that, don't you?'

As they parted, Susannah turned to David and that timbre of motherly sarcasm returned to her voice. 'So?' she said. 'Are you going to tell me or do I have to phone the man myself and—'

'Weeks!' David blurted out. 'A few weeks.' Then, more quietly,

11

he said the words again and started breathing heavily as if recovering from the effort.

Susannah's eyes glazed over, then spent a few silent minutes wandering around the room, looking everywhere except at her son or daughter. David and Judy looked to each other but both remained tight-lipped, waiting for their mother to break the silence. When she did speak again it was with a frailty Judy had only occasionally heard before.

'It's a good job I've said all of my goodbyes, I guess. I can't complain that I haven't had time to get my affairs in order.' She looked at both of her children in turn, then shrugged and said, 'Some people don't get that opportunity.'

It was then that Judy started to feel overwhelmed, and within seconds was gasping for breath, taking small gulps and holding a hand over her face. There was an urge to give her mother another hug, which she gave in to, this time almost falling onto her body and swamping her. Her mother's arms pulled her in with as much strength as they had, and when they parted Judy sat back and saw that her mother too had tears to wipe away.

As they both relaxed, still looking at each other, David's phone went off again, and Susannah let out a loud *tut*.

David stood up and walked over to the far end of the room. 'No,' he said. 'No, it isn't. That's just not good enough. We need to reach thirty thousand *at least* on the Berkley portfolio.' He held his spare hand onto his forehead for a moment. 'Look, I can't, Gary. Not now. Just do whatever you need to.' He closed the call, sat back down, and apologized.

'That's all right,' Susannah said. 'I know life has to go on.'

On hearing that David's eyes now moistened too. He glared at his mother, and for a moment it looked as if his face was about to crack open.

And then it did. He choked and gasped and covered his eyes,

pretty much as his sister was doing. And then Susannah's hand reached out and held his, and smiles broke through the tears for all three of them.

'Just think,' Susannah said. 'I'll see your father again.' She pointed a crooked finger at David's business suit. 'You know I used to joke to him about your dress sense. I always told him he should be worried because you were too neat and smart to be a son of his.' She paused as David spluttered a laugh, then continued, 'I'll bet he's as scruffy as a hobo without me to look after him. I expect his shoelaces are undone and his tie's all crooked, and he needs me and misses me every bit as much as I do him.'

She paused again while David gulped and Judy sniffed.

'And don't worry, I'll pass on your regards to him,' Susannah said, which made her children smile. Then her face lit up ever so slightly, looking tighter and younger than it had any right to. 'You know, I'm not scared,' she said softly. 'Not at all. Everything passes in time, and I'm no different. I've seen plenty of countries, married a wonderful man, given birth to two of the best children in the world. And that's not bad for a little Jewish girl from Berlin.'

David looked at her and blinked away a few tears.

'I'm happy,' Susannah added. 'I lived to see my eightieth birthday.'

David and Judy passed each other a glance. Judy nearly said, *Even if it wasn't actually your birthday,* but it wasn't the moment, and hearing those words would have upset her if not her mother.

But Susannah had that magical motherly understanding, almost hearing her say it anyway. 'I'm sorry about the birthday thing,' she said. 'It doesn't matter anymore but I guess I made too big a deal of it at the time.'

'Mother,' Judy said, speaking slowly and tentatively. 'About your birthday. Did you find out about it?'

Both David and Judy looked to her expectantly for a few seconds.

Eventually Susannah nodded slowly. 'I guess I learned a thing or ten.'

'So . . . what happened when you were in Europe?' David said after a few moments' silence.

'There was a war, my darling, a mighty big one. Millions of people died, and the Germans . . .' She stopped on seeing the reprimanding looks of her children.

David's face cracked a smile. 'Jesus, Mom. You did a lot in your life but why weren't you ever on the stage?'

'I'm sorry,' Susannah said. 'You always were on the receiving end, weren't you?'

'I don't mind,' David said. 'I don't mind at all.'

Judy knew not to push it, and reckoned David did too. Their mother knew damn well they both wanted to know, and if making a joke of it was her way of saying she didn't want to talk about it, then that was fine by them.

But then Susannah's face took on a more serious expression, almost studious. 'I *was* going to tell you,' she said. 'But not immediately. I was waiting for the right moment.'

'Well . . . now's a moment,' Judy said.

Susannah opened her mouth and gave a little shrug of the shoulders before she started speaking. 'Yes,' she said. 'And, after all, I guess the two of you, just like me, deserve to know the truth – everything.'

'So?' David said.

She turned to him. 'How long do you have?'

David gazed at her for a second, then reached into his pocket, pulled his phone out, and switched it off. 'I have all the time in the world for you, Mom.'

'Listen,' she said. 'Why don't you fix us some milk and cookies and then we'll talk?'

'I'll do it,' Judy said, standing up.

14

'It's okay,' David said. 'I can—'

'No,' Judy answered, stepping between him and the door. 'You stay right where you are. And don't you dare start without me.'

CHAPTER FOUR

The truth was that Judy needed a break. Something about the events of the previous few months told her she needed a few minutes alone to prepare herself mentally for her mother's travelogue.

Milk and cookies had been a common childhood treat for her and David, a balm for all worries great or small. And as she crept downstairs into the kitchen – where she'd learned to eat almost fifty years before – the memories of those years started hurling themselves back at her.

Of course, she'd regularly returned home to see her parents for thirty years – and her mother alone for the last three. It had always held a special place in her heart the way any childhood home should – the long narrow kitchen with its ridged-oak set of table and chairs her father had made before she was even born, the living room with the large window overlooking the back yard (and with the crack in the ceiling that drew the eye to the scene outside), the hallway with cheap pictures of everyday birds that had somehow stood the test of time and changing fashions. All of these and everything else about the place had now taken on a tinge of sadness for Judy. Sometime soon strangers would buy this house and change all of these things,

the things her mother had kept just as they were in order to comple-
ment her memories.

But what of Judy's own memories? Now she was comfortably
settled into middle age all misdemeanours that might have been
were long forgiven and forgotten. But being in that very state of
middle age – and bringing up her own children – had also made her
reappraise her own childhood with unbridled honesty. And it hadn't
quite been the idyllic time everyone tried to pretend. Sure, she felt
secure and loved; she'd grown up to be happily married with two
awkwardly normal children, but there had always been something
about her mother that seemed different from other mothers. There
seemed something of an emotional gap between them too, and
there had been plenty of odd behaviour of one sort or another on
her mother's part that hinted at deep-rooted problems. There was
the occasion Shirley Carlton from across the road told Judy she'd
heard her parents whisper that Judy's mother used to be an alco-
holic, which was something Judy knew to be untrue (so much so
it didn't upset her in the slightest at the time). However, it seemed
to pulse away in her mind like unpalatable thoughts often do when
you aren't quite 100 per cent sure and that tiny percentage threatens
to spread like a virus.

There were the medical prescriptions that her mother kept
locked away in a cupboard – even when Judy was in her twenties.
There were those very vague memories – so faint Judy could never
be sure of their veracity and had never told anyone about them, not
even her husband. Memories of her father telling her to stay away
from the bathroom for an hour or more because her mother was in
there, and she wasn't to tell anyone about it or ask what her mother
was actually doing in there. Only once did Judy disobey those
orders, and ended up having a very short conversation through the
locked door with a woman who didn't seem to be her mother at
all. And she remembered how surprised she'd been, when she first

started visiting school friends' houses, at how little food they had in – fridges merely three-quarters full, some cupboards with space left over; no tins, bottles or jars stacked up in the corners of garages.

There were also the distant family members – aunts and uncles, great-aunts and great-uncles, cousins and second cousins – that everyone but the Morgans seemed to have. All the Morgans had were Paul, Helena and Reuben in North Carolina, and a few Scottish relatives of Father whose names they never remembered because they hardly ever met.

Then there were the occasional looks of stark terror on Mother's face when there was a knock at the door – even in the middle of a bright afternoon – when Judy knew not to ask questions or do anything that might upset her. That fear of asking – never a fear of Mother herself – meant that even when Judy reached that inquisitive age she automatically filtered out questions on certain subject areas.

But the childhood memories that simply wouldn't loosen their grip on her mind were those of the arguments between her mother and father that she was sure had happened when she'd been around four or five years old, ones she'd asked David about once when she visited him at college. He just closed his eyes, shook his head, and told her very firmly and very finally to read up on her history, which she didn't understand at the time.

When she finally did 'check her history', what she found merely confirmed that this was something best left alone to wither away. On the few occasions that the family heard or watched news stories about the aftermath of the war – for instance, the trials of the Nazis – all mouths stayed shut and waited for the issue to pass. Once, when David was in his early teens, he asked his mother what she thought about the penalties handed down to the SS officers. She replied that sometimes it wasn't a good idea to think so much, that he should get on with his life and study and work hard, and leave the past in the past. But he persevered and asked what she thought of how the German authorities had behaved over the issue, while in the background Judy stilled her breath all the better to hear what Mother's reaction would be. But Mother simply replied that there was good and bad in every group of people and he should stop getting all obsessed with it. However, it was clear from her short breaths and the tremble in her voice that it was a case of 'do as I say and not as I do' – or even just 'shut up'. And, as far as Judy could recollect, neither of them ever raised the subject with their mother again.

It was only later on, when Judy was at college herself, that she started to understand what David was trying to get at – at least she guessed so, for they never discussed it. Their mother had always been unable to talk about any aspect of her own childhood, except to say that she'd been born in Germany as Susannah Zuckerman. Beyond that the only glimpse of their mother's ancestry had been when David and Judy had come home from school and – for some long-forgotten reason – Judy had asked her whether they were Jewish. Her mother gathered both of them in close the way only a mother can and told them with a calmness she seemed to struggle with that they should be proud of the half of them that was Jewish, the half that was Scottish, and the fact that they were also as American as anyone else in the country. It was something never mentioned again, and when Judy later studied the history of the Second World War it was something she pushed away to a dark, cold corner of her mind. She simply couldn't connect her own mother with what had happened there – or didn't want to – and couldn't even phrase the question in her head that she'd always pondered on but never obsessed about: why she and David hadn't been brought up as Jews.

Once, while her mother was sleeping, she checked her arms for tattoos. There were none, which only made her more curious about her mother's background. But still, she knew not to ask outright about her experiences in Germany – or wherever – during the war, and resigned herself to never knowing the truth.

When the man who was later to become Judy's husband casually asked about her mother's background, she told him it was something they simply didn't talk about because Mother found it too upsetting, which effectively ended that conversation for good.

It was only in middle age, with the rage and passion of youth extinguished but still giving off wisps of smoke, that David and Judy learned just something of what had happened to their mother. It had leaked out when Father became ill, when he knew he didn't have long to live and, it seemed, wanted his children to know at least a little about their mother's history. And there lay the contrast between them. Father had spent the first twenty-four years of his life living in the same house in Glasgow, and if anyone wanted to know about his years working in the Govan shipyards they only needed to ask – then pretty soon they'd be wishing they hadn't. On the other hand, Mother had always hinted at having such a varied and interesting life but clammed up whenever she was asked to talk about it.

Which was where Father helped. In his final days he told David and Judy that their mother had been brought up in Berlin, but had moved around Europe in her teens – so much so that she couldn't quite remember the place names – and had ended up in Bergen-Belsen concentration camp. She'd been nicknamed 'The Lucky One', partly for escaping death when so many others hadn't, but mostly because the camp had been liberated on her birthday. Soon after recovering she'd come over to America with Paul, Helena and Reuben – also all from Berlin – and settled in Wilmington. And after that they never wished to live anywhere else.

Three years after Father's death, that was still the sum total of Judy's knowledge of her mother's childhood. There had been the occasional moment in those three years when Judy had relived a few of those faint memories from her own childhood, and found that they were starting – but only starting – to make some kind of sense. The ups and downs of her own life, however – and a fear of upsetting the family equilibrium – always managed to get in the way.

Judy poured out three glasses of milk, emptied some ginger and orange cookies onto a plate, and put the lot on a tray. She went to pick the tray up but paused as she glanced out through the back window, her eyes settling on the banner stretched across the lawn celebrating Mother's 'Big Eightieth' birthday.

The banner had been there for three months now. It was tired and sagging in the middle but still hanging on, and the sight of it immediately threw Judy's mind back to earlier that year, when the whole thing had started.

CHAPTER FIVE

S usannah's 'Big Eightieth' birthday party had taken place on 15 April 2009.

God had granted the town of Wilmington, North Carolina, a day that was cloudy but easily warm enough to spend most of the day outside. The fragrances of freshly cut cedarwood and roasting hot dogs mingled to produce an effective deterrent to whatever early-bird insects were around at that time of year and might have wanted a piece of the action.

On one side of the back lawn was the most complex and ornate bird-feeding station in the county by all accounts; a solid square trunk was concreted into the ground, and struts and beams of various ages and types of wood were bolted on at a range of heights. And, in turn, what looked like hundreds of smaller rods – the 'twigs' – were connected to those. Hooks and snags and the odd flat surface abounded to hold whatever titbits people managed to get up there. The story of how it came to be had been told to friends and neighbours so many times it was etched in Judy's mind. Her father had made the contraption two years after he and her mother were married – about the time she'd suddenly got interested in attracting birds into the garden. Much later on, when, as an adult, Judy

2/01/2017
D/C Settlement Genealogybk
$36.66

2/01/2017
Pre Auth Genealogybank
$70.32

debits to my account —
866-641-3297 FL

$36.66 s/b credit
DC settlement

Conf # BA5484 B
~Shakigh
— Bill —
Manager

had got to know some of the family friends who still referred to it as Archie's Knot-Tree, she heard talk that it had been more of an obsession than an interest, and once overheard a whispered aside that Archie didn't have any choice in the matter because any new obsession of Susannah's couldn't possibly be worse than the old one. Whatever that meant, it was obvious to Judy that her father had been intent on building those sparrows, wagtails, bluebirds and meadowlarks the biggest and best feeding station possible. He once told Judy that while he was building it he kept moaning that he didn't understand what was wrong with a goddam tree. When Judy asked the very same question he told her that a large tree cost a whole lot more than the waste offcuts from the boatyard he worked at, and Judy's mother simply wouldn't wait for a small one to grow. Judy knew the two sides to the story didn't quite match up, but didn't think anything of it.

On the other side of the lawn was a large shed, the shed Father had used as a wood-turning workshop right up until a few weeks before he died.

And early on the morning of their mother's eightieth birthday Judy and David had snuck out and strung a huge banner up high between the shed and the bird-feeding station, a banner with the appropriate number of years daubed in words Mother said were so large they were 'loud enough to wake up Roosevelt'.

Susannah said that using Archie's shed was a fitting use for the old goat's hideaway because he wouldn't have wanted to completely miss out on her – or indeed any – party.

Throughout late morning and early afternoon the back lawn was lively with neighbours, relatives and friends old and new. David and Judy and their families stayed all day, with a steady mix of people dropping by throughout.

Those who didn't yet know about Susannah's recent diagnosis were put right in no uncertain terms by David and Judy, with strict instructions on how to behave in front of her. They were not to cry or frown or pity or say, 'Physicians? What do they know?' or advise, 'My Uncle Jerry was told he had cancer three years ago and the old dog's still alive today.'

It was left for David and Judy to bear those particular bombardments of 'poor Susannah' sympathy.

It happened at about five o'clock in the afternoon.

Judy noticed her mother starting to wilt outside – perhaps overwhelmed by the occasion or attention she wasn't used to – and also it had become just a little chilly, so she insisted on taking her indoors for a rest. She settled her down in an armchair facing the back yard, so she could still see the banner and the guests gathered on the lawn in her honour, then fetched her a drink of warm lemonade and asked her if anything was wrong and whether she was enjoying her birthday.

It was then that her mother said it.

Only four words came from between her thin, cracked lips, but Judy couldn't have known the significance of those words at the time, and what an effect they were to have on her mother's life and on Judy's understanding of her own.

Although Judy heard it clearly, she asked her to repeat it because she didn't quite believe it. Her mother did, and Judy told her not to be so silly. It was then that Judy saw a look in her mother's eyes she'd never seen in all her years; those dark-brown saucers seemed so full of secrets they were about to overflow, and Judy felt fear crawling up her spine.

Judy told her to stay where she was – hardly a rational statement given her mother's physical condition but a reflection of her state of mind at the time – and hurried outside and down to the end of the lawn to where David was.

'There's something wrong with Mom,' Judy said after she'd pulled him aside from the guests.

'Did you call a doctor?'

'I don't mean physically,' Judy answered, struggling in her mind to work out how to categorize it.

'Has she been . . . ?' He lifted up his glass of wine rather than say the word.

'Drinking?' Judy asked, feeling puzzled at the suggestion. 'What makes you think—?'

'No,' he said. 'Forget I said that. Just tell me what's happened.'

'She's . . . she's acting strange.'

'I noticed she's starting to hoard food again.'

'It's more than that this time,' Judy said. 'She's getting delirious, imagining things.'

David shrugged. 'Is it the drugs she's on?'

'She isn't on any drugs,' Judy said, her face dropping a little. 'There's no point, and you should know that.'

'No. I'm sorry.' David peered up at the back of the house, squinting to see their mother through the window. 'Well, perhaps it's nothing to do with her illness; she *is* getting old.'

'Don't say that, David. We both know her mind's like it always has been – sharp as a brand-new pin.'

'A cut-throat razor more like,' he mumbled, placing his glass down on the table. He paused for a second, then set off for the house, leaving Judy hurrying to keep up. 'So what's she saying, exactly?'

Judy grabbed his arm and said, 'She's saying today isn't her birthday.'

David halted. 'What?' He shook his head a few times. 'Jeez, trust her to spring a stunt like that on us today of all days.'

They both started striding again towards the house.

'You think it could be because she knows it's her last one?' Judy asked.

'We don't know that for sure.'

'Come on, David. You heard what the oncologist said as well as I did.'

The words caused David to stutter his gait for a second and part his lips, but his sister's assertion went unchallenged, and he started off towards the house even faster.

CHAPTER SIX

Judy was almost jogging to keep up with David as he strode through the back door, only then deadening his pace and ambling with an exaggerated air of nonchalance into the room that overlooked the back lawn.

He smiled at his mother, then stood next to her chair and jammed his hands into the pockets of his jeans, while Judy knelt down next to her.

'Feeling any better?' Judy said.

'I've had a tiring day,' Susannah replied, still gazing ahead.

'What are you looking at?' David asked.

'My feathered friends,' she said. 'They help me relax, get things into some sort of perspective.'

David and Judy looked out too for a moment, at the birds that hopped to and from the feeding station in spite of the people gathered below. Then David asked his mother whether she was feeling dizzy or weak, whether she was tired after meeting all her friends in one busy day, and whether she wanted to go for a lie down.

'You made me so happy when you got married,' was the reply.

David's face froze. He glanced at Judy for a moment, then looked to his mother. 'What?'

'You left it a bit late in life, of course. Your father and I thought you were never going to settle down and give us any grandchildren.'

'Well . . . you're welcome.' He drew breath as if to give notice of important words to come.

'Of course,' Susannah said, 'more would have been nice.'

'Mom. Listen to me.'

Still she stared straight ahead. 'Only one child, not even average.'

David bent down to get a closer look at her face. 'Are you sure you're okay, Mom?'

Now she pointed her sagging jowls to him. 'I have cancer. Does that count as okay?'

Then Judy moved to be in front of her too. 'Mom. I told David what you said earlier, about today not being . . .'

'It makes no difference,' she said. 'I've done a lot of thinking since I saw the medical man.'

'The oncologist.'

'Yes. The medical man.' She lightly slapped the cloth armrest of her chair. 'And I'm as sure of it as I am of anything.' She spoke the next words slowly and carefully, like a politician's slogan: 'Today isn't my birthday.'

For a few moments the only sounds were of children playing outside and the slight whistle of Susannah's chest sucking air in and out past her cracked lips.

'What . . . what does that mean?' David eventually said.

Her shrunken shoulders gave a twitch. 'You don't understand English, now?'

He took his glasses off and pressed the heels of his palms over his eyes.

'I'm sorry, son,' she said. 'I'm teasing you. Habit of a lifetime.'

'Why are you saying that?' David said.

She struggled to find the words, needing three attempts to start her sentence.

'I . . . I say it because it's the truth. I'm not eighty for another few weeks yet. I've always known this isn't my birthday. I just . . . I just seem to have forgotten exactly why.'

'The oncologist said you might be getting delusions,' David said.

Susannah shook her head and gave him a pitying look. 'No, he didn't.'

'Okay, so he didn't. But . . . today's your birthday, Mom.' He tried an encouraging laugh and added, 'It always has been.'

'You remember,' Judy said. 'You remember why you were called "The Lucky One"?'

A reflective smile drew itself on Susannah's face. 'How could I forget? More importantly, how could *we* forget? April fifteenth. It's a special date for me, for sure. But my birthday?' She gave an upturned smile and shook her head slowly.

At that moment Alex, David's young son, trotted in from the back yard carrying a football. As soon as he saw the three of them, his ruddy, playful face dropped half an inch. 'What's wrong, Dad?' he said.

'Nothing at all, buddy,' David said. 'You okay?'

Alex bounced his knuckles on the ball. 'Thought we could . . . play soccer?' The words were spoken in a downbeat manner, as if a rejection were a foregone conclusion.

'One minute,' David said, ushering his son back out with a stroke of his hand.

Half of that 'one minute' was wasted in silence.

Eventually Judy spoke. 'We can talk about this later, Mom. It's not important. What's important is that you enjoy your day, birthday or not.'

David nodded and edged towards the door. Judy followed.

Then Susannah turned her face towards her children once more. 'Oh, and there's one more thing you need to know.'

David and Judy glanced at one another out of the corners of their eyes before looking back to their mother.

'What's that?' Judy said, trying to stop the waver in her voice.

'Well, last night I had a dream – one I haven't had in a long time.'

David nodded slowly and said, 'Oh–*kay*.'

'But this time it was different.'

Judy and David glanced at each other again. David simply shrugged.

'This time it left me asking myself questions.'

'You're not making sense,' Judy said.

'Oh, I'm making perfect sense, dear. Like I said, I've been doing a lot of thinking, and I've made up my mind. I'm going on a vacation.'

'What?' David said, with a short explosion of laughter. 'No, you're not.'

'I'm going to Hamburg.'

David shook his head, folded his arms, then unfolded them, and gazed nowhere in particular.

'Hamburg?' Judy said. 'But I don't understand. Why?'

Before she could answer David waded in. 'Mom, you're being stupid. You don't need to do this; if you need somewhere peaceful to spend your—'

'My final days?'

'Please. Mom. If you need some time someplace else, I can drive you there. Somewhere more peaceful. How 'bout that?'

'And if I say no, you ask me again and again until I agree?'

'But you shouldn't fly, not with . . .'

'Not with cancer?'

David groaned and shook his head.

'I wish you wouldn't joke about it, Mom,' Judy said.

'Who's joking? If I said, "I'm not flying with cancer – I'm flying with United Airlines." Now *that's* a joke.'

30

David drew rigid fingers through his thinning hair. 'Judy's right, Mom. Please don't say things like that.'

'So tell me, if I can't joke now, when can I?'

'And stop trying to change the subject. You're not making sense. Why do you want to go to Hamburg?'

'And who are you going with?' Judy added.

'Nobody. And that's out of choice. I need to go on my own.'

'No, Mom. I'll come with you, David too. I can get time off work and I'm sure David can leave his business at arm's length for a while.'

David hesitated before nodding. 'Sure, of course. But you have to tell us why. Why do you want to go there?'

Susannah held up the palm of her hand. 'I know you mean well, but your father wouldn't have been interrogated by his own children and neither will I.' She sliced the air with the edge of her hand. 'I *am* going, I'm going on my own, and that's an end to it.'

Judy turned to David. 'Hamburg? Isn't that near . . . ?'

He shrugged. 'Don't ask me; you're the geography major. I know it's in Germany but—' And then his face dropped. 'Oh, no. Please, God, no.'

'I don't expect you to understand my reasons,' Susannah said. 'I *do* expect you to respect my wishes.'

David's knees cracked as he knelt down next to her. 'Please, Mother. You should be spending time with your family. You haven't got long, six months if you're lucky.'

'But you forget, David. I *am* lucky, I always have been.'

Judy could feel her breaths, heavy with fear, and stifled the tears that were screaming to escape. 'And don't you remember why?' she said. 'You've been called "The Lucky One" ever since you escaped from that goddam place. Why do you . . . ? I mean . . . there must be something wrong with you to even . . . to want to go within a thousand miles of that hellhole.' She shook her head and turned away. 'David, tell her.'

David opened his mouth, but only air came out.

'Judy. David. Listen. I know I moan and beef at you both, and you both know I don't mean it and I love you more than I love myself. A mother couldn't have wished for better children than you two. You're only trying to look after me, I know that. You're so good to me when we all know I'm no longer much use to anyone.' Then the wrinkles across her face seemed to stiffen. 'But please. This is one thing I must do for myself. I have to go there. And I *am* going to do this, with or without your blessing.'

'But why?' Judy said, now having to wipe away a stray tear. 'If you could just tell us, we might understand.'

But Susannah simply held on to her stern expression, and for a few seconds the room was filled with more of that uneasy silence.

David went to speak, but stalled, then tried again. 'Mom. If that's what you really want, then I'm sure we could work something out.' He glanced at his sister. 'But don't you think Judy has a point? Why the fascination with that place? It's morbid.'

'You expect me to explain it? The whole thing? Here? Now?' She started to shake her head in dismay, then stopped and leaned forward towards him. 'No, wait. I can try. Do you remember that stupid football game you and your father used to talk so much about? The one he took you to for your sixteenth birthday?'

David gave a thoughtful smile. 'The Super Bowl.'

'Yes. That stupid football game. And I used to say I never understood why it was such a big deal, didn't I?'

'Sure.'

'And you always frowned to me, put on your grown-up-man voice, and said, "Mom, you just had to *be* there."' Susannah's eyebrows, faint and wispy, nudged themselves upwards for a second, and she settled back into her chair.

David took a few steps sideways, back and forth, then stomped out of the room, mumbling, 'I gotta go to the john' as he left.

'Men!' Susannah said. 'Is this what they mean when they talk about them having their brains in their pants?'

'He's concerned,' Judy said. 'We all are. You're sick and getting worse.'

Then Susannah looked at her daughter again and Judy got the impression she was looking straight through her rather than at her.

'You call this ill?' she said. 'My dear, you have absolutely no idea, do you?'

'So you really think you're well enough to travel?'

'Remember, Judy, there's one heck of a lot of sitting around involved in travelling.'

'I'm just thinking of the stress,' Judy said. 'And the planning, the paperwork, the—'

'The excuses?'

Judy stopped there. She was no match for her mother and they both knew it. And Judy also knew in the back of her mind that her mother was searching for something – something that, perhaps, Judy wanted her to find every bit as much.

'You never were quite as headstrong and stubborn as your brother,' Susannah said. 'You always took after your father more, a little more understanding and thoughtful, always willing to view things through others' eyes.' She suddenly reached forward and grabbed her daughter's hand. 'That's a good thing, Judy. It's a *good* thing. And I know David has that quality too, he just has a side salad of pig-headedness with it.'

Then David returned. He looked at Judy, then turned back to his mother. 'I've decided,' he said.

Susannah laughed. 'No, you haven't, David. *I've* decided.'

'Whatever,' he said. 'If that's really what you want, then that's what'll happen. Just promise you'll ring one of us every day?'

'I promise. You can have it in writing if you want.'

They both looked to Judy. She couldn't think straight for a

moment; all she could do was examine her fingernails. 'Okay,' she said after a few seconds. 'If you really, really have to, I guess.'

'I do,' Susannah replied. 'I need to know certain things, and I . . . I must see what death looks like before I meet it.'

David shrugged, then held his mother's hand. 'I don't understand what that means, but I do know that tomorrow I'm going to book you on a first-class flight and into the best hotel in Hamburg.'

And that was how it all started – the trip to Europe and everything that followed; with Judy's mother insisting that the day on which they had always celebrated her birthday wasn't really her birthday at all, and with neither David nor Judy having a clue what she was talking about.

Judy picked up the tray of milk and cookies and went upstairs.

In their mother's bedroom David had already made a flat area on the bed for the tray and all three of them settled down, Judy and David in the armchairs either side of their mother.

'Are you sure you're okay with this?' David said, as they each took a cookie.

'Oh, yes,' Susannah said. 'Every bit as much as I was about going to Europe in the first place.' She took a tiny sip of milk. 'Especially with something to wet my throat.'

'I was just thinking about your party earlier this year,' Judy said. 'When you told us it wasn't your birthday.'

'And I guess that's as good a place as any to start.' Susannah's yellowing teeth broke off a chunk of cookie. 'If you remember, that was when David kindly gave me permission to go.'

David smiled wryly but said nothing.

Then, as they all ate and drank, Susannah began to tell her story.

The person lying in bed in front of Judy was the Susannah that had been her mother for forty-nine years. But the more she listened, the more she realized there was also a Susannah she hardly knew at all.

PART TWO
The Flight and the Fleeing

CHAPTER SEVEN

It turned out to be a whole five weeks after Susannah's birthday-that-wasn't that she flew out to Hamburg. And they were difficult weeks, during which David and Judy knew better than to try to talk their mother out of it again, but at the same time they made it clear they would rather she didn't go. This entailed asking her in depth about what the physician had recommended – which meant quizzing her on things they already knew. According to Susannah she had the all-clear to live a relatively normal life in the short term, as long as she didn't exert herself, so she told her children that while she was in Germany she would try her utmost to go easy on the booze, the drugs, the all-night raves and the sex – well, just for a few days.

Judy took her to Wilmington airport and stayed with her until she was called to the departure lounge. During that time Judy twice went through a checklist of items her mother should have packed, and three times told her to ring either her or David each day. And four times Susannah told her daughter not to fuss so much, that she wasn't an invalid, that she could look after herself, and that it wasn't her brain that was diseased.

It was only when Susannah was called to the departure lounge that a little of her self-confidence dissolved and her speech started to waver. And when Judy told her yet again to be sure to ring home every day and grabbed her for a final hug, she knew it showed. She was now unsure for the first time whether she really was doing the right thing, and held onto her daughter for what seemed like half the flight time. Then the flight was called again and she drew back, holding onto Judy's hands for a while longer, examining her frame and features as if it were the last time she would ever see her. She knew that was a real possibility.

She nodded farewell to Judy, keeping tight-lipped so as not to show again that fear in her voice, but giving her daughter one last hug – a gentle understated one this time – before turning and leaving for the departure lounge.

Susannah settled herself onto her seat and smiled politely at her neighbours, which led to them striking up a conversation.

The young couple was touring Europe and was starting with northern Germany, followed by Denmark and the Netherlands, then on to France, where they were planning to spend a lot of time as they were keen wine aficionados.

Beyond France Susannah only half followed their itinerary; after all these years there was something not quite right to her about someone wanting to tour Europe. Archie had always been interested in exotic places and cultures, and they'd travelled widely together after the children had reached the age where parents were little more than an embarrassment. However, even he knew better than to suggest visiting Europe; that was a lesson he had learned from their early years of marriage.

෴

Susannah had met Archie Morgan for the first time at a dance in Miami while holidaying with her Uncle Paul and Aunt Helena.

She'd been attracted to men before, but there was something different about Archie. There was the physicality, for sure; he was tall, but not too tall, strong but in a sinewy rather than a bulky fashion, and he was good looking, with thick, slightly rubbery lips and warm eyes. But it wasn't so much those that attracted her. His blond hair had a distinct red tang and refused to be controlled no matter how much wax and combing was employed, and his clothes always had a crooked appearance, as if they were specifically 'tailored not to fit', Susannah thought. Also his shoes were always scuffed, and his laces kept coming undone. Somehow she found that air of vulnerability attractive, but above all he was kind in an uncomplicated way and gentle whenever he kissed her, which almost made her faint on the first few occasions it happened. She concluded that love was love whatever, and when Aunt Helena cautioned that she shouldn't dive into things, that only served to make her mind up. She couldn't think of a better experience in life to dive into than the attentions of a loving, kind-hearted man. It was only now, looking back, that in spite of the many happy memories of married life, she realized that the 'diving in' attracted her almost as much as Archie Morgan himself did. She was aware, more than anyone else she knew, that sometimes life was for living – not for taking time to judge and plan and weigh things up.

They became pen pals, and Archie regularly travelled up to North Carolina to see her. When he eventually made the effort to move up to Wilmington, it settled things for Susannah and very soon they got married. They started out in a new home in the suburbs, where Susannah looked after the house while Uncle Paul got Archie a job at one of the many nearby boatbuilding yards. All was well for a few months, and Susannah thought she was happy. She looked after the house, tended the garden, and went shopping.

On an unusually chilly January morning she went out to get some groceries – in truth they didn't really need food, but it was good to have some extra supplies in the house 'just in case' and the routine kept her busy. She collected the usual items and a few that weren't, and left the store. Mr Abrahams, a retired neighbour, gave her some kind of polite greeting but she didn't hear the words; all she heard was his dog barking. It was on a lead and it barked only a couple of times, but it felt to Susannah like it was pointing its snout directly at her, preparing itself to pounce. She dropped her bag of groceries where she stood, ran to her car, and jumped two red lights to get home. Once she'd bolted the door shut she opened the kitchen cupboard, fought her way past the pile of groceries that Archie always said was big enough for them to open their own mini-mart, and found the gin.

That settled her.

In fact, it settled her enough to completely ignore for a moment the fact that the gin bottle she'd bought only two days before was almost empty.

And Archie didn't drink gin.

CHAPTER EIGHT

On the plane Susannah tensed her muscles as firmly as any woman of her age could and tried to concentrate on the words of that same young couple who happened to be sitting across the aisle from her, how they were planning to spend some 'work time' learning about viniculture in France – because the pipedream was to acquire enough land to start their own vineyard – after which they would hire a car and mosey on down into Spain for some 'play time'. However, they were flexible and knew plans were no more than that because sometimes – when unforeseen events occurred – you couldn't always go where you intended to.

And then, just as Susannah was getting interested in the hopes and dreams of others, they turned to the 'oh, but we must be boring you' excuse and stopped talking.

Susannah leaned back into her seat, closed her eyes, and thought of her own hopes and dreams of years gone by.

࿂

It was two months after being upset by Mr Abraham's dog that Archie confronted her about the number of empty gin bottles in the trash.

Susannah dismissed his concerns with a frown that could cut and a yell that could maim. Archie didn't mention the subject for another eight months.

They had good days and they had days when tempers were tested, but it wasn't until Thanksgiving that he tried again. They'd been to spend the evening with Susannah's Uncle Paul and Aunt Helena, who lived ten or so miles to the north. Susannah didn't drink while she was there, but when they got back she reached for the gin bottle as soon as she was through the door – before she'd even taken her coat off, in fact.

It was then that Archie let her have it.

'Susannah,' he said. 'I have to tell you something, something really important.'

But whatever it was it was never going to be important enough to stop her unscrewing the top of the bottle.

'Please put that down,' he said.

'I need a drink.'

'No, you don't.'

She poured a slug into the nearest thing to hand – a coffee cup. Archie rested the palm of his hand over the top of it and pressed down. 'Please,' he said. 'Just . . . just leave it for tonight.'

But she snatched the cup away from his control and threw the contents into the back of her throat.

'You have to stop this,' Archie said.

She grabbed the bottle and poured more into the cup. He grabbed the bottle too and there was a brief tug of war; he obviously wasn't going to let go as easily as he had the cup.

'Just stop it!'

'I won't sleep,' Susannah said. 'And you know that.'

Archie wrenched the bottle away and poured the contents down the sink. 'So see a doctor.'

'You think that's the only one?' Susannah said, with a cackle.

Archie placed the empty bottle onto the side. 'Why do you do it? I mean, for Christ's sake, what's the point?'

'I told you. It helps me sleep.'

'No, it doesn't. Can't you see? It's getting to the stage where you're depending on it. It's like—'

She cracked the cup down onto the wooden table. 'Fine, so I can't live without it. Happy now?'

'*And I can't live without you, Susannah!*'

She stood frozen for a moment, then said, 'Is that what it's all about?'

'What in God's name is that supposed to mean?'

'Perhaps you want to live without me. Perhaps you have someone else.'

'You're crazy,' Archie said quietly.

'*I know the signs!*'

Archie stepped closer to her and spoke softly, his eyes glassy with tears. 'Why do you keep saying things like that?'

'I thought . . .' Susannah gulped and placed a hand over her eyes. 'I thought you were going to leave me.'

'But I married you,' Archie said, his face a mixture of sorrow and confusion. 'I love you. Why would you think . . . ?'

Susannah dropped the cup, which shattered on the floor, fragments darting to all corners of the room. She flung her arms around him and started sobbing quietly. Archie held her tightly for a few minutes, until her crying eased off, then slowly manoeuvred them both to chairs at the table. He took off her coat, then his, and sat down next to her.

'You can't go on like this,' he said, holding her hand in his. 'You're killing yourself.'

Susannah looked into his eyes, then around the room, but couldn't find the words.

'You want this for the rest of your life?' Archie said. 'Ask yourself. Could you ever consider living a normal life like this? We both know you want children, but you can't.' He gave his head a languid shake. 'You can't – not like this.'

Susannah's gaze dropped down to her hands. She said, 'But . . .' and no more.

'You're not well,' Archie said. 'And . . . I know it's hard to accept, but you need to see the doctor again.'

Two days later she did just that. It didn't help that he wasn't her normal doctor, even less that he looked fresh out of medical school. It was apparent within seconds that he came with a head full of textbook.

'You're still not sleeping?' he said.

'I can't.' She shook her head. 'Not without . . . help.'

'You can't drink your way to mental health, Mrs Morgan.'

'You don't know what it's like,' she said.

'But I *do* know what happened to you in years gone by, Mrs Morgan. It's all in your medical records. You have no lasting physical damage. And you look fine to me too, that's always a good sign.'

Susannah leaned forward on the desk between them. 'But I can't live without . . . without something. Sure, I'm all right now, sitting here talking to you. But if I'm on my own, or if I have a bad day, if the . . .' She paused and took a couple of deep breaths.

'Go on,' the doctor said. 'If what?'

'I have bad thoughts. Sometimes the . . . the memories get to me . . .'

'You mean, you *let* the memories get to you.'

She stared at him for ten seconds, her expression somehow turning from anger to pity. 'My, my,' she said. 'You sure learned good at medical school, didn't you?'

'Actually, Mrs Morgan, with the greatest respect, this is known to be the best way of overcoming any traumatic incident.'

Susannah narrowed her eyes. 'Did you say "*incident*"?'

The doctor's voice rose slightly in volume. 'You have to leave the past in the past. It really isn't helping you to dwell on bad memories.'

'Dwell?' Susannah said, almost shouting the word. '*Dwell?*'

'Mrs Morgan, we can't change the past. If your memories are getting in the way of living a healthy life, then the best way to deal with the problem is to forget all of that ever happened.'

She leaned in closer and whispered to him, almost breathlessly, 'You really think I haven't tried something so simple?'

The doctor swayed his head from side to side, as if deciding between a cream soda and a milk shake, Susannah thought. But he didn't speak.

'This is part of me,' Susannah said slowly, her voice gaining strength, her finger prodding the centre of her chest.

'All I'm saying is that you have to try to forget all of that and think about the here and now – your future with your husband.'

'I cannot forget!' Susannah shouted. 'I cannot forget! I cannot forget!' She leaned back, rested for a second, then again said quietly, 'I. Can. Not. Forget.'

The doctor sighed and reached for his prescription pad.

'And I don't want drugs,' she added.

'Mrs Morgan, if you won't let me help you . . .'

They stared at each other for a few moments. Susannah saw no vestige of humanity in the man's eyes; he couldn't have been less helpful if he'd had a uniform and a helmet on.

Without a word she grabbed her coat, stormed out of the doctor's, and stopped on the way home to buy a fresh bottle of gin.

CHAPTER NINE

Susannah changed flight at Charlotte and was on her way to Hamburg. Now there was definitely no going back. She found it difficult to relax, her concern for what she might find there keeping her awake for most of the journey. Inflight movies of fighting and destruction really didn't help. It was only towards the end, when her 'concerned self' accepted that she was definitely doing this whatever those concerns might have been, that she was able to settle down and try to get some sleep, and as she closed her eyes and became alone with her thoughts she tried to forget those painful memories of the early years of her marriage. But memories sometimes beget more memories – often worse ones, and she fell into the ambush just like she had so many times before in her life.

A young woman in a cold, dark cabin shrinks her frame and turns her face away from the darkest of visions. Dirt floor. Bare walls. Live ghosts.

But she cannot ignore expressionless faces that have mislaid their owners, eyes that are past pleading, cheeks like dirty craters.

The mass of shaven heads don't jostle – there's no point. The SS guard barks a tune – 'Clothes. Shoes. Glasses. *Off.*' – and they *danse macabre*.

Subhuman silhouettes shuffle past her, cowering, their eyes facing the blood-spattered dirt but their minds long devoid of meaningful thought.

'*Time for shower!*'

The butt of a rifle on her breastbone stops her joining them.

'Not for you. I'm told you're "The Lucky One".'

She stands silently, ignoring the stench of mildew, disease and human waste, as the *Untermenschen* drop their fetid rags, indifferent to their cadaverous nakedness, and leave the dim cabin.

'You would prefer to go with them?' the guard asks her.

She ignores the jet of spittle that hits her as he cackles. She doesn't answer.

'Of course not,' he says. 'Because you are "The Lucky One", is that not what they say?' He turns to kick the legs of the last *Untermensch* to leave, who drops his wreck of a body to the floor, then crawls out of the room. He hooks his rifle on the door edge and swings it shut, its clang echoing in the dank emptiness.

He steps towards her, places the butt of his rifle on her shoulder and nudges.

'So, tell me, why are you different, so special? What is it you do?'

She keeps her head low, swings it left, right, left. Then she feels her shoulder being shaken, again and again.

'Tell me! Why are you called "The Lucky One"?'

She feels faint, losing consciousness in spite of the guard's unrelenting interrogation.

⁓

'Excuse me, madam?'

Even in waking Susannah couldn't escape the pain of the rifle nudging her shoulder – except that now it was being used more gently, not hurting quite so much.

'Could you put on your seatbelt please, madam,' the voice said. 'We're about to land.'

In that no-man's-land between sleeping and waking, Susannah looked up and gasped as she saw someone in a perfectly pressed field-grey uniform bearing down on her, giving her orders. After a shocked blink she looked again and sank back slightly, seeing now that she'd made a mistake; the figure standing over her was a flight attendant dressed in light-blue garb. She almost cried out, *Where am I?* but her natural reserve held judgement just long enough for her to glimpse the polite smile, and she let out a long sigh, then another.

'Oh, yes,' she replied breathlessly. 'I'm sorry.' Then she obeyed the order – no, she *complied with the request.*

It was another moment before she could answer her own unspoken question: where was she?

'Hamburg,' she muttered. 'Of course. That's where I am.' And then the loudspeaker announcement confirmed the destination. It took another moment for her to consider the question that followed on in her mind: why was she here?

Within minutes the unsettling judder of the rubber tyres on the runway made her give the question more thought. *Yes. Why, exactly, was she here?* Guilt? Hardly. Perhaps seeing again how unlucky so many others had been – how a whole generation had had their lives and dreams stolen from them – would remind her how lucky she'd been to escape sixty-four years ago. Of course, in the immediate aftermath of the war those questions had dominated her life. Why had she escaped? What was so special about her? Why had God spared her and not some of the younger children? Would she have been better had she been with them? Those thoughts and feelings had controlled her life for many years – and had almost ended it once. But she'd fought and beaten those demons – together with the bottle – to leave those memories well and truly behind, and had all but straightened herself out by the 1950s. She'd had to in order to have any kind of normal existence, to share what had been – all things considered – a happy home with Archie, David and Judy. There had been aberrations during those years – of course there had – but she'd learned the tricks of how to cover up, how to project those feelings of guilt and regret inward, how to brick up the wall when those memories came marching back into her fractured world.

Guilt? After all these years? Of course not. But perhaps this visit would help her put her life – and in particular the fact that it was nearly over – into some sort of perspective. Yes, perhaps that was what it was – seeing *that place* again might bring her some sort of closure (that was a modern term she hated but she had to admit it had an accurate ring to it).

And no, it wasn't about finding out why she was really called The Lucky One, but it might just possibly make her final months on this planet more peaceful ones.

As the plane came to a halt and the passengers started standing up and gathering their hand luggage, Susannah did likewise – albeit quite a bit more slowly – and turned to the aisle.

She let out a small shriek as she locked eyes with a gaunt, shaven-headed man inches from her face. A dry swallow turned to breathless panic as her eyes were drawn down to the grimy blanket covering his paperweight frame. She fell back into her seat, squeezing her eyes shut.

'I'm sorry, love,' the man said. 'After you.'

She opened her eyes again, and between deep breaths saw him

step back and wave a hand to invite her into the aisle. Yes, he was bald, maybe a little slim, and a scruffy grey T-shirt hung limply down over his jeans. But the accent was English and the face was clean rather than dirty, healthy rather than covered in scabs and pockmarks.

'No,' he said, with a kindly smile. 'Go on.' He stayed back to give her time to get to her feet, then said, 'You sure you're all right?'

She nodded. 'I'm sorry, yes, I'm fine, thank you. It's these . . . these inflight movies, they send me to sleep and I have . . .'

'You get nightmares, eh?' He laughed and held out an arm for support as she stepped into the aisle. 'I know exactly what you mean. Come on, love.'

CHAPTER TEN

S usannah waited inside Hamburg airport for her luggage to arrive, waited some more, then found a nearby bench where she could keep an eye on the carousel in a little more comfort. She glanced around her.

This was the first time she'd been back to Germany since 'then'. If her children had had their way she wouldn't even be here now. And the urge inside her was to book the first plane back to the States – or to anywhere, in fact.

But she'd spent a lifetime suppressing urges – that particular skill was as useful now as it always had been.

She took a few deep breaths of the horrid plastic air and looked around the interior of the airport once more, making mental notes on anything and everything her eyes fell on. Her attention flicked swiftly from porter to passenger, from burger kiosk to clock to glassy granite floor tiles, all glaring and shiny from the throw of lighting that was as artificial as the air.

And then those bad thoughts were gone.

Now it all looked so normal. Perhaps the interiors of German airports looked pretty much like those of every other airport in the whole world; it certainly seemed that way.

She peered across to the carousel, but no, no luggage yet. So she looked around once more.

Her eye caught the word 'Berlin' on one of the destination displays. Sure, she'd seen the word a hundred times before, at airports around the world from Tokyo to New York. Somehow this time it was different, because this time she wasn't viewing the words from the safety of a different country.

Anything more than dull memories of the first eleven years of her life were hidden in the corners of her mind, but now that she was back in the same country – hearing the accents and seeing everything written in her native language – more details started to force their way through.

The thoughts started to come back.

❧

Susannah remembered a very happy early childhood. Those dull memories were mostly the things that could have happened in any child's world: playing in the playground of her first school with skipping ropes or games chalked on the yard; a few close friends – names long forgotten – plaiting each other's hair on a Sunday evening to be smart for school the next day; a few vacations to the sea, where it was usually much too cold to swim; playing – and too often fighting – with her younger brother, Jacob.

She spent the first eleven years of her life in the same tenement apartment in the Jewish quarter of Berlin. Quoting the names of streets was beyond her, but she definitely remembered the three large stone steps leading to the front door, steps she struggled to climb as a very young child. Her father was an engineer at a local factory, and Susannah remembered him coming home every night in his smart suit and changing into his old creased suit – the one with patched elbows – to play with her and Jacob either in the apartment or at the nearby park. She couldn't remember the official name of the park, but everybody called it Rose Park on account of the floral displays throughout early summer. And that explained why for the rest of her days, whenever she smelt a sweet sherbet rose, the little girl in her started running through Rose Park again.

Like the rest of the community the family celebrated Passover and Hanukkah and ate lots of matzo balls and hamantashen. Even the plain old chicken soup had a Jewish feel to it. On Fridays at sundown, surrounded by blessed candles and good conversation, they ate a Shabbat meal, which was usually egg bread followed by gefilte fish. On every Saturday and holy day Mother and Father took the family to the local synagogue, and Susannah always knew when they were about to go because Mother put on her best dress and Father wore his kippah. Susannah got the impression it was about tradition, and was an excuse to meet people and share collective ideas for a fulfilling life as much as it was about the worship itself.

Susannah didn't give much thought to the idea of being Jewish in the early years, only really becoming conscious of it when she had to change to an all-Jewish school even though she was perfectly happy where she was, and then having to make sure she sat only on the yellow benches whenever she went in Rose Park, which wasn't such a big deal even though she didn't see how using the other benches should cause a problem.

Uncle Paul and Aunt Helena, together with their son, Reuben, lived just a short walk away, and would visit every weekend. Uncle Paul was her favourite relative; she was attracted by the way he resembled her father, albeit a little taller and slimmer, with silver-threaded hair that had started to thin. But the most striking similarity was the way his jaw took on a square shape whenever he smiled, again just like Father, which meant he was a friend.

Whenever they came around Paul would greet her by tweaking her ears and tickling the sides of her belly until her legs collapsed underneath her, whereupon he would pick her up and pretend to throw her away. At some point the two Zuckerman families would split into their accustomed groups. If it was dry Susannah would play with Reuben and Jacob in the park across the road, otherwise they would play inside, usually pretending to run a sweet shop. Aunt Helena and Mother would retire to the kitchen to talk or cook or make curtains, and Father and Uncle Paul would do little more than sit in the living room and talk.

It was all happy, and only in hindsight did Susannah realize her parents must have shielded her from what was happening in the country at the time. But she knew something serious was happening because of the arguments Uncle Paul and Father used to have. Sometimes Susannah would come into the room at the wrong time, and the two men would look at each other and huff a little, and would always manage to say that it was nothing whenever she asked what they'd been talking about. But as time went on they stopped making excuses and simply carried on arguing in front of the rest of the family. And everybody got the general idea. Uncle Paul always seemed to be complaining; it was always: *The Socialists are doing this*, or *The Socialists are planning that*, or *Soon it will be illegal for us to step outside of our homes.* Father always seemed to dismiss the concerns; he used clever words like 'unreasonable' or 'paranoid', and kept saying that it wasn't so bad, that there were many strong-minded, intelligent Germans. He said that the government was only trying to make Germany a stronger country, and that sooner or later they would come to their senses and realize that Jewish people could help with that. He kept talking about having faith in the German people. And whenever he did say these things, that was when Uncle Paul would get really upset and use more words Susannah didn't understand, like 'deluded' and 'persecution', and would have to cough and rub his face to try to disguise how angry he was.

But, in time, all of those heated discussions would be put to one side and the two families would eat together and play cards and talk before parting.

CHAPTER ELEVEN

Susannah's memories of her childhood years in Berlin were of mainly blissful times, but those heated discussions between Father and Uncle Paul on the politics of the day weren't the only dark stains on the social tablecloth.

Three specific events from those years stuck particularly firmly in Susannah's mind in spite of the passing of almost seventy years.

The first was when the two Zuckerman families were spending the day together, and Uncle Paul and Father had been talking all afternoon while Mother and Aunt Helena took Susannah, Jacob and Reuben to the park. They returned to find the two brothers in the middle of a particularly bitter argument. They could hear the shouts through the door, but the exchange stopped as soon as they entered.

For once Uncle Paul didn't give Susannah that square-jawed smile or tweak her ears or give her a playful tickle. In fact, his face looked a little scary, like she'd never seen it before. He looked almost weary, with sweat beading on his ruddy brow as if he'd been chopping wood.

'I hope you all kept to the yellow benches,' he said, the stress in his voice evident even to a child. Reuben looked to his mother and started welling up; his father's fear had been conveyed to the boy's mind in an instant.

'Leave the children out of it,' Susannah's father bellowed. He marched over and stood in front of Susannah and Jacob.

'Open your eyes, for God's sake,' Uncle Paul replied, matching the anger in his brother's voice. 'What sort of country do you want your children to grow up in? I tell you, we should all—'

'We're not going anywhere,' Father shouted across. 'We live here. It's our country as much as anyone else's.'

Then Susannah felt the firm touch of her mother's hand on her shoulder, and all three children were shepherded into the kitchen, where they stayed with Mother and Aunt Helena, listening for a few seconds as the argument raged on next door.

'Milk,' Mother said, forcing a smile and opening a cupboard. 'And some biscuits, yes?'

The two mothers talked and drew pained, sickly smiles on their faces, and kept asking whether the children had enjoyed playing in the park. Susannah didn't feel like speaking, and evidently neither did Jacob or Reuben.

And just as it all went quiet in the next room and Mother's shoulders started to relax, the door was flung open and Uncle Paul stepped into the room. He looked to his wife and nodded to the door. They both had frowns that aged them and a sad redness around the eyes. Soon they were hugging Susannah and Jacob, and Mother and Father were hugging Reuben.

Then Susannah's aunt, uncle and cousin were gone. They never came back to the house in Berlin again, and Susannah knew better than to ask what had happened to them.

The second event happened late in 1938. Susannah had had difficulty getting to sleep, with noises outside that Mother and Father just told her to ignore. But eventually she slept, only to be woken up with a start in the dead of night by a hammering noise at the front door that sounded like people running along wooden boards.

Soon she saw light streaming into the bedroom from the hallway, and heard her father swear, which was very unusual for him. Then she saw his shadow break the light and heard the front door creak open. She pulled her bedclothes higher against the cold November air that crawled into the bedroom, and listened.

'What is it?' Father said. 'What the . . . ?'

'You need to come and see, Mr Zuckerman. The synagogue . . . our businesses . . .'

Then there was a silence. There was also a hint of smoke in the air that stilled Susannah's breathing and made her heart race.

Father cursed again, then said, 'I've been hearing things happening all night.' He spat the words out in anger. 'I never thought they would go through with it.'

'You heard the talk?'

'Of course I did!' Then he apologized for shouting at the man and said, 'I . . . I just . . . didn't want to accept it.'

A few more terse exchanges were whispered before the light went out and the door closed.

In the strangely silent darkness Susannah sensed something else in the air. But this wasn't something she could describe, like a sound or a smell; for the first time in her young life she knew real and life-changing fear.

Father hardly spoke for days after that night, and more importantly he didn't go back to work. He spent his time simply sitting in the corner of the living room, his face looking more like a well-worn glove every day, his fists clenching and unclenching with resentment. Only when Susannah was alone with him and asked whether he was feeling well did he relax a little and paint a sad smile on his face – just for a moment – before sighing and fixing his gaze on the far wall.

It was then that she took the chance to confront that fear she'd had days before. She knelt down next to him as he was deep in thought. 'Father,' she said softly. 'When are you going back to the office?'

He glanced to her, then quickly pulled his eyes away and back to the wall. 'Something happened to the office. I won't be working there for a while.'

'But—'

'Susannah,' he said. 'It is better that you don't ask.' Then he glanced down to his fingers, fingers he was rubbing together like two fire sticks, and looked at Susannah again. Then he called Mother and Jacob into the room from the kitchen.

'Listen, all of you,' he said in a slow deliberate tone that held a threat. 'You're not to go outside alone.' He looked to Mother.

'You must do as your father says,' she said. 'Just for a while.'

'Yes,' Father said. 'Just until things . . .'

'Improve?' Susannah said.

Father's lips stayed sealed, and he simply blinked a few times.

'Yes,' Mother said. 'We'll see what the New Year brings.'

As it transpired, the New Year brought the third significant event Susannah could remember from those Berlin years.

The strongest memory she had of her time there – the kind of memory where she could distinctly remember the emotion on people's faces and her own grim awareness that this was no game of hide-and-seek or a scold for spilling a drink – was when Mother and Father sat her and Jacob down and asked them whether they would like to see their Uncle Paul, Aunt Helena and cousin Reuben again.

Susannah had reached that age of awakening, but knew Jacob was too young to understand and wasn't going to answer, so she said that yes, of course she would like to see them again. Only then did Jacob nod agreement. So Father told them that they could do that, but it might mean them not seeing their school friends for some time.

Susannah remembered saying she would miss all of her friends (although now, almost seventy years later, she couldn't even remember their names) but in truth she missed Uncle Paul and would have agreed to anything just to see him again. Her parents told her it wouldn't be for ever and promised they would all return home one day. They could even think of it as a long vacation to the place where Paul, Helena and Reuben now lived – a place called Amsterdam, which was near the sea in the Netherlands. Mother also told them they would all be safer there, that she and Jacob could play again with Reuben outside, and – even better – that they would make many new friends and play in new and exciting places, that they would explain to them when they were older what it was all about, and that they were not to get upset or cry or ask questions because life was difficult enough as it was.

So Susannah didn't ask.

She just kept repeating in her mind those words of her parents: the promise that they would all 'return one day' to Berlin.

❧

Susannah, still sitting on the bench at the airport, and still gazing at the hypnotic luggage carousel, allowed herself a reflective smile at her thoughts – wondering whether her luggage would 'return one day' to her.

And then, as if on cue, her eyes fell on the large wheeled case as it made its appearance, and she eased her stiff frame off the seat and made her way towards it.

The kind couple who had been telling her all about their European trip helped to retrieve her luggage and set up the wheels and the long pulling handle. She thanked them and left to look for a cab.

CHAPTER TWELVE

S o this is Hamburg,' Susannah said as her cab set off for the
hotel.
The driver took the bait and struck up a one-way conversation in perfect, if clipped, English, telling her about some of the
usual tourist attractions. She didn't have the heart to tell him she
wasn't really interested in how many museums, theatres, art galleries and restaurants he could recommend. She hadn't come for
those. Apart from inserting the occasional 'yes' or 'I see' between his
words, she occupied her mind taking in some of the city scenery.
And thinking. She mainly thought about how the city resembled
any modern US city more than it did a 1940s German city, what
with the cars, the architecture, the clothes, the advertising hoard-
ings for McDonald's, Porsche, Coca-Cola, Mercedes and many
more. Then again, the world had changed so much since she'd last
been to Germany, so what else did she expect?

Indeed, what *was* she expecting? Why was she wasting her time
– that precious time evaporating like water from a frock in the summer sun – visiting old ghosts here, even torturing herself?

It occurred to her that perhaps she'd made the most monumen-
tal mistake of her long life. She looked up to the street signs, and

even the sounds of the words on them seemed harsh and brutal as she spoke them in her head. It was then, waiting at a set of traffic lights, that she heard the sharp snapping of dogs barking, and for a few seconds her heartbeat felt stronger than it had for years. She cleared her throat, gasping for air as if the hauntings of the past had stolen the breath from her lungs, and tapped the driver on the shoulder.

'Excuse me?' she said, almost shrieking the words.

The driver turned to her, and in a few seconds she ran through the scenario in her head. She would ask to turn back, he would ask why, she would say she'd forgotten something at the airport, he would tut and huff, but she would have to sound angry and insist. Then he would turn back.

'Are you okay?' he said with a softness that startled her and brought her mind back to reality.

The lights changed. They looked at each other for a moment.

Then a horn sounded from behind them and Susannah glanced over her shoulder. 'It's nothing,' she said. 'Let's carry on.'

'You look ill,' the driver said. 'I mean, if you don't mind me saying. Are you sure you're all right?'

There seemed genuine concern in the man's eyes – two almonds that seemed to understand.

'I'm fine,' she said. 'It's the jet lag. I just need to get to my hotel and have a lie down.' And after he'd turned and driven on for thirty seconds she said, 'But thank you for asking.' It only seemed right.

As soon as she got into her hotel room she collapsed, fully clothed, on the bed and felt herself drifting off to sleep.

No, that wouldn't do.

And, anyway, she'd now recovered. Furthermore, one thing – one realization – kept her from sleeping: it was clear she would have to be a lot stronger than this over the coming week. If a barking dog upset her there was little hope when she got to . . .

She dismissed the concern with a sigh and slithered her feet over the side of the bed and onto the floor. Yes, courage was needed here. She hung her coat up, popped her head between the curtains to see the street scene outside, then took a few calming moments to peruse the rest of the room. En suite, check. TV, check. Well-worn leaflets on Hamburg tourist traps, check. Mini-bar . . .

She stepped over to it and opened its clean and shiny bright door, then cast a crooked finger along the row of drinks.

Mini-bar.

The word sounded so innocent.

And so too the sign above it in four different languages: PLEASE HELP YOURSELF!

That sounded so . . . well . . . helpful.

She took a final look at the bottles before shutting the door on them.

Judy.

She had to phone Judy and tell her she'd arrived safely.

In the event, telling was pretty much all she did. She told her daughter that, yes, she'd arrived safely; that, yes, she was feeling fine; that, yes, the hotel seemed nice and the room was clean and spacious; that, no, she hadn't eaten yet but soon would; that, yes, she wouldn't hesitate to contact someone from the lobby or even an ambulance if she started feeling ill; and finally that she was tired and in a bit of a rush so she would call and have a proper talk tomorrow.

And she prayed Judy wouldn't ask whether there was a mini-bar in the room.

She knew – she'd known for years – that Judy had heard the rumours. And Judy probably knew that she knew. So that was it; if they both knew there was no need to talk about it.

*

She ate a small meal at the hotel, had a long soak in the bath, then went to bed.

She turned out the bedside lamp. Now it was just her and the darkness.

No, it was her and the darkness and those voices – barked orders, malevolent questions and whispered threats alike projecting themselves from the ether.

For a split second she tried to visualize where the mini-bar was relative to her.

No. She was past that – although not past thinking about it. She was safe where that particular form of assistance was concerned – and had been for years.

And, anyway, was she even still in the hotel room? If not, then there was no mini-bar to tempt her.

As her eyes became accustomed to the darkness, the scene before her started to reveal itself. Yes, she was still in the hotel room. So, yes, there was drink. But she knew it wouldn't help. Nothing could help her – she had to let the past flow, not the drink.

For Susannah the past had always flowed.

And now, alone in a foreign country – *that* foreign country – recollections of the past came so easily. The walls of Germanic accents at the airport and within the hotel were now starting to kick all of those fears and sinister memories towards her. She was afraid of those memories – especially the ones that were waiting for their moment to cause trouble. But at the same time she knew that perhaps that was exactly the reason she had come here – to confront them.

So the voices were there, she might as well accept it.

She nestled her head deep in the pillow and tried to relax.

Relax? Maybe.

Sleep? Unlikely.

CHAPTER THIRTEEN

I t was on a sunny morning early in 1940 that Susannah and her brother, mother and father prepared to set off on the journey from Berlin to Amsterdam. While their parents packed as much as they could fit into eight suitcases, Susannah and Jacob spent some time having a last play with their friends in Rose Park, telling them they would see them again soon, that it was almost like going on a long vacation and they might even bring something back to show where they'd been.

When they got back to the apartment Susannah tried to help her mother squeeze the last few items into the two smallest suitcases – the ones Jacob would be carrying. Her mother was very quiet, and didn't seem to want to look straight at her, preferring either to look down or to concentrate on the job in hand. Then there was that frown on her forehead that had taken up residence two or three days before and refused to move on. She hadn't smiled at Susannah since then either – well, unless you counted the artificial half-smile that seemed to pass straight through her.

And Father didn't seem much better, also speaking only when he had information to convey, such as what the others should do or where they should go. The rest of the morning passed quickly, and in no time they were all standing together outside on those stone steps Susannah had had so much trouble clambering up for her first few walking years. Father checked that all of the suitcases were with them, and took one last look at the exterior of the building. Mother and Father embraced with a tenderness Susannah had seen only once or twice before, and then turned away from the front door in unison. They all tightened their coats against the winter chill, lifted their suitcases – two large ones each for the two adults, small ones for Susannah and Jacob – and started walking to the railway station. Very few words were exchanged between them.

Susannah had been to the station a few times before, but now there was a different atmosphere – as if the air was bad. In fact, it might as well have been a different station: there were not only more people, but they seemed more pensive too; there were no conversations as such – just the occasional questions and single-word answers. Even at the ticket kiosk there was very little talk; passengers stated their destination and handed the money over, then took the tickets and their change and stepped away.

A station that had previously whisked the family away on days of joy and togetherness now seemed stark and unfriendly. Today the station layout seemed to positively pull the cold wind in and funnel it along the platform. Mother protected Jacob and Father protected Susannah from the worst of it, but it still seemed to sum up the day. Their last day in Berlin was never going to be one to look back on with any element of fondness.

Susannah's mother had shown little emotion during the few days leading up to their departure. She'd had to keep moving because things needed doing, and she'd done those things with a gentle and coaxing efficiency, with no time for sentimentality. However, as soon as the train pulled away from the platform – with nothing for her to do but look and think – her face seemed to contort. She pursed her lips, as if putting all of her effort into the muscles around her mouth, controlling it, keeping it shut.

When that resolve broke, Susannah initially thought the outburst was a cough, but then there were a few convulsive splutters, and she watched with reflected pain as her mother turned and placed her face against Father's chest. Jacob's face took on a quizzical look, and he looked to Susannah and opened his mouth to speak. She narrowed her eyes a little and gave her head the tightest of shakes. They sat, not making a sound, and watched Father curl those long arms around Mother and hold her gently as her head trembled. He kissed her hair, stroked it a few times, and rocked her back and forth.

Susannah remembered a guard coming into the carriage to check the tickets when most of Mother's cries had subsided but she was clearly still upset. He ignored her tears – ignored *her* – and asked Father what the purpose of their journey was. Father replied that they were going to spend a short amount of time with his wife's mother, who was very ill, hence the grief.

Susannah remembered knowing that Father was lying but not knowing why, and feeling upset at this because such behaviour was so uncharacteristic of him.

When the guard left the carriage Father gave Susannah a smile and tousled her hair. She smiled back at him. Then, as he kept a comforting arm around Mother, his face cracked slightly. Susannah could tell that it wasn't a real smile.

By the time they arrived in Amsterdam with their lives packed into eight suitcases, the sun had long since set and the streets shone with lamps reflecting on settled rainwater. It was then that Susannah felt that fluttering in her stomach once more, the feeling she'd had when the fires had happened in Berlin, the sense of fear. It might have been because of the time of day, or the weather, but Amsterdam looked bleak and claustrophobic, with a low, heavy sky.

Simply not a nice place to be.

She had the urge to tell Father she wanted to go back home – no, that she desperately *had* to go back home because she didn't like it here; she didn't know why, she just didn't. But she saw Mother's red-rimmed eyes and ruddy cheeks and knew that such talk would cause upset, so she kept the words to herself, repeating over and over again inside that one day she would get to go back home. Jacob looked very much the little boy lost – he wasn't exactly in tears, but his face was full of fearful confusion at the new streets and buildings. Father must have spotted the signs because he took a suitcase each from Mother and Jacob – wedging them under his arms – so that Jacob could hold onto his mother's hand.

And Jacob didn't once let go for the whole of the long walk to the other side of town.

When they did eventually reach Uncle Paul's and Aunt Helena's apartment there was an immediate improvement in morale. There were hugs and smiles all round between the two families, and Uncle Paul went out of his way to tweak Susannah's ears and tickle the sides of her belly for longer than usual. But throughout all of this she could tell that Father was again using one of those make-believe smiles he had shown her on the train. It was clear to her that he didn't want to be here any more than she or Jacob or Mother did.

After hot drinks and detailing of where the local shops and the secret synagogues were – interspersed with some reminiscences of their days in Berlin – they all got up and the new tenants were shown to their room. Although Susannah didn't take part in the talking, the whole discussion made her feel safe once more; it was normal, as if she could think of this apartment as a part of Berlin that had somehow got lost and turned up in Amsterdam. And she felt even better when she saw the room they were to sleep in. A large mattress lay on the floor along one wall, with two small beds on the other side at right angles to each other. There was nothing else in the room because there was no space; only a passageway threaded between the beds for access.

Good, Susannah thought, they would all be sleeping in the same room. If anything happened here Father would be within reach and would protect them all.

'How does that all look?' Father asked.

Susannah nodded and said, 'Cosy – just like at home in Berlin but smaller.'

Her father knelt down and gave her a hug, then did the same to Jacob. He looked up to Susannah's mother and smiled. And Susannah thought she saw that his real smile had returned.

That was a good sign. Perhaps they would be happy here.

'I'm sorry,' Aunt Helena said with a slight grimace, 'but you'll have to store all of your clothes in boxes here in the hallway; nothing else would fit in the room.'

'Please,' Father said. 'There's no need to apologize. What you've done for us is enough.' Then he stood up and glanced around. 'Is Reuben out with friends?'

'No,' Helena said.

Father peered into the doorway of the other bedroom. 'But . . . will he be sleeping in your room?'

Helena looked to Paul for an answer.

Paul coughed to clear his throat and said, 'Reuben has gone away.'

'Away?' Susannah's mother said.

'He . . . he had the chance to go away. His friend at school – his family, the Berwalds – they said they were going to America. They offered to take him and we thought it best for his future.'

Helena covered her face with her hand, and very soon her head was quivering and clear droplets were dripping from between her fingers.

'Oh, no,' Susannah's mother said, holding an arm around her shoulder, guiding her into the other bedroom.

Susannah heard her aunt whimper and stammer out the words 'I miss him', and then again, 'I miss him so much', before the door closed.

There were a few seconds of awkward silence between Father and Paul, then Paul drew breath and said, 'I . . . I miss him too.' Then he plunged his hands in his pockets and bowed his head. 'But it was for the best.' It was intoned as a question, as if pleading for support.

Father looked at his two children and pulled them to either side of his torso. 'Of course it was,' he said to Paul with a firm nod. 'You've done the right thing.'

After that Aunt Helena and Uncle Paul rarely spoke about Reuben.

The weeks and the months in Amsterdam passed by, and Susannah gradually got used to the cramped conditions of the apartment compared to their house in Berlin. She made new friends at school, and came to accept the evenings gathered around the radio listening to people talking. They talked mainly about the political situation, which she knew was important but didn't fully understand.

After two years in Amsterdam, old friends in Berlin were no more than faint memories in another, distant life. The Dutch city had almost become home, and those two years turned out to be two of Susannah's happiest. She and Jacob were now used to the apartment, the city and their new school; they had found a public park a short walk away where they could play. The climate was a little milder than back in Berlin, and there had been time for a few trips to the coast, which wasn't far away. Most importantly, Father and (especially) Mother both seemed to have become happier with the passing of time, and that made Susannah happy. The six of them whiled away most evenings – after they had listened intently to the news on the radio – playing cards; Uncle Paul had a book of games and they played what seemed like every game ever invented.

But in spite of all this, Susannah still hadn't forgotten Father's promise that one day they would all return to Berlin. Jacob showed few signs of emotion, but then again he always was more likely to cry when he fell over than when he felt scared. He never mentioned Berlin, apparently possessing a natural toughness that Susannah envied.

In Amsterdam, between the two of them, Susannah and Jacob celebrated four birthdays.

These were important as pointers; it was only in hindsight that Susannah realized that each of those birthdays was slightly less joyous than the last, and that the food and presents – even though they were laughable by twenty-first-century standards even at the beginning – had turned to mere tokens by 1942.

Jacob's eleventh birthday that year was the last they would celebrate in Amsterdam – in the apartment that was now home.

Susannah could remember little of their final night there. But the few details she could recollect were all that were needed.

It was a dry night blessed with a full moon.

Mother and Father woke her and Jacob and told them to get dressed.

'Are we going back to Berlin now?' Susannah asked.

'Not yet,' Father whispered. He kissed Jacob and Susannah, then pulled them both into his chest. 'But some day we will,' he said. 'I promise.'

CHAPTER FOURTEEN

The next morning, after taking breakfast, Susannah freshened up and phoned David. She told him that, yes, she did have a good night's sleep, and that, yes, she would look after herself, and that, no, she wouldn't do anything likely to stress her out or make her upset. After that she left for the railway station.

She joined the queue at the ticket office, but as she got nearer and nearer to the front her mouth started getting dry and her pulse quickened. The voice that came from her mouth when she eventually reached the counter was weak and croaky.

'How do I get to . . . to . . . ?'

And now her mouth wasn't merely dry – it was scared to even speak of the place.

The woman leaned forward. 'Yes, madam?'

No, no. This was stupid, she was a grown woman. 'I need to get to . . . Bergen-Belsen,' she said eventually. 'Or Belsen. Or whatever you call it now.'

'You mean the memorial?'

The woman said it so matter-of-factly, as if it were a stately home or a theme park or a good restaurant. Susannah had to take a deep breath before confirming that, yes, that was where she wanted to go, and immediately regretted her choice of words; it wasn't so much that she *wanted* to go there, more that she *had* to.

'There's no station at the memorial site, madam.'

'Are you sure?'

'Well . . . yes.' The woman had a puzzled frown on her forehead.

'But . . . there used to be,' Susannah said. For a split second images flickered into her mind: steam clearing to reveal the hazy shape of those field-grey uniforms – with rifles rested across and shiny black boots below – alongside slavering hounds with piercing stares.

'That's right,' the woman said. 'But that was a very long time ago.'

More images flashed themselves to Susannah, of wrought-iron gates and of wire fences, tall and striding into the distance. She took a moment to banish them. 'Yes,' she said. 'I guess it was.'

'The best way to get there is by coach. Do you know where the coach station is?'

Not quite up to lucid thinking, Susannah half nodded and half shook her head.

Then the woman darted a hand to her side, to a place hidden from view. Susannah disguised her flinch from the woman's action with a cough. But the woman's hand reappeared with nothing more dangerous than a leaflet, which she handed over the counter to Susannah.

Susannah thanked her, coughed again, then stepped – almost staggered – away and found a seat in a quiet corner of the station to rest her shaking legs for a few moments.

It had taken all the courage she possessed to queue up here; now she had to do the same all over again at the coach station.

In a way, queuing up and having to queue all over again was a bit like moving to a new city, getting used to it, making the effort to get to know people and places and make it a true home, only to find you then had to move someplace else and do the same all over again.

❧

Susannah couldn't recollect the name of the isolated farm that the six Zuckermans had moved to under cover of darkness in 1942. No, the reality was she couldn't have remembered because she didn't know it even at the time. What she did remember was the pattern in the sky on that night: a murky moon that lent an unreal appearance to a sky streaked with pipes of dirty grey cloud. The land around the farm was flat and featureless apart from a seemingly endless patchwork blanket of fields and a cluster of trees that appeared to be huddling together for warmth and security.

They'd been crammed together for hours in a car, during which Susannah fell asleep a couple of times. So she didn't know whether the driver spoke at all during the journey, only that she never heard him utter one word, and that as soon as they had all stepped out into the muddy farmyard Father thanked him and he replied with nothing more than a nod before speeding off.

There were four buildings around them. The biggest was a long stone cottage with shuttered windows and a chimney at the far end, its black plume rigidly stuck to the vertical above it and getting hazier the higher Susannah looked. And then there were three out-buildings, made of rough stone blocks and having only gaps in the walls by way of doors.

The door of the cottage opened with no noise whatsoever, and an elderly couple walked out and greeted them all. They were dressed in boots and dirty grey overalls, and seemed to be asking lots of questions of Uncle Paul.

Susannah wasn't sure what was being said because she was more interested in the views of farmland – a murky green in the moon-light; and breathing in the air – clean and fresh with a distinctly salty element to it. And as she looked to the distance she noticed small shapeless forms – lots of them – drifting around the fields that surrounded them like ghostly shadows.

Just as she locked her eyes onto one of the shapes, the talking stopped. She looked to the elderly couple, who had taken a step back from Uncle Paul and were whispering to each other. Eventually they nodded, first to each other and then to Paul. The woman pointed to one of the rustic outbuildings, the one that had a lone tree standing in front of it, almost as if it were making a pathetic attempt to camouflage the building.

They all started walking across the muddy yard to the outbuilding, and Susannah and Jacob were told they should call the couple who lived in the cottage Maria and Erik.

Within days, Susannah learned that these were not their real names, as she heard them using different names when they talked to each other.

But that was far from the most important secret here.

The couple said that the three rustic outbuildings were milking sheds, which explained the drifting dark shapes Susannah had seen in the fields all around them. They went on to explain that the one they were now approaching – the one guarded by the lone tree – was not all it seemed.

From the outside it looked to be a perfectly ordinary milking shed. It was only by looking up from within that anyone could see that the ceiling somehow didn't match with the roofline as viewed from outside. Inside there was a distinct – but not overpowering – smell of cow dung. Somehow that smell seemed natural to Susannah, almost pleasant even. At one end of the interior, behind the wooden fence that held the cows still for milking, bales of straw were neatly stacked right up to the ceiling. The adults had to squeeze to get behind the bales, although the children could almost saunter through, and there they found a steep and narrow wooden staircase – actually little more than a ladder – wedged in place. Susannah and

Jacob giggled to each other as they clambered up the stairs; it was as if the subterfuge was liberating.

The stairs led up to a hatch door, above which was a single long room. The room was split into two by a large blanket hung over a length of rope tied between the two longer walls. Those two rooms were to be home for the six of them – for how long Susannah had no idea. The rooms were not very high, but that was only a problem for Paul, who was almost six feet tall and could stand up straight only along the centre. The shed had a water supply – just a single cold tap – and easy access to the nearby slurry pond for emptying chamber pots.

Yes, Susannah thought, it was going to be exciting living here. It seemed such a fascinating place to make your home – and such a contrast to the noise and grime in Berlin or Amsterdam.

But it only took one night for the lustre of excitement to tarnish. It wasn't because Susannah didn't sleep well – she did, in spite of being cold and being able to smell that bucolic air that wafted up from below. But in the morning she and Jacob were told that they were never to leave the two rooms. It was also explained to them that it would get even colder when winter came, and that the sole source of heat would be bricks heated by Maria and Erik in the main farmhouse and carefully carried up to them in a leather bag.

Not having to go to school seemed a side effect to be celebrated – and for a few days it was. After that, spending all their time indoors became more of a penance, as if they were prisoners. They'd brought some books and packets of playing cards with them, but there were only so many times Susannah could read the same books and get excited, and only so many times she could play cards without getting bored. She complained to Mother, who answered that she understood, that at her age she should have been making friends, developing her mind with education, even learning a little about boys. But Mother looked weary and haggard whenever she spoke like this, as if there was a great weight on her shoulders, so Susannah decided she would have to try to keep her frustrations to herself.

However, Mother must have talked to Maria and Erik, because things improved a week later; they started bringing up a modest but regular supply of new books and newspapers – and Susannah tried to read every single word of every single one of them.

Susannah and Jacob and their parents slept on a blanket, which lay on a large bed of musty hay strewn over the wooden floorboards, while Uncle Paul and Aunt Helena slept on a slightly smaller version in the other 'room' on the other side of the dividing blanket.

The food was fresh and good in quality if not in variety. It was usually bread and vegetables, occasionally meat and cheese. Throughout the icy winter months the highlight of the week was the Sunday hot meal. Fresh milk, so creamy it almost had to be chewed, was always plentiful, and served hot every day in winter. But whatever food was delivered, Susannah's parents told her and Jacob never to complain or be ungrateful, and that they should feel lucky to have such good friends as Maria and Erik. Rules about keeping to kosher food and observing Jewish celebrations were relaxed out of necessity but – as Uncle Paul kept reminding them all – not forgotten.

Susannah and Jacob played and fought and argued as much as they always had, but it was always forgotten within the hour and they started playing again. Likewise the seasons visited and left just as they always had. Cold winters that felt even colder in a draughty stone shed seemed to pass more quickly than the bright spring and summer months. At least whenever Susannah left the building in winter the flatland breeze told her to seek shelter, but when she stepped outside in the warmer months it took every ounce of her willpower to resist the temptation to chase butterflies through the hazy fields, or bury her feet in the mess of leaves blowing from the nearby cluster of trees, or simply bask in the sunshine.

That would also have been a way to escape from the arguments. By the time the farmhouse had been Susannah's home for almost two years she was approaching her fifteenth birthday, and her emotions were maturing along with her body. She was becoming less interested in playing with her brother and more interested in the relationships between the four adults she was living with. Sometimes, instead of reading, she pretended to sleep and listened closely to what was happening between them, and started understanding the nuances of their behaviour. Apart from Father's and Paul's political disagreements she'd never really witnessed an argument between any of them, but now there always seemed to be two people out of Mother, Father, Paul and Helena who snapped at each other, or who didn't talk to each other at all – sometimes for days on end. It never seemed to be about anything important, and was always started by someone complaining about who had eaten the last slice of bread, or who had woken who up in the middle of the night, or who was taking too long reading the newspaper. And the worst thing was that the arguments never seemed to get resolved.

Whenever she asked Mother or Father about this – why they were always arguing – she was told that things were difficult, that this was bound to happen while they all lived together.

Once Father told her that when rats were trapped in a cage they would fight with one another, but then he told her to forget he'd said that.

CHAPTER FIFTEEN

It was early in 1944 that one of those rats at the isolated farmhouse started to bite.

There was another argument. Just like the rest, the seed of the disagreement seemed to be petty. Maria had brought some home-baked shortbread biscuits for a treat – perhaps, Susannah thought, she was trying to defuse any tension. Paul doled them out as if they were keys to heaven and he was an archangel. Everybody had two each and returned to their beds, but half an hour later Mother pulled the dividing blanket to the side and started looking at the boxes and clothes that were scattered around Paul and Helena.

'What is it?' Paul said, his eyes following hers.

'Biscuits.'

'What?'

'Where are the rest of the biscuits?'

Paul sighed and shook his head slowly. 'They're for tomorrow.'

'But where did you put them?'

'Does it matter?'

'But I want to check them,' Mother said, her face starting to redden.

'You want to . . . ?' Paul let out a forced laugh. 'You think we've had more without telling you?'

'I didn't say that.'

And then Father appeared behind her, standing up as straight as he could in the eaves of the building, and put a hand on her shoulder. 'Let's calm down,' he said.

'Don't speak to me like that,' she replied, her voice now trembling. 'You're supposed to be on my side.'

Then a voice said, 'There are no sides here.' It was Helena, who sat up on the makeshift mattress next to her husband.

'I wasn't talking to you,' Mother said. 'Have you had any more biscuits?'

'Paul,' Father said. 'Can't you just show her the biscuits so she can see you haven't had any?'

Paul's face creased up. 'You don't believe your own brother?'

'It's not that.'

And so it went on. Within minutes the argument came to a head when Mother knelt down and started rifling through Paul's and Helena's few personal possessions. Father held her arms back, pulling her to her feet, but she wrenched them away. She shouted at him and struck out, hitting his chest and making him take a step back.

'Don't touch me!' she hissed. 'I'm *sick* of this.'

'And you think you're the only one?' Paul said.

Mother looked around for support but none came, which just seemed to increase her anger, which she now directed at her husband. 'How long do you expect us to live like this?' she said. 'Another year? Three? The rest of our lives? We're living like *animals*.' The last word was shouted, and on the other side of the room Jacob started to cry. Susannah could feel her heartbeat pulsing faster; she'd never seen Mother speak to Father like this before. She put an arm around Jacob and held him close.

'Listen,' Father said quietly. 'We have to—'

That was all he could say before Mother interrupted, her face now a deep red and her hair shaking as it was tossed from left to right. 'We have to do this, we have to do that, we can't do this, we can't do that. You never give anyone the *choice* to disagree. I read the papers too. There are camps set up for people like us – with proper beds instead of straw, with meals every day instead of once a week, even things to do and—'

'No!' Father said, silencing her. '*You must not believe it.* Can't you see? It's all propaganda. It's lies. I'm telling you we're better off here; it's not pleasant, but at least we're free.'

'Ha! *Free?*' Mother picked a cup up from the floor and threw it at Father. He turned a shoulder but it missed him anyway and smashed against the stone wall behind him.

Jacob let out a shriek and Susannah rocked him, for her own benefit as well as his.

Father looked to Paul and Helena for support, then turned back to Mother, now speaking in more gentle – even pleading – tones. 'Listen to me. Whatever else we do, we must stick together on this. And as long as three out of four think we should stay hidden . . .'

And as he paused for breath a lone voice, calm and reserved, said, 'I think she's right.'

It was Helena.

'What?' Paul said to her, almost roaring out the single word.

'It's not working out,' she replied. 'I've had enough too. She's right; this is no life for an animal, let alone a human.' She bolted for the trapdoor in the corner of the room.

'Are you mad?' Paul said.

'Yes,' Helena replied. 'Mad is exactly what I am. We're all mad, but some more so than others – too mad to see it. I can't go on like this.'

She lifted the door and disappeared down the staircase, the

wooden rungs thumping with her desperate footsteps. Paul went to follow but Mother stepped in front of him and said, 'Let her go.'

Paul went to speak, but no more than a grunt came through his clenched teeth. He turned away and slapped the stone wall.

After watching and listening to all of this Susannah's mouth was arid dry, and she dared not speak even if she could think of anything to say, so she just watched the three remaining adults pace and sit, then stand up and pace some more.

When Helena came back half an hour later the atmosphere had calmed down a little; there were no raised voices but the air was still hot and stuffy with tension.

'So?' Paul said, standing directly in front of her.

She pushed him to the side and lay down on the straw bedding. 'So what?'

'Where did you go? And did anyone see you?'

'I just wanted some fresh air,' she answered. 'I walked to the woods.'

'But did anybody see you?' Father asked, both men now crowding around her.

She turned onto her side and closed her eyes before answering. 'Of course not. There's nobody about. I don't know why we have to stay inside.'

It was stalemate: two adults against two adults. All four of them talked and eventually Paul and Father accepted that, in spite of the dangers of being seen outside, it might be worth the risk if it stopped them tearing each other apart. They got Erik to take them around the farm grounds on the tractor to check for other buildings or roads. There were none with a direct view of the milking shed, so they all agreed that instead of spending twenty-four hours a day inside they could now leave the building at dawn and dusk only, as long as they walked no more than a hundred paces away. Father told Susannah that she was now nearly an adult, and that he was trusting her to obey the rules and make sure Jacob did too whenever they went out together.

For Susannah and Jacob, after being cooped up for so long, those first days of freedom in the spring of 1944 felt like paradise. They were careful at first, venturing out only after taking a good look around the buildings and along the farm track, savouring the cooling breeze, the brushing of long grasses against their legs, and the songs of the birds that flitted in and out of the nearby wood.

But as Susannah was maturing, so she was starting to have her own mind on what she should do. For weeks there was not even a hint of another person, and so the one hundred paces rule became stretched to two hundred. What the adults didn't know wouldn't trouble them, Susannah reckoned, and before long she and Jacob were venturing even further. Then dawn became early morning, dusk late afternoon. They walked through fields of tall grasses, always ready to duck down and hide if they heard anything that resembled a voice or a vehicle. But there was nothing, and they always got back to the shed within an hour. Then one day they followed the birds into the shade of the wood. That was a shelter in itself, and no more than a few hundred paces from the shed, so they often went there to play hide-and-seek, climb trees or paddle in the slow-moving stream that lay at the far end.

It was during those months that Susannah noticed the change in Jacob; just as she was growing up, so was he. Although he was younger and smaller than her, he could now run as fast – and climb trees faster. There was also a swagger of sorts in his walk, and occasionally a deep croak to his voice. She wondered whether he, too, had the urge to do something more than play games in the woods – even to meet people. Still, anything was better than being stuck in the milking shed.

As the hot days of summer came, the stream became their favourite place to play – racing twigs along its length, or splashing each other and running off, or simply lying down in the shallow, clear waters that were as cool and refreshing as an iced dessert.

It was on one of those sultry afternoons, when Susannah and Jacob were busy splashing each other, that Jacob suddenly stopped responding to her playful flicks of water. He was frozen, the only movement or sound coming from the swirls of water around his bare feet. And he was staring at her – no, he was gazing *straight through her*. She turned. In the distance was a boy, perhaps Susannah's age, perhaps a little older. Like them, he was standing in the cooling stream, and for a wishful split second she thought it could be some sort of distorted reflection of Jacob.

But no.

Mother and Father had told them to avoid contact with people – no, more than that, to stay out of sight of *anyone* other than Maria and Erik. They had broken the rules by visiting the wood and the stream – but being seen was another level of rule-breaking entirely.

Should they run? Susannah felt short gasps blow from her mouth as she waited, fixed to the spot, not knowing what to do. The staring contest continued for what seemed like minutes. Then she gathered her strength and started walking towards the boy, that clear water splashing further up her legs the faster she walked.

Then she stumbled on a slippery stone and almost fell down.

When she looked up the boy was gone.

She scanned the scene, the glimmering stream stretching to the horizon contrasting with the dark shade of the clusters of trees on either side.

Had she dreamed him? Had it been a vision?

For a moment her throat felt dry, her breathing shallow like the stream she stood in. With a start she turned and began running back towards her brother, his eyes still transfixed.

'Hurry!' she cried out, pausing only to pick up their shoes as she ran into the wood. There were no more words, just puffs and pants and footfall breaking the forest silence as they raced back, matching each other stride for stride, to the safety of the milking shed.

There Susannah looked behind, then all around them, scanning the horizon, searching for any human form.

There was none.

'Don't tell,' she whispered to Jacob, who said nothing in reply but whose face almost bled with panic. 'And don't cry,' she said to him. 'It will be all right.'

She tried to give him a brief hug, and he resisted. 'I don't cry anymore,' he said.

She nodded to him and they took a few more minutes to recover their breath before going into the shed, behind the bales of straw, and up the staircase.

As they entered the room, Father gave them both a suspicious glance, and opened his mouth to speak.

Another voice got there first.

'Is there any bread left?'

Father turned to see Helena swiping the hanging blanket aside.

'No,' he said. 'I gave the last of it to Jacob for breakfast. I'm sorry if—'

'But it was supposed to last all of us until Saturday.'

'Well, there was only one slice left; we didn't think it was worth keeping . . .'

Susannah didn't hear the rest. Her mind was racing with thoughts of the forbidden contact she'd just experienced. She lay down on the thin straw mattress with Jacob and kept her eyes firmly shut, praying Father would not ask where they'd been.

She was lucky; the argument about the single slice of bread seemed more important.

Two days later, just as the sun's first rays were lighting up the single window in the room, Susannah was woken by the sound of engines – at least two of them – drawing to a halt outside.

She opened her eyes to a shadow in front of her face.

'Stay in bed,' Father whispered. 'Don't say a word.' Then to the side, 'You too, Jacob. Don't make any noise.'

Susannah shot a glance to Jacob and placed a single finger to her lips. He nodded back to her. *He understood.*

But Susannah wanted to speak; she wanted to say it a thousand times, to shout it and scream it into those evil corners of the room that were laughing at her.

She wanted to say how sorry she was.

But the more she stayed silent, the more she thought that perhaps – just perhaps – her fears were unfounded. Then they all heard shouts from outside piercing the calmness of dawn – angry, questioning ones echoing around the farmyard. And soon after that came the pleadings of Maria and Erik, then more shouts and some wailing.

Then came the drumming of boots on the sun-packed mud that lay between the buildings, and more shouting and barking. Susannah looked around to see the shadows of Mother, Father, Paul and Helena rising from their beds and standing up.

Susannah stayed down and turned away, covering her face with her hands. A few tears forced their way out into the stupid, stupid darkness, just as the barking and shouting started to come from directly underneath them.

After what seemed like split seconds of confusion in the half-light, the trapdoor was open and the room was flooded with light from lamps and echoed with triumphant cries. The soldiers pulled Father and Uncle Paul to one side, slamming them against the stone wall, and started asking questions. Father was angry. Mother was crying. Susannah couldn't remember anything about Helena or Jacob because it all seemed to happen so quickly.

The soldiers allowed them to pack one suitcase each before forcing them outside, where they were prodded with rifles towards one of the trucks. Between her tears Susannah saw Father and Paul being knocked over and kicked, and then everyone got on the truck.

This time Susannah didn't ask whether they were going back to Berlin; that place was now a distant memory that had faded to the palest of greys in her mind. She was more concerned with the smell of the dirty inferno that had been the farmhouse up until a few minutes before. And as it burned into the dawn, the sails of flame matching the yellow of the early-morning sun, the trucks sped off, and she wondered where the people she called Erik and Maria were now going live.

ᘐᕒᕒᕘ

In the ticket office of Hamburg railway station, Susannah stood up slowly, taking time to stretch her back up straight, and walked out onto the street.

She spent a few minutes studying the leaflet the woman had given her, occasionally looking up and around to get her bearings. After a moment she gave a satisfied sigh, then set off in the direction of the coach station.

But she didn't get there.

She walked fifty or so paces, then realized the moment had gone. After the effort of preparing herself to make plans for visiting the place – to make herself actually utter the words, 'I want to go to Bergen-Belsen' – she simply felt too tired.

She returned to her hotel to lie down. A painkiller might help too.

On the bed she let her body go limp and closed her eyes.

She opened them again only when the bright and ghostly shapes dressed in white that slowly drifted towards her became filthy skeletal figures who were pleading with her and reaching out to touch her.

CHAPTER SIXTEEN

A fter waking up with a start, Susannah let out a few tired gasps of relief, then threw her hand out to the bedside clock and checked the time.

Another hour wasted.

But hold on. She was in Hamburg for a week. That was plenty of time. Why the rush to visit Bergen-Belsen?

Perhaps the cab driver had been right. There were so many museums, theatres and other attractions in Hamburg. It would be a shame not to visit any of them. And, of course, there were the shops. She hadn't come for all of those, but now she was here she might as well take the opportunity to get a flavour of the place.

Yes, that would do. She was an old woman, after all. She should be taking things easy, avoiding stress. If she couldn't enjoy life now and do exactly as she pleased, then when could she? Why was she torturing herself by committing herself to visiting *that place*?

For the next few days – and thoroughly pleasant ones they were – she tried to ignore that question. She even considered flying straight back home on more than one occasion – that would have ignored it permanently. But the question stuck with her every bit as stubbornly as that bout of bronchitis had done the winter before last. The unpalatable fact was that she'd flown out here for a reason, and that although her clock was ticking she needed answers more than she needed time. She'd spent long enough milling around shops, art galleries and museums on her own. She needed to know more about The Lucky One. Much as she hated her memories, she knew the urge to find out what had happened all those years ago would haunt her to the bitter end if she did nothing.

The struggle in the back of her mind played itself out to a conclusion, and she eventually became sure of the right – the brave – thing to do. It was only on her final day in Hamburg, after a large breakfast to give her strength, that she took the short walk to the coach station and started looking for the coach that would take her to Bergen-Belsen – or, at least, to where it once had been.

Her search was interrupted by a short session of palpitations, and she had to find a bench and rest for a while. It must have been the walk tiring her ancient legs. Or the hearty breakfast unsettling her stomach. Yes, that was probably it.

When the palpitations had given up trying to frighten her off she got up and started looking again, checking the destinations on one or two coaches. Then she realized she didn't really know what she was looking for. The woman at the railway station had mentioned the new name for it but now she'd forgotten it. And then she found it – the coach with WAR MEMORIAL on its front.

Of course, that was it. That sounded so much more acceptable than EXTERMINATION CAMP. Who in their right minds would get on *that* coach?

Her throat almost choked with rising fear as she asked for the ticket, and for a moment she thought her legs would be too weak to carry her to the coach, but after leaning against a wall to gather strength – and with some help from the attendant – she hoisted herself on and settled into a window seat.

The coach set off and she realized that this was definitely, unequivocally, the point of no return. However, she couldn't stop her mind wandering back in time again, and the expectation of what she might find at the 'war memorial' provided the fuel.

༄

Susannah didn't know the name of the isolated farmhouse she'd been taken from at gunpoint all those years ago, but she never forgot the name of the place she'd been taken to.

The two soldiers that accompanied them in the truck sat in a silence that nobody dared challenge, and soon after leaving the farmhouse the vehicle stopped and one of the soldiers jumped out, the other still motionless, staring ahead, gripping his rifle. Ten minutes later the soldier returned, handed each of the two Mr Zuckermans a sheet of paper, and sat back down.

Only as the journey restarted was the silence broken. It was broken by a single word – the first word spoken since they'd left the burning farmhouse – and it was spoken by Uncle Paul. He read the paper and uttered that one word, quietly but clearly: '*Westerbork.*' Susannah recognized the word. It was one of the places Mother said were created for 'us'.

The rest of the journey was just as noisy and uncomfortable, and the two soldiers still said nothing. When they eventually came to a halt and the engine was switched off Susannah could hear faint shushing noises – noises that, under other circumstances, might have been calming. But the noises were interrupted by a few sharp shouts, and an occasional bark.

When they were ordered off the truck it was obvious where they were. The shushing noises were now louder, accompanied by huge plumes of steam reaching for the skies. Initially everything seemed utterly chaotic outside the railway station, but it was soon made clear to the six Zuckermans where they should go – a row of soldiers with rifles casually slung over their shoulders was funnelling them to a doorway at the station entrance. Father and Uncle Paul led the way, and when they reached the doorway they showed their papers to the soldiers who stood there.

There was no time for a toilet break or a rest; they were ordered straight through the station building and onto a platform towards a waiting train. In the confusion of barking dogs, soldiers shouting orders, and steam swirling all around them, Susannah got separated from the rest of her family. For a moment she panicked, gasping and struggling to reach them, but found herself being shoved through the open door of a carriage and was told to sit on the floor. At first she ignored the order and stepped back towards the platform, her eyes glaring out through the throng of figures in the mist. Then she yelped in pain as she felt her wrist being pulled and twisted. She fell down and cowered as she saw the butt of a rifle being readied to come down on top of her. But the guard moved on to the next passenger and she started frantically looking around, scanning the carriage she was in and then staring through the connecting door to the next one. Was that the top of Uncle Paul's head? At first she wasn't sure what she was seeing between the bustling bodies, but then she definitely saw Jacob, and then the others. *Oh yes!* They must have come in through the next door. She started scrabbling on all fours across to them. A pair of jackboots appeared in front of her eyes and a shout told her to get back. This time she did as she was told.

At least they were all on the same train.

She sat on the hard wooden floor, never taking her eyes off her family, and started massaging her wrist. *As soon as the guards left she would go across to them.* She watched them kick and shove the prisoners, occasionally feigning a blow with their rifles. Within minutes the carriage was full, and, as soon as the guards left, Susannah prepared to go.

But then a man sat down next to her. Although he looked young he had the unsteady physical actions of a much older man. 'There's no need to cry,' he said.

Susannah froze, torn between going to her family and talking to this man. She took a moment to study his appearance. His body was long and rangy, the sort that was naturally fit and sporty, and he had a long coat draped over him like a blanket. His lip was bulging and bloodied on one side, his cheekbones were scuffed and red, and one eye was badly bruised.

'I . . . I want to be with my mother,' she said, pointing into the other carriage.

The clank of the doors slamming shut made them turn their heads.

'It's all right,' the man said quietly. 'They won't be leaving the carriage.'

'But I'm scared,' she said. 'This Westerbork place . . .'

'Westerbork isn't so bad,' he said. Then he half smiled at her, the bulging side of his lips not moving.

Reassured a little by his smile, Susannah took a last look at her family before sitting down next to the man. 'Well . . . that's what I've read in the newspapers, but . . .'

'No, really,' he said. 'It's almost like a mini-town. It was especially built for Dutch and German Jews. The food and accommodation is reasonable, and it even has sports facilities.'

'Honestly?' Susannah said, frowning.

At that the man's friendly smile dropped, his jaw stiffened and his nostrils twitched. 'I'm nothing if not honest,' he said wearily.

'I'm sorry,' Susannah said. 'I've heard there's a doctor, even entertainment. But I . . . I don't know who to believe anymore.'

The displeasure left the man's face as quickly as it had arrived. He seemed to run his eyes over her face, causing her to look away for a second.

'I'm Franz,' he said, offering his hand.

'Susannah.' She shook it, feeling the warm crust of blood on its palm.

'What you probably heard is all true,' he continued. 'There are choirs and, yes, even a theatre of sorts that runs cabarets. And also a small hospital, a hairdresser's and a postal system.'

'So the newspapers didn't lie?'

'That depends,' Franz said. 'Did they mention the barbed-wire fences that surround this mini-town, and the dread people have of being transported away to places much worse?'

Susannah thought about that for a moment. Even with all the barbed wire and fencing, and with the fear of being moved on again, and even though she was sad to leave the farm and worried for Maria and Erik, a part of her looked forward to living at the camp, mixing with new people, joining in sports and entertainments. Perhaps there might even be some handsome boys there. At that moment she made up her mind that the first thing she would do when she got to Westerbork was go to the hairdresser's and have her hair styled like Greta Garbo.

As Susannah was picturing herself with a new hairstyle, the carriage jerked into motion with a screech, forcing her shoulder onto Franz's arm. He grimaced and pushed her away, holding his arm tenderly. A tear squeezed itself from his eye and ran over the dark-blue bruise below.

'I'm sorry,' Susannah said. 'Have you hurt yourself?'

His grimace turned in an instant to a resigned laugh. 'Yes,' he said with a smile. 'I've hurt myself. My ribs. My arm.'

'And your face.'

'Yes.'

'At least you'll be able to go to hospital at Westerbork.'

Franz opened his mouth to speak, then stopped, closed his eyes tightly shut and bowed his head.

'What is it?' Susannah said.

When he looked up at her his expression had changed again, to one of despair and fear. He shook his head and looked straight at her for a moment. She could see inflamed blood vessels in the white of his bad eye.

'Not for me.' He sniffed, and drew a hand across his eyes, collecting a little wetness along the way. 'There's something else the newspapers haven't told you.'

'What's that?' Susannah said. 'Is it something I need to know?'

'There are . . . there are special arrangements for . . .'

There Franz broke down and wept, covering his face with a hand that was brown with dirt but also streaked in dried blood. Susannah stayed silent until he spoke again, now with brittleness in his voice. 'You see, I was there for a year, then I escaped back to Amsterdam. They caught me, and now they'll class me as a "Convict Jew". I'll be put in a punishment block. I'll have to wear wooden clogs on my feet and a uniform instead of my own clothes. They'll shave all my hair off and give me the very bare minimum of food.'

'That's terrible,' Susannah said, reaching a hand out, holding his.

'But there's more,' he said, now crying freely and not caring to hide his face. 'We're the first to be selected for transportation.'

Susannah wondered whether that was so bad. Surely transportation meant simply being moved to another camp – possibly a better one. She'd read about other camps just like Westerbork. Some were bound to be better, weren't they?

Just then the man pulled his knees up and buried his face between them.

Susannah placed a hand, tenderly, on his shoulder and said, 'I'm so sorry.'

He stopped crying and looked up for a moment. And then Susannah saw the tautness in his skin, the whiteness of his teeth, but mostly the innocence in his eyes. She saw that it could well have been Jacob in a few years. This was no man, merely a boy, perhaps a year or two older than her. She placed an arm around his shoulder. He started to cry again, then turned to her and hugged her. She let him, and held onto him for the rest of the journey.

Perhaps getting her hair styled like Greta Garbo wasn't quite so important after all.

CHAPTER SEVENTEEN

The train slowed down and Susannah saw the signs for Westerbork flash past the opposite window. She would very soon find out the reality of her new home – whether it really did have those facilities. As they drew to a halt she gave Franz a tight-lipped smile and stood up. She told him she had to be with her family now, and made her way over to them. Yes, now she had to think of herself and her own family – of her own kind. Westerbork would be good. Not free, but good.

Through the window she saw more soldiers holding guns and more barking dogs. She was scared, but strangely not as much as she thought she would be – perhaps she was getting used to all this moving around.

They were all ordered off the train, and although there were more orders, Susannah didn't listen; she didn't need to, because for her and the rest it was simply a case of following the herd. Again, steam billowed all around them, heightening her senses, as if something hidden within it was sniffing them out or hunting them down.

Yes, she felt a little less scared, but somehow different too. Thinking of her own kind; following the herd; being hunted down. Yes, that was it: she was starting to feel like an animal of some sort.

The thought made her shiver.

They all queued at the entrance, with guards ever watchful but at the same time never looking directly at them. Susannah stayed close to her father, just like her mother and Jacob did, with Paul and Helena not too far behind. She looked over to the camp itself, her eyes searching for the hospital, the recreation buildings, and especially the hairdresser's.

She was still looking when they reached the front of the queue. A wide desk separated them from a uniformed officer with a ream of papers in front of him. Susannah's father passed the sheet of paper to the officer, who studied it for a second. Then he checked his own lists and his soulless, efficient eyes glanced at the four of them in turn. The corner of his mouth flicked upwards and he gave an almost imperceptible shrug.

He handed the papers back to Father and said only five words: 'Hiding. Convict Jews. Punishment block.'

'Punishment?' Susannah's father asked, slightly shocked, looking to the sides as if requesting a second opinion. A guard, rifle gripped in fidgety fingers, stepped in front of him, their faces inches apart.

'All right, all right,' Susannah's father said, holding both hands up and taking a step back.

Susannah could remember little else of that introduction to Westerbork.

But she could recollect the disappointment in her heart on realizing that, for her, there was to be no theatre or sports. And also that within two hours the hair she dreamed of being styled like Greta Garbo's lay in worthless clumps on the dusty earth.

By the middle of summer 1944 Susannah had served two months at Westerbork, all of it in the punishment block. Her hair – shaved back to the skull on her first day – had now started to grow back. It seemed as if she was spending every waking hour in the workroom taking apart old batteries, which made her hands weak and left them covered in cuts and patches of skin irritated by the chemicals.

Like all her fellow inmates, Susannah had blisters and calluses on her feet from the wooden clogs they were made to wear, and her skin had started to turn pale and scaly from the poor diet. She'd lost some body weight – but not as much as Mother and Father, who always gave some of their food to their children. All of their clothes were very dirty by now.

Animals? They were even starting to smell like them now.

The saving grace was that they were allowed to stay together at night, all four of them, and more importantly for Susannah they were allowed to talk during the working day as much as they wanted. After the relative solitude of the last few years she thought it almost worth the physical pain to be able to strike up conversations with people outside her family, and she gained something of a reputation for chatting.

It was during one of those chats with fellow inmates that she learned about the Tuesday transportations – the weekly round-up of inmates who were taken away to other camps. Nobody seemed to know what these other camps were like, but on one occasion an elderly gentleman told her, his whole face quivering with fear, that they were much more severe than Westerbork. When she asked him how he knew this, his mouth clamped shut, his head bowed, and he started prising apart the battery in his hand with the vigour of a man thirty years younger. Susannah didn't ask further, but wondered whether it was possible for a camp to be worse than this one.

She made a mental note to ask him again but never got the chance. Just after dawn on the next Tuesday – the day inmates feared as much as death itself – as they were preparing to drag their weary bodies to the workroom, Susannah, Jacob, Mother and Father were told to gather their possessions.

They were leaving.

By this time their belongings were little more than the dirty, smelly clothes they stood up in. Mother kept a spare set for each of them, but they were hardly much cleaner. Father kept a packet of playing cards and two books.

They all had their heads shaved again, and were ordered onto a train and told they were going to a better camp – either Bergen-Belsen or Auschwitz-Birkenau. Susannah asked Father how they decided. He replied that they probably tossed a coin.

Uncle Paul and Aunt Helena didn't go with them. Susannah didn't know whether they were going to one of the same two camps on a later train or staying at Westerbork – and nobody dared ask. Only then, as she sat with her family on the bare wooden floor of the carriage, did Susannah realize how much she was going to miss them. She cried a lot on the journey, as did Mother. Even Jacob could disguise his feelings only for so long, eventually burying his head in the crook of his arm. Father didn't cry, but he didn't utter a word for the whole journey either.

PART THREE
Terror Through the Fog

CHAPTER EIGHTEEN

The coach journey from Hamburg to the Bergen-Belsen Memorial took a little more than an hour. At first Susannah enjoyed the scenery – mostly wide expanses of farmland. And yet there was something that unsettled her. She looked at the other passengers; it was no party atmosphere – that was for sure – but they all seemed to be enjoying the views of the pleasant countryside too.

Only towards the end of the journey did Susannah work out why she wasn't enjoying it quite as much as the other passengers seemed to be; unlike just about everything else, the views out onto the patchwork fields were much like they'd been all those years ago when she'd seen them through the carriage window. In fact, what she saw was far too similar for comfort, and she felt a seed of panic fall into her mind.

However, it was only when the coach turned onto the minor road leading to the memorial itself that her palpitations returned. Again, the scenery was too familiar; the road seemed to dive into a forest, which, Susannah felt, signified that her moment of reckoning had come. She would very soon have to step off the coach and face that place – and her worst fears – once more.

But what would actually be there? What was left of the place? More importantly, how would she react? Would she find what she was looking for, whatever that was? Or would the blind panic take over like a devil sitting on her chest, holding her down?

The coach pulled into the car park and the heavy scrunch of its tyres on the gravel pulled her away from her fears for a few seconds. She looked around – the place was so nondescript it could have been any car park in the world.

Perhaps that was the idea.

She stayed in her seat and took some time to take a few deep, calming breaths while everyone else got off. She looked through the coach window to the edge of the car park.

Was this really the same place?

It didn't look familiar apart from the surrounding pine trees; perhaps there had been a mistake. Then the driver walked along the aisle and said something in German, pointing to the door. Susannah's German was encrusted in sixty years of rust, but she understood the words 'we are here'. She took one last deep gulp of air, got to her feet, and slowly headed in that direction. At the door she gripped her handbag tightly with one hand and the handrail with the other. She wondered why they had to make these steps so large, and then made one final effort to set her foot down onto the gravel.

It was then that the invigorating fragrance of pine hit her and transported her back to a time when that smell had been the smell of hope and horror all at once.

❧

Her foot is not that of a woman in her closing years who has spent most of her life in civilized North Carolina, but that of a fifteen-year-old girl who was once full of hope and optimism but is starting to feel numb and worthless. She isn't getting off a coach in a gravel car park but alighting a train – a train at Bergen-Belsen camp station.

She smells fresh pine but that delight is soon forgotten. Wherever she looks a fog of steam shrouds the view. Half-hidden dogs bark louder than ever. The guards don't need to shout – but they do, as if it's the only way they can possibly communicate.

All occupants of the train get off with the same bewildered, frightened expressions, and they automatically drift to the gates of the camp as if accepting of their destiny. There are wire fences around the perimeter with lookout towers at intervals. Susannah looks up to one and can make out an armed guard silhouetted against the blue sky beyond. Barbed wire appears to be everywhere – at the top of the fence, at the base of the fence, and in parts making up the fence. As Susannah gets closer a guard shouts out the word 'Electric!' and she jumps, then quickly moves back to her family.

But the shouting doesn't stop – not for a moment. The guards holler and point in the direction the prisoners are moving anyway, as if they're shouting for the sake of it. Or for enjoyment. Even the dogs seem to relish the undercurrent of terror they create.

Susannah sees a scene reminiscent of a cattle market, bodies being shoved and prodded in whatever direction the farmers desire, across a muddy farmyard, penned in by electrified fences, with only the most rudimentary of facilities. But here the bodies do not belong to rotund animals, but scrawny humans, and the 'farmers' control their 'livestock' with guns and aggressive dogs and very real threats of using both. Susannah realizes quite quickly that there will be no facilities here like there were at Westerbork.

Father calls Mother, Jacob and Susannah in close and they join the queue, which leads them into the jaws of another building and ends at another desk.

The man behind the desk snatches the papers from Father,

spends only a few seconds reading them, then says, 'Star Camp,' and waves them away. A guard leads them to another room and gives each of them two pieces of cloth – one a yellow star badge and one a number. He tells them to sew these into their clothing, and they do as they're told. The guard notes down the numbers and tells them never to remove them under any circumstances. Then he leads them out of the building. He doesn't look at them or say anything else, but points to a gate and shoves Father towards it with his rifle.

Father leads them across to the gate, where they wait with others, standing in the soft mud, moving from foot to foot to dull the ache in their legs. At one point Susannah goes to sit, but Father tells her not to, and after about an hour they're all let in. Inside, they stumble over yet more rutted muddy earth to join another queue, and again they wait. What seems like another hour passes. Susannah's feet hurt to the bone, her legs threaten to buckle due to weakness, her back aches. She can tell others feel the same by the way they stand. A woman goes to sit on the floor, but a guard motions to strike her with the butt of his rifle and she gets back up.

Jacob looks up to Susannah, his face obviously straining to hold back the tears. She puts an arm around his shoulder and squeezes gently. As a glum smile starts to appear on his face he gets pulled away by a guard. Susannah holds onto him for a few seconds and shouts, 'No!' – but then a rifle is aimed directly at her and she yelps and releases him.

She looks to Mother for help but then notices Father being shoved away at gunpoint too. She runs towards him but Mother gets to her before the guards do, and tells her they're just taking them away to the men's cabins.

'But when will we see them again?' Susannah calls out.

'I don't know,' Mother says, holding her close while watching Father and Jacob leave, the alarm etched on her face too. 'I just don't know.' She turns to another guard and asks whether the males and females mix during the day. He says, 'Of course,' and then laughs as he turns away and tells the women to follow.

After a short walk the guard points to their cabin and then to their toilet block before leaving. Susannah and her mother are both desperate to relieve themselves after their journey and head for the toilet block, rushing inside together. Then it becomes difficult; they both squeeze their noses shut to the stench that seeks to overpower and humiliate them. The building houses long wooden benches on either side, with large holes drilled along their lengths at intervals of about two feet. The raw sewage piles up underneath in two trenches. There's no paper, but more importantly for Susannah and her mother, there's no privacy. Mother steps back out, telling Susannah to go first, then she will go afterwards.

Susannah relieves herself, then comes out to let Mother go in. Their faces are both emotionless but, as soon as Mother leaves, Susannah is on her own, and her face breaks, letting the tears dribble out.

Then she hears a childlike voice from behind her.

'Are you new here?'

She turns to see a young girl, much smaller than herself. She has hair flecked with dirt, a body that is plumper than it's polite to mention, and spindly legs. She bobs up and down with enthusiasm, and Susannah thinks she looks like a wagtail.

Susannah says nothing at first, then wipes her nose and sniffs a few of the tears back. 'How do you know I'm new?'

'Because I know everyone around here and I haven't seen you before.'

'Are you German?' Susannah asks.

The girl shakes her head. 'I'm from Groningen, in the Netherlands, but my parents were from Frankfurt so I speak good German.' Then she looks to the top of Susannah's head and giggles, causing Susannah to instinctively cover her prickly close-shaven scalp with her hands.

'Why are you laughing?' Susannah says. 'I look horrible.'

'No. You look funny.' The girl clamps a hand over her mouth and her shoulders rise up as she suppresses more laughter. Then, slowly, her joy dissolves and she straightens her face. 'I'm sorry,' she says. 'But hair isn't important. And it will grow back before the cold months come.' She lifts the sleeve of her blouse. 'This will never go away.'

Susannah looks closely and sees a long number tattooed onto the tender flesh on the inside of the girl's forearm. 'That's terrible. Doesn't it hurt?'

The girl shakes her head. 'Not anymore. I don't like it but I don't really care.' Her eyes have a fresh sparkle that Susannah has not seen for many years. It's like the eyes are happy, even though they have no right to be.

'Look,' Susannah says, showing her arms. 'My family, we didn't get those.'

'Not everybody does. Some have it on their chests, most on their arms. Some don't have it at all. It's probably because you're German. They make them sew the number into their clothing instead.'

Susannah shows her the number on her blouse but she prefers to glance at Susannah's head again and have another giggle. Susannah wonders how another prisoner – a girl at that – can be so cruel about shaven heads and numbers branded on flesh like animals. But then she notices that sparkle again and splutters out a small laugh herself. She realizes how long it's been since that's happened; it's a release of sorts, and it makes her belly feel warm.

'I'm Ester,' the young girl says. 'I was twelve last month.'

Susannah finds that difficult to believe because she's so small, but nods and likewise introduces herself.

Then Mother comes out of the toilet block.

'I'll see you later, *Susannah*,' Ester says, and scampers away.

Mother smiles to Susannah, then nods towards the cabin and they go over to it, stepping inside tentatively, as if it's a dark cave.

Inside there is indeed very little light, and also the air is heavy with a stale odour – the smell of sickness. The room is crammed full of bunk beds, but also people lie on the floor. A few eyes dart in her direction, but there are no greetings. For the second time in a few minutes Susannah tries not to breathe through her nose, so says nothing and concentrates on suppressing her nausea.

Their feet pick their way between the bodies until they find a spare bed. Then she talks, whispering for fear of waking the women and girls lying all around them. 'Mother,' she says, 'I don't want to stay here.'

Mother sighs. 'But . . . you have to.'

'I mean, I just *can't*.'

Mother sits down. 'Susannah. Listen. This isn't like Westerbork. I don't see any choices. So please don't make an example of yourself by saying anything out of turn.'

'But . . .' Susannah wants to say she can't bear the idea of sleeping for one night in here no matter what the punishment might be, but she bows her head and sits down next to her mother.

Mother puts an arm around her and gives her the briefest of embraces. 'Always remember what your father tells us all,' she says. 'One day the country will come to its senses, all of this will be over, and we can return to Berlin.'

Susannah looks at the rough wooden floor and twirls the tip of her shoe across it. Mother talks some more, but Susannah has already dragged her mind away. She doesn't focus on her mother's well-meaning words, or the other women in the cabin, or the tears that are running down her cheeks – but instead stares at the cabin door. Then she jumps off the bed and runs out through the door, almost tripping over the bundles that lie on the floor. Outside she sees Ester, but doesn't want to talk to stupid, stupid Ester. She turns and runs around to the back of the cabin, then kicks the wooden panels at the bottom. She collapses on the floor and starts weeping uncontrollably.

She tells herself she would rather die than live here.

A few minutes later, when the salty stream has run dry, Susannah wipes her face and exhales the last whimper of her cry. She tries to prepare herself mentally for doing what she knows she has to do – go back into the cabin – and looks to the side. The familiar figure of Ester is there, in a coy pose, playing with her hands.

'I'm sorry, Susannah,' she says.

Susannah turns her head away.

'Do you want to be alone?' Ester says.

Neither of the girls speaks for a few minutes. Then Ester skips over and sits down next to Susannah. 'Do you want me to tell you about the camp?' she says.

'I hate the camp,' Susannah says.

'It's a home of sorts.'

Susannah looks at Ester, sees that effervescence in her eyes again, and shrugs. 'It's the only home I have,' she says. 'So I suppose I need to know about it.'

They talk – or rather, Ester talks.

Ester says her parents are in another camp, so she never sees them. Susannah finds out that there are, in fact, many separate camps within the Bergen-Belsen complex, each separated by more fences and more barbed wire. She's at least relieved to find out that the guard was telling the truth – that Father and Jacob will be close by in the same camp, sleeping in separate accommodation but able to meet Susannah and Mother every day. Ester tells her about work, food, roll-call, and more.

They talk for half an hour, then Susannah says she has to return to her mother, who will be worried. Reluctantly she trudges back to her cabin, and to Mother.

When she gets there Mother sits her down and says, 'I didn't come after you. I'm sorry. But I didn't know what more I could say. It's difficult for everyone else too, Susannah. You're starting to grow up, you must realize these things. You must accept what is happening.'

Susannah already has. The place is starting to feel like home already. She wonders whether that's a good thing.

CHAPTER NINETEEN

It only takes a few weeks for the process to complete. As far as Susannah is concerned the Star Camp of Bergen-Belsen is now home.

She gets used to the stench that once made her feel nauseous – there seem to be simply too many people and hence too many dirty, smelly clothes. A few women are incontinent with dysentery. The cabin is made of wooden planks, with large gaps between them. This is good now, giving some ventilation – the smell would be unbearable otherwise. Susannah says nothing to Mother, but worries what it will be like when it gets colder. For now all prisoners have a single blanket each, but Susannah thinks that perhaps in the winter months someone brings in hot bricks to provide heat, like they did in the milking shed.

And with Ester's help, day by rotten day, she gets used to camp life. First thing in the morning is roll-call. Whether it's wet or dry, cold or warm, all prisoners must quickly put their clothes on, run out into the courtyard and line up in the correct order to be counted. Nobody is allowed to move, and if there's a discrepancy the counting starts all over again. Sometimes this takes hours. On some days, during this roll-call, horses pull carts right in front of them. The carts are full of dead bodies. Some have their necks twisted at unnatural angles, some have dark red streaks across their torsos. All of them, like the living, are very thin. The guards laugh at the corpses and strike them with whips. They proudly announce at the top of their voices that these are the bodies of prisoners who have tried to escape, or who have disobeyed orders, or who have tried to organize rebellions. Occasionally there are bodies hanging from the fence throughout the roll-call; these are the ones who have flung themselves onto the electrified fences rather than live.

The first time the bodies were exhibited Susannah felt sick, and managed to stay standing only by calling on every last ounce of her willpower. The second time was the same, the third a little easier. Now, weeks later, all she can think is that she's glad Mother and Father made her do as she was told.

At one corner of the camp is a large pool, which is used for washing clothes. Susannah helps Mother with the washing because it's close to the perimeter fence, which is close to the pine trees that smell clean with an almost citrus-like freshness. It's a welcome change from the vile smell of the cabins. She always wants to stay longer, but as soon as a guard approaches they speed up their washing and leave.

All prisoners – apart from the younger children – have to work for most of the day, and for this they get extra food. For most of the women that means the shoe tent, where worn-out shoes from all over Germany are brought and piled into a mountain as high as the cabins. The job of the prisoners is to undo the stitching of the shoes and separate the materials. Leather, fabric, waste. Leather, fabric, waste. Leather, fabric, waste. There are tools to do this, and because some of the tools are sharp there are always armed guards near the tables they work on. Father and Jacob often carry out heavy labour, chopping wood and making more cabins, but also sometimes work in the shoe tent. Mother usually works in the kitchens, peeling vegetables and making bread and soup.

After Susannah's first few days at work her hands are red, blistered and painful, but calluses soon form where once there was tender skin. The pain in her knuckle joints leaves after a few weeks too, and she quickly becomes skilled at the job.

And working means extra food. The prisoners spend more time talking about food than actually eating. The standard rations are as degrading as the sanitation. For breakfast they get a kind of weak coffee drink with a chunk of bread. For lunch they have another chunk of bread and a bowl of watery soup made from root vegetables – usually potato or turnip – and supper is the same as breakfast. Workers get an extra chunk of bread each day. There's no other food. There are rumours that some prisoners get meat that's stamped 'not for human consumption'. Very soon Susannah dreams of such a treat, as all four of her family lose even more weight. The time after the last meal of the day is the only time Susannah looks forward to – the mixing time when the whole family can be together. However, it's always a long time coming and over as quickly as a child's birthday.

A regular group of guards is allotted to Susannah's section of the camp. The guards are dangerous and Susannah is repeatedly told not to look any of them in the eye unless being addressed. Three of them seem to cover most of the shifts at the shoe tent; Susannah gets to know all three by name.

Müller is one of the few female guards. She's stout with bulbous facial features, a blank stare and a permanently downturned mouth. She walks and stands with her shoulders back and her head high. She looks more like a man than a woman, the only different feature apart from her chest being long blonde hair tied at the back.

Jung shows himself to be dangerous every day. He looks you in the eye and smiles frequently, which makes him seem approachable and friendly, but on more than one occasion Susannah has seen him beat women as well as men for simply saying the wrong thing.

The third regular guard is Keller, apparently new, with young, taut skin. Susannah is very wary because appearances – as in Jung's case – can be deceptive. Keller is just a little more unkempt than the others – no, not unkempt, that isn't allowed. But he never has his tie completely straight, has tufts of hair poking out at various angles from under his cap, and has frequently been scolded by Jung for having scuff marks on his boots or stains on his jacket. Out of all the guards Susannah dislikes Keller the least because he somehow seems more human, less like a machine. Although Susannah doesn't understand the ranks of the SS, she knows from the way the three interact that as well as being the youngest and newest, Keller is also the lowest in rank.

Susannah has learned very quickly from what she sees and from talks with others in the cabin to keep a low profile.

One day, while the families are mixing, she also finds out that anyone who is different tends to get taken away. They are alerted by a commotion outside the cabin and, one by one, carefully venture out to see what has happened.

A man is arguing with Jung. He says that three days ago a doctor came to visit his son, who is deaf. He says the doctor told him he would take the boy away to cure him of his deafness. But he hasn't returned. The man is shouting at Jung, saying he wants to see the Kommandant to find out what happened to his son. At first Jung simply smiles, but the man continues and so Jung raises his voice and tells him in an understated monotone to be silent. The man carries on complaining about his son. Jung strikes him across the face with the butt of his rifle. The man's head gets sharply twisted to the side and he cries out in pain, but then looks at Jung with wildness in his eyes and starts shouting again. Jung, his face now starting to redden, adjusts his hold on the rifle and strikes the man more strongly. He falls to the ground and curls up, covering his head with his arms. Now he's quiet and still but Jung hits him again and again. Then Müller rushes over and strikes the prostrate figure with her rifle too. Together they continue to smash their rifle butts down onto the man's head, back and legs. The man is still and quiet, but five or ten more blows come before the guards stop and look up to the crowd. Every prisoner who catches a glare immediately turns, and the onlookers all shuffle away to their cabins. The last thing Susannah notices before she pulls her head back into the cabin is Keller on the far side of the courtyard, looking across to the incident but standing still.

The next day Susannah sets off for the shoe tent, but halts abruptly as she sees the man who was beaten. She sees but can hardly bear to look; his clothes are coated in a shell of mud, he has blood all over his hands, and he walks with the heaviest of limps, dragging one leg behind him. She trembles at the sight and hurries as far away as she can – towards the perimeter fence, or as close to it as she dares. She takes a moment, holding her head in her hands, to compose herself, before continuing on to the shoe tent.

As she approaches it she hears a familiar voice from behind her.

'I forgot to tell you about that,' it says.

Susannah turns. 'Ester. I . . . I was . . .'

'It's horrible, I know.'

'You know what happened?'

'To Mr Vega's son? Of course I do. There's a lot of that.'

'A lot of what?'

Ester pauses, then shrugs before speaking. 'A lot of . . . people who are different being taken away. I mean, I don't know why – I don't know what they do with them, but they never bring them back.'

'What do you mean, *different?*'

'Just unusual. A few weeks ago new people arrived in my cabin. A woman had twin girls. The doctor came to visit them, and the next day the twins were gone.'

'Gone where?'

Ester shrugs.

'I don't know how much I can take of this,' Susannah says, shaking her head. 'Every day, when I think I'm getting used to it, something else horrible happens, and I feel I . . . I want to . . .'

'You must keep hoping,' Ester says, now holding Susannah's arm and shaking it. 'You must do your best to survive and hope that things will get better eventually. Otherwise there's nothing – no point in living.'

'If . . . if you say so.'

Now Ester squeezes Susannah's hand. 'Don't you want to leave here?' she says.

'Of course I do. Doesn't everyone?'

'Then don't give up.' Ester tilts her head in a carefree way and looks to the greying sky beyond the lookout tower. 'You have to think of your dream and hold onto it with all your strength no matter what happens.'

'I can't dream,' Susannah says, her face feeling slack. 'I can't see any way out of here.'

Ester shakes Susannah's arm again, imploring her. 'You must have a dream. What about when you're free? Think of what you'll do when you leave here.'

'When I leave here I'll go home to Berlin,' Susannah says. 'All of us together. My father has promised it.'

'Then that's exactly what will happen,' Ester says. She speaks slowly, and Susannah notices – and is jealous of – her wide-mouthed smile, bright eyes and hair almost down to her neck.

Susannah lets out a sigh, then starts walking again. Ester follows, with her usual mixture of hopping and skipping.

'So, what about *your* parents?' Susannah says. 'Will they take you back to the Netherlands?'

For a few moments Ester's skipping gait falters, the smile falls away, the eyes drop to the muddy earth. Then she nods, says, 'Of course,' and runs away, leaving Susannah to face the shoe tent.

Susannah never hears Mr Vega speak again. And his son is never seen again.

CHAPTER TWENTY

As the coach drove off Susannah took a few steps towards the gates of the Bergen-Belsen Memorial.

After all these years there was little structure remaining of the original site apart from the entrance gate. And it looked as if nature had covered and smothered everything that hadn't been torn down. Creeping ivy, climbing brambles and a sprawling lawn of moss had all played their part in trying to bury the place in a green and peaceful grave.

The other tourists spent a few minutes taking photographs, then headed straight for the Visitor Centre, but Susannah stayed at the gate, looking up, and was soon alone.

And in a flash the clear blue sky was hidden by clouds of hot ash swirling and billowing up above the trees, the perimeter once more formed a barbed-wire cage, and she could hear little over the drone of military vehicles. Then she heard boots approaching behind her.

'Excuse me?'

The accent startled her.

'Are you okay?'

The man was dressed in chinos and an open-necked shirt. His smile kept with the smart-casual theme.

Casual is good, Susannah thought. 'Yes, thank you,' she said. 'I was just . . . going in, just steadying myself.'

'You're American, yes?'

She looked once more to the gates. 'I guess I am. Do you work here?'

'Yes. In the Visitor Centre.'

She pointed beyond the gates to the path as wide as a street. 'Perhaps you can tell me where all the buildings are?'

'Buildings? No, there are no buildings. They were all burned by the British to get rid of the typhus.'

'Oh.'

'I know there's not much here, but please, go to the Visitor Centre, listen to the talks and see the displays in there. Once you've done that it's a little easier to take a walk through the site and . . . well, use your imagination.'

She nodded and smiled politely. 'Yes, thank you. I think I might manage to do that.'

She followed the man, and when she entered the Visitor Centre a talk was under way, an elderly man telling a group of twenty or thirty people, including children, of the events that took place in times Susannah had long ago forced into the darkest corners of her mind.

Behind the speaker pictures of a slide show faded in and out. There were photographs of the camp as it had been during the war, with wooden cabins in regimented formation. There were also thousands of faces, all gaunt and pleading to the camera, all belonging to people now long, long gone. And Susannah just knew that every single one of them once had dreams of returning to their homes and their normal lives, just as she once did.

She took a seat in the back row and started listening to the speaker talk of how many men were held in the camp, how many men died, how the men suffered.

'Excuse me?' she heard herself ask in a confident but fractured tone. 'But weren't there women prisoners here too?'

'Oh yes,' the speaker replied. 'A lot of them; there was even a special women's camp.'

'Why did they imprison women?' a young girl at the front asked.

'Well, because they were Jewish,' the speaker replied.

And it was then that Susannah started to remember events with a clarity that made her pulse race. Uneasy, almost in tears, she went to stand, but stopped as the girl spoke again.

'Were they treated the same as the men?'

The speaker nodded slowly. 'I . . . I guess so. Except, of course . . .' He blushed, glancing to the children and lowering his voice. 'It's difficult to explain. The female prisoners, they had, shall we say, other uses to the guards.'

'You mean, as informants?' the girl asked.

'Okay, Lisa,' the woman sitting next to the girl said. 'Enough questions.'

'No, no,' the speaker said. 'That's quite all right. The girl is correct. Some of the younger women were very popular with the guards, and those who became, shall we say, good friends with the male guards went on to become informants, telling them which prisoners were causing difficulties, perhaps those who were likely to lead any rebellion or plan an escape.'

'You mean they were on the side of the Nazis?' the girl asked.

'No,' he said firmly, then hummed a pause. 'Well . . . in what they did, possibly. But never in what they thought. Never.'

'So why would they do that?'

An awkward, sickly smile grew on the speaker's face. 'Because it spared them,' he said.

Susannah now stood, a hand went to cover her face, and she shuffled away, trembling.

At the door a member of staff placed a consoling hand on her shoulder. 'Are you okay, madam?'

Susannah kept her head down and gave a single, almost imperceptible nod.

'I know it's hard sometimes. Bad memories are common around here. Your feelings are nothing to be ashamed of. You've been here before, yes?'

She shook her head and wiped the dribbles from the end of her nose. 'No,' she said firmly. 'Not me. Never. But thank you.'

She stumbled out into the daylight and sat on a bench for a while, but could not settle. She got up and soon found herself blindly meandering along the main paths, beneath the pines that towered overhead.

The man conducting the talk had been right. Apart from the Visitor Centre there were hardly any buildings, just wide open spaces covered in that spreading ivy and bramble, and also with heather and wild flowers sporadically breaking through the long grass. It could have been a nature reserve.

Almost.

CHAPTER TWENTY-ONE

It's now late 1944. With summer no more than a warm memory, cold winds have started to whip through the cabins at Bergen-Belsen. Prisoners huddle together for warmth, as many in a bed as will fit.

But there are the occasional mild days too, when the wind dies down and prisoners venture out of their cabins and stand facing the sun, as if worshipping it. Their thin and wrinkled skin feels a slight burn. It's a welcome burn.

A lot of prisoners have now stopped working in the shoe tent through illness, meaning they get smaller rations. But Susannah still works there, even though the extra chunk of bread hardly justifies the effort. And because there are now fewer workers, there is usually only one guard on duty. Susannah senses a change of mood in the camp – on the part of the guards as well as the prisoners. A lot of the prisoners are lifeless, physically and mentally. There are few smiles – in fact, few facial expressions at all. A lot of them are simply waiting. If they still exist tomorrow, then so be it. If not, then their torture is over. The guards have started to relax certain rules – or have given up caring, but the brutality is still there, even if it's intermittent and random. Perhaps the uncertainty is getting to them too.

Susannah finds it difficult to concentrate on the work. Her hands are weak and she works slowly. She speeds up when Jung or Müller are on guard, but slows down when it's Keller's turn. His tie is still crooked and his hair is now longer and becoming even more unruly, with the odd stray curl dangling from under his cap.

By now Susannah can recognize which guard is approaching by their footsteps. Jung announces his imminent arrival with that distinctive regular stomp of his jackboots, as though he's trying to kill a rat with every step. Müller's noise is much the same but her steps are smaller and more frequent. Keller has a slow loping stride, almost casual. Whenever Jung or Müller come to relieve Keller they always start by checking the prisoners are hard at work – as if it's something they don't trust Keller to do. And then they scold him about something – his hair or a stain on his jacket or a scuff mark on one of his boots. Susannah now almost likes Keller – she can relax when he's on duty. She occasionally even looks him in the eye, but turns away if he looks back.

As the days get shorter they also get darker, and afternoons of clear blue sky when the sun is strong and reviving are getting rarer. On one such afternoon Susannah and Ester are washing their clothes by the pool. The air feels thin and the cold water has turned Susannah's hands numb – which hardly matters as she's got used to ignoring that particular pain, and now the rest of her is warmed by the sunshine.

She tells Ester about her father, his work in Berlin, how he used to come home in a smart suit and change into his 'home' suit before playing with her and Jacob, often in Rose Park. Ester says nothing to all of this.

Then Susannah says, 'You still hear no word of your parents?'

Ester shakes her head. They both spend a few minutes squeezing and pummelling clothes underwater to rinse out the soap.

'In my cabin there's talk of war being over soon,' Ester says eventually.

'I'm sure you'll meet your parents then,' Susannah says. 'When we're all free.'

Ester stops squeezing for a moment, then says, 'Father told me he would always come back for me.'

'I'm glad my family are all kept in the same camp,' Susannah says. 'Father says you should be able to be with yours too.' She forces a smile. 'Father says you should ask the Kommandant which camp they're in.'

Ester's big childlike eyes look up to Susannah. For a second they're moist and glassy. Then the muscles around her sockets tighten fit to burst.

'*Father says, Father says, Father says,*' she hisses. 'I hate your father.'

Susannah hears but doesn't believe. 'What did you say?' she asks.

But Ester has thrown down her clothes into the water, spun away from Susannah and is now running to the fence. Susannah's first instinct is to look around for guards, to see who is on duty. Surely no guard would shoot a small girl running to the perimeter fence?

She chases Ester down, her larger strides meaning she grabs her before she reaches the fence. She pulls her back, and sees thorns in her eyes – eyes which up until now have only shown happiness, hope and optimism. Her face is scarlet, a dribble of saliva breaks her lips, and her breathing is heavy and shallow.

'What do you mean?' she asks Ester.

'I hate your father. I hate your mother. I hate Jacob. And I hate *you.*'

'But . . . but . . .' Susannah cannot squeeze any more words out. As she stands open-mouthed at these words, which have replaced her friend's usual endearing joy, they both hear boots running towards them and turn to see Keller approaching.

'Away from the fence!' he bawls. 'Away! Back to your washing!'
'Can't you see she's upset?' Susannah says back.

Keller looks to Ester, then his face stalls.

Susannah glares at him. 'She misses her parents.'

Keller quickly glances all around him. 'I'm sorry,' he says, now
quietly, almost softly. 'But . . . but you must move away from the
fence.'

Susannah and Keller stare at each other for a few seconds.
They're disturbed by more shouts and both turn to see another
guard approaching.

Keller stands up straight, and waits for the other guard to get
closer before starting to shout at the girls again. 'Move away!' His
voice strains for volume. 'Back to your washing!' The other guard is
Jung. As he arrives, breathless from running, Keller places the butt
of his rifle on Susannah's arm and shoves her and Ester away.

'Trouble?' Jung says.

Keller shakes his head. 'I've dealt with it.'

As Susannah puts an arm around Ester and leads her back to
the washing pool, she sees Jung becoming angry with Keller, slapping his rifle. She hears him telling the younger guard he has to
shoot if anyone goes near the perimeter fence again.

Then she stops listening to turn her attentions to Ester. She
wants to reassure her that one day her mother and father will return
and take her home to the Netherlands. But she thinks better of
mentioning it again, and, although she tries hard, she can't think of
a single positive thing to say. They both gather their washing in their
arms and head for their cabins in silence.

Inside Susannah's cabin Mother and Jacob are curled up on the
bed. Father lies next to the bed, only straw between him and the
wooden floor. 'Father,' Susannah says, gently shaking his shoulder.
It doesn't need much effort to shake him now; there isn't much
weight to move. 'I've done the washing.'

He sits up, resting his back against the bed, and caresses her face with a weak, trembling hand. 'Well done.' He whispers the words but Susannah isn't sure whether it's through weakness or in order to avoid waking Mother and Jacob. 'You shouldn't have to do your parents' washing,' he adds. 'Nobody should. You're a good daughter.' The last few words are delivered with a tremble in his voice.

'How are you feeling?' she says.

'A little better. I think I can walk now. But Jacob and your mother aren't so good. I think the lice and the stomach cramps are getting to them.'

Susannah looks over to Jacob and Mother, curled up together like rats in a nest. 'There's . . . there's talk of the war being over soon,' she says.

She doesn't know whether Father takes any notice or even hears. She sees that his eyes are now dull and grey, and the bone of his nose is more prominent. His chest sinks slightly and he covers his face with his hands and starts to weep.

This is the first time in her life Susannah has seen her father cry.

CHAPTER TWENTY-TWO

By November 1944 winter has locked itself into the camp. There are so many prisoners that there would seem to be a shortage of guards to control them. So now there are kapos.

The kapos are trusted prisoners – but never Jews – and are considered traitors by the rest of the prisoners. They have the clothes of prisoners but the arrogant air of guards; they also appear to have the authority – if not the rifles – to back up their orders. But what they lack in firearms they make up for in open brutality.

Disease continues to attack like swarms of ravenous locusts devouring all before them. Every day bodies are removed from Susannah's cabin by prisoners on the instructions of the kapos. Every day, however, more prisoners arrive to replace them. Susannah has heard rumours that the weaker prisoners are starting to die in the other camps as well, and that they too are being replaced by more inmates. *Where are all these people coming from?*

There were brief spells when Susannah was accompanied by her father or mother in the shoe tent, but now she's mostly on her own again. Only about twenty or thirty prisoners work there now; the others are too sick, or too weak, or simply can't see the point in working for the meagre extra rations the work gives them. Prisoners have started stealing food from one another, but Father says they shouldn't, so Susannah works when she can to earn food. It isn't enough – everyone is losing more weight – but at least the rations slow down the rate of loss.

One day, while Susannah rips shoes apart, her mind wanders back to the days in Berlin, to her schooldays, to playing in Rose Park with her friends, to when Father came home from a hard day's work, hungry for food, eager to play with and talk to his children, to when Mother kept the house clean and tidy and ensured her children were healthy, well fed and well educated. It seems such a long time ago – in another lifetime even. *What was the point of it all?* Now, it seems, she hardly speaks to Mother, who leaves the cabin only when she's ordered to work in the kitchens.

She gets shaken from her thoughts by a distant rhythmic thudding noise – Jung's jackboots. And the noise is getting louder. She also hears him laughing raucously. She glances to the doorway of the tent. Next to it Keller is motionless, staring straight ahead.

Susannah's gaze drops to the floor. She sees that one of Keller's bootlaces is undone. She holds a hand up. She cannot hold her fingers out straight because of the pain in her knuckles, but she leaves her hand up until he notices.

'What is it?' he says, stepping forward to her. 'Why have you stopped working?'

She says nothing, but points to his feet. He opens his mouth wide and takes a breath, as if to shout, but glances to where she's pointing and holds back when he notices the offending bootlace. His face turns red, he scans the interior of the tent and takes a quick look outside; the footsteps are getting louder. He fixes stern eyes on Susannah for a moment, then drops down to tie up his bootlace, standing back upright and back in position seconds before Jung enters.

Jung walks straight up to him and looks him up and down, giving his face and jacket a cursory examination, then drops his gaze to check his trousers and boots. He nods approvingly. 'Very good,' he says, making his surprise plain in his tone. 'Now you can go.'

Susannah watches Keller turn to leave. There's definitely a fraction of a second when he catches her eye. She doesn't know whether it's a *thank you* look or a disapproving glare, but he definitely looks.

And at the same moment Jung shouts out, 'You!' causing Susannah to drop her knife. Jung steps towards her. He shouts at the other prisoners, tells them to stop gawping like stupid pigs and carry on working.

'What were you looking at?' Jung says.

Susannah frowns and shakes her head. 'Nothing.'

'Pick up your tool,' Jung says. 'Carry on working.'

'Thank you.'

'My pleasure,' he answers with a sturdy smile. Then he turns to Keller, who loiters at the tent opening.

'So what are you waiting for?' he says. 'Go!'

Keller doesn't reply, but merely turns and leaves, his languid, light footsteps contrasting so much with those of Jung.

And Susannah carries on working, but senses the tiniest glint of hope.

Perhaps this is the hope Ester spoke of.

CHAPTER TWENTY-THREE

At the memorial Susannah continued her walk along the pathways, meandering between the grassy mounds with signs that said, '10,000 buried here' and '5,000 buried here', wondering how many of those she knew in a different life.

She tried to tell herself that the distress she'd suffered while listening to the talk was a fuss over nothing – that she was being small-minded in letting herself get so upset over mere words and pictures after the very real things that had happened to her (and to those at peace under those grassy mounds) all those years ago.

Somehow that didn't work; she still felt agitated, as if something or someone was creeping up on her – hunting her down.

Perhaps coming back here had been a big, big mistake.

Only the paths were left to remind anyone of the original camp layout. Like the Super Bowl, if you hadn't been there at the time you simply wouldn't understand. To look around without knowing the history, these could have been the ruins of a complex of factories or farms. Susannah was unsure whether this disguise was something to be grateful for or not. But at least she'd recovered her composure and started to appreciate the afternoon sunshine warming her face. She'd done that a few times before – except that back then it had been almost sumptuous rather than merely pleasant.

'Sixty-four years,' she mumbled to herself, looking at the empty spaces. 'And I could be in a different city. Or country.' She inhaled the scent of pine for a few minutes, and listened to nothing but birdsong.

Then her shoulders jolted at the gunshot and her head dipped instinctively. She looked up and saw not lofty pine trees but lattice-work lookout towers; she turned to the side and saw not open space but a pit, and smelt not the heady freshness of pine but something that made her cover her mouth and turn away. She hurried as much as her antiquated joints allowed, keeping to the paths that took her as far away from the pit as possible, until after two or three hundred yards she stopped, breathless.

She looked around her and saw no other visitors. Nobody.

But she saw one building.

She stared, then turned around, stumbling, almost falling, but blinked and saw nothing but barren space. She looked behind her, to where she'd just seen a building – *that* building. But again there was merely open space. She shook her head in dismay and headed back to the Visitor Centre. She needed a strong coffee and a sit down.

Twenty minutes later she was sitting in a quiet corner of the cafeteria with a cup of coffee on the table in front of her and her phone in her hand.

'I can tell you're upset,' David said.

She wasn't sure how he knew – she'd waited for her nerves to settle before ringing to give him an update. She'd started off by asking for the latest news on how his business was going, but he ignored the question. She was beginning to regret ringing.

'I'm fine,' she said.

'You know what the doctors said. You shouldn't upset yourself.'

'I'm not upset. It's this line coming halfway across the world. It's not my fault if my voice comes out all distorted.'

Ha. That was very true.

'So you're enjoying yourself?'

'Mmm . . . well . . .'

'Sorry, Mom. Stupid thing to say.'

'I'm . . . making progress.'

'Good. I'm glad for you, but . . .'

And then Susannah mouthed the words in a yacking fashion – *Why you want to be there I'll never know* – lolling her head from side to side as she did so.

But he didn't say that, he said, 'Please, Mom. Just don't overdo it.'

'I know, David. You don't want the cost of flying home a coffin airfreight.'

'Oh, *Mother.*'

The word was groaned down the phone. And Susannah had to admit he was right to groan.

'I'm sorry,' she said. 'But I'm all right, really. I can look after myself.'

'Just make sure you do.'

'So how's business? Are you going to tell me?'

'It's . . . okay.'

'Not so good then.'

'Just ring me tomorrow, Mom. Please.'

'I will.'

A few minutes later she was beginning to regret saying those things. Especially the coffin gag. David deserved better than that. Then again, she always had been an impulsive sort, from as far back as she could remember.

She pulled her coffee cup closer and placed her hands around it, faint wisps of steam swirling as they rose, almost hypnotizing her.

The last time she'd been here the only nutrition available had been watery soup with a faint flavour of potato or possibly turnip – they never could tell which. It tasted like the water had been taken from the washing pool or the gutter. But it was hot, it replaced fluids lost to diarrhoea, and obviously had some calories hidden in it somewhere. But not enough.

∞

For a brief period early in December 1944 Susannah falls ill, and spends a few days on the straw covering the wooden floor of the cabin, being looked after by Mother and Father. Ester comes into the cabin every day to talk with her, telling her that she will get better and that one day she will be back in Berlin.

Ester keeps apologizing for the unpleasant things she said about Susannah's family, and Susannah keeps telling her to stop apologizing.

When Susannah recovers she's pleased to find that the rest of her family are now in relatively good health too, meaning the dysentery has abated and they're not bedridden. This means they can all work, which means more food.

But still not enough.

Every inch of Susannah's skin seems permanently cold, and the rest of her family regularly voice the same complaint. They spend most of their non-working time huddled next to each other, covered in all the clothes they possess, or lying on the bed or the floor covered in the few dirty blankets that haven't been stolen by other prisoners. The bed isn't always available, because in spite of people dying the cabin is more crowded than ever due to the influx of new prisoners. They try to play cards together once or twice, but it's a muted affair; it's not the same when nobody cares whether they win or lose. It's as though people have given up all hope of anything positive. They invite Ester to join in, which helps. Ester is back to something approaching her normal self – always cheerful no matter what. Even though she's lost weight she doesn't seem to have lost hope. However, she can't play cards very well, and Susannah has to help her a lot with the rules.

Playing cards reminds Susannah of Uncle Paul and Aunt Helena, of the many years they spent playing bridge together in Amsterdam and in the farmhouse. She wonders what's happened to them. Mother and Father just shake their heads when she asks if they know anything. Perhaps they'll find out something when they leave Bergen-Belsen camp.

Then Father falls ill again, and Mother looks after him and Jacob, meaning Susannah goes to the shoe tent alone.

Inside it's as quiet as ever, apart from the slicing and ripping of leather. Susannah tries to catch Keller's eye. She's heard stories that the foreign forces are making advances. Such rumours are rife in the camp, but nobody really knows how much truth is in the stories. Perhaps Keller knows more. Perhaps if Susannah strikes up a conversation with him he'll tell her what's happening outside. Even if he wouldn't tell her deliberately his expression might give something away. Susannah is desperate for any news whatsoever, and now she's almost an adult she feels she can judge character better – especially of people not much older than herself like Keller.

She looks towards him. He looks straight ahead. *Did he glance at her for a split second just then?*

She keeps her eyes on him, now fearlessly – she wouldn't dare stare at any other guard.

And then she does it.

She thinks she can work without paying much attention, but with tired hands and a blank mind the knife slips and its blade – blunt and jagged though it is – runs across her other hand and scrapes off a small flap of skin.

She yelps in pain, drops the knife, and clasps her bloodied hand. As she starts to cry, she looks around. Nobody takes any notice. In fact, nobody even looks. Keller still gazes straight ahead.

She lifts her hand to assess the damage. If she can't work there will be even less food for her family. As she examines her hand something casts a shadow over it, and she feels a strong hand lift hers.

'Let me look,' Keller says. He's furtive, passing glances every few seconds to the opening of the tent. He pulls a rag out of his pocket and wraps it around her hand. 'That will stem the flow of blood for a while,' he says.

Susannah doesn't feel pain anymore; she's thinking of Keller, of why he's helping her. Perhaps there is hope after all.

She thanks him, still breathing heavily, and looks up at him. Even now he won't look directly at her face, only her hand. Is that an expression of pity or shame on his face? And if pity, then for whom?

Then Keller's name is shouted from the tent opening. It's Müller; somehow she's crept up on them.

'What's happening here?' she says, then turns and shouts Jung's name out of the tent opening. Within seconds Jung appears, and Müller explains to him what she's seen. Jung steps towards Keller and strikes him across the face with a gloved hand.

'What the hell are you doing?' he shouts, his face as close to Keller's as he can get without touching.

'I cut myself,' Susannah says.

Jung's head flicks sideways to her. 'Silence!' Then back to Keller. 'Well?'

Keller's face has turned a solid pink colour. He struggles to speak.

'I . . . I noticed she cut herself.'

'So?'

He shrugs. 'She's . . . she's a good worker. She produces a lot of leather and fabric. We need good workers.'

'Well, let's see how good she is.' Jung turns back to Susannah and says, 'You. Carry on working.'

'But I've cut myself.' She offers up the hand wrapped in the now bloodied rag.

Jung slaps her across the face once, twice, three times. With a manic twitch he grabs her hand, pulls the rag off and throws it away. He points to her knife on the floor and tells her to carry on working.

Susannah, still feeling the sting on her cheek and the ache in her jaw, obeys, and slowly starts working.

'Faster!' Jung shouts to her, almost screaming the words in her face.

'I'm only human,' she mumbles.

'What?' Jung grabs her grimy blouse and gives it a shake. A long rip appears in the thin material. 'What did you say?'

'Nothing,' Susannah says. Their eyes meet; she sees madness in his, and looks away after a second.

He lets go of her roughly and crouches down, picking up a handful of sandy dust from the floor. 'You see this?' he says, standing tall and looking around to show he is now addressing Susannah, Müller and especially Keller. He lifts his hand up, opening it slowly, letting the dirt fall back to the ground. There's an air of the theatrical to his display. Then he faces Susannah, glares at her, and lowers his voice. 'You people are nothing more than dust,' he says. 'And you are one mere speck of that dust.' As the final grains fall he blows them into her face. 'That is the truth. Never forget it.'

He wipes his hand on his trousers and looks to Keller for a response.

For a moment Keller's face has a puzzled expression. Then the confusion disappears, leaving a straight, stark nothingness. He steps forward.

Susannah sees his head jerk, then feels the splash of his spittle shock her face. Then she hears him say, '*Untermensch!*' The single word is hissed but also loud and clear.

She freezes, her mouth open, her throat locked shut. She has to wipe Keller's spittle away with the back of her hand before she believes what he's just done. Then she bursts into tears and races out of the tent.

She hears angry shouts coming from behind her, telling her to stop.

She doesn't care.

If they shoot, they shoot.

CHAPTER TWENTY-FOUR

The Star Camp is at the edge of the Bergen-Belsen complex, and so has a perimeter fence to the outside world.

Those who approach it get away from the stench and the dull drone of prisoners talking and groaning in the cabins. The nearer they get to the barbed-wire fence, the more respite they have. There it smells of grasses and pine and freedom, and the sound is of a heavenly peace where they can even hear birds chirping.

But the perimeter fence is a double-edged sword. Those who approach it also risk looking as if they're trying to escape, and so risk being shot or hanged or perhaps only beaten.

However, when Susannah runs to the fence and collapses next to the barbed wire none of this matters to her; she has long since given up thoughts of freedom and doesn't care if bullets pierce what little flesh she has left or fracture her weary bones.

And the cut on her hand is little more than a fading sting.

So when she hears jackboots thumping the earth behind her she doesn't turn to see which guard has given chase. That forces Keller to step around in front of her.

'Go away!' she shouts to him. 'I hate you!'

She wipes the tears from her dirty face with her dirty coat

sleeve and pulls the coat around her body as a shield against the cold wind.

'You have to come back to the shoe tent,' Keller says, nervously glancing back there.

'I thought you were . . . my friend, perhaps.'

'Your *friend?*' Keller says with a puzzled frown. 'But . . . I'm a guard.'

'But you're different from the other guards; you know how hard life is for us. I know you can see that.'

Keller runs a finger around the inside of his collar and pulls his face straight. 'You must get back to the tent. You could get shot if you stay here.'

Susannah bows her head and her fist hits the ground, blowing up a cloud of cold dust. 'Oh, what's the point?' she says.

Keller crouches down next to her for a second, then checks himself and appears to realize what it could look like. So he stands up again and points his rifle at her. 'Don't worry,' he says. 'This is in case someone is looking. I'm not going to shoot.'

Now Susannah looks up to him for the first time. 'You really think I care?' she says. 'What hope do I have? What's the point in doing anything here? This . . .' She looks around her. 'This is hell. It's not even worth being alive here.'

Keller sighs and relaxes his grip on the rifle. 'You know, when I started here a year ago things were better. Things are only getting so much worse because they force more and more prisoners in here day after day.'

'Oh, *I apologize,*' Susannah says, spitting the words out like a jilted lover – like someone who has had the chance to find and lose love. 'I'm *so sorry* if we're making life difficult for you.'

Keller's frown returns. He looks all around him, his gaze lingering at the shoe tent. Then he lowers his voice. 'You know,' he says, 'you're not the only one who's sorry.'

'What do you mean by that?'

She waits, but Keller says nothing more.

'Are you telling me *you* are sorry?' she asks.

'I'm telling you that many Germans aren't happy about what's happening.'

'And you?'

Keller pauses as he rolls his tongue around his mouth for a moment. 'I'm sorry about what I did to you in the tent.'

'And everything else?'

Keller looks to the ground. His face twitches once or twice before he nods.

'So . . . why do you do it?' she says. 'Why are you a part of this, doing these things to us?'

Keller shrugs and hesitates to answer, then looks up and left to the sentry guard some distance away. 'Because there's the hope that someone will see what's going on and realize what madness it is, and because it's my job.' He looks back to the tent, and now Susannah senses despair in his voice. 'Also because if I say these things to any other guards I know what will happen to me.'

Susannah stares at his face, trying to judge. Is he playing games of some sort?

She thinks not. Perhaps there's a tiny ray of hope after all.

'Please,' Keller says. 'Come back to the tent.'

'And if I do as you say, then what can you do for me in return?'

He almost laughs. 'What do you want me to do – help you escape?'

'That would help,' Susannah says, speaking the words slowly so there's no chance of it being taken as flippancy.

'You know, I don't think it would,' Keller replies. 'You would be captured and at the moment that means you would be shot. And so would I.'

'Or you could . . .' Susannah hesitates to say it. He could say no but he could also do any number of things. Yes, now is as good a time as any to ask.

'I want some extra food for my family.'

Keller looks shocked. 'You know I can't do that. I'd be shot. And food is now scarce even for Germans.' He nods back to the tent. 'Come on. I'll try to make things a little easier for you when Müller and Jung are not here. But that's all I can do for you.'

Slowly Susannah gets to her feet, her joints feeling stiff and tired even though they're young, and starts walking. Keller points his rifle at her back, and as Jung and Müller step out of the tent he prods her with it.

'What took you so long?' Jung says.

Keller says nothing. Jung strikes Susannah across the face again and shoves her over towards the pile of shoes. She picks her knife up from the floor, wipes the blood off her hand, and takes a shoe from the large pile in front of her.

She keeps her head low, and she works.

CHAPTER TWENTY-FIVE

In the memorial cafeteria Susannah finished her coffee and thought about what had happened to her earlier, about her vision of the building, about seeing the cabin that was no longer there.

That was easier – thinking about it was easier than going out and facing it again.

She looked down to her tray, to the two empty sugar sachets. She stared at them for a moment, then looked around to see if anyone was facing in her direction.

Nobody was.

She picked up one sachet and poked her finger into the hole, ripping the miniature bag apart. Then she glanced around to check again that nobody was looking before lifting it to her mouth. She gave the paper a lick, tentatively at first, then quickly, almost in ecstasy, flicking her tongue, squeezing its point into the corner folds of paper in case they held a hidden grain or two. She didn't check to see if anybody was looking when she picked up the second sachet and did the same. Only when she'd cleansed this second scrap of paper of every speck of the sweet powder did she stop, think, and quickly place it down.

What the heck was she doing?

Her mind was falling apart. Yet another sign that coming back here had been a mistake.

But no – she was upset, that was all. And why shouldn't she be? This was never going to be easy. She was here searching for answers to difficult questions.

And she wasn't going to find those answers by drinking coffee.

She puffed out a long sigh and braced herself to go outside again.

There, she slowly made her way back – close to where she thought she'd seen the cabin she lived in all those years ago.

Lived?

Ha! It was hardly living.

She stood still and concentrated for a few seconds. Then more details came back to her. Now she could see the cabin again, and this time it wasn't quite as frightening. After all, it had been her home for something approaching a year.

∽

The conditions in the camp have now worsened, and so too has the prisoners' mental resolve. In September a traditional ram's horn shofar was smuggled into the camp in a coffee cauldron at great risk to those involved. To celebrate Rosh Hashanah it was sounded – very softly so as not to alert the guards – spreading hope and pride. Similarly, to celebrate Yom Kippur in October, candles were smuggled in – and some manufactured through scraps of fat saved from the desperately short food supplies – and clandestine prayer services took place. By December, however, the mood had changed along with the weather. When Hanukkah arrived there was simply no appetite to do anything more than observe the holy days by saying silent prayers.

Now 1944 has turned into 1945, and an already bitter winter

hardens further, cracking skin and making bones ache. In the cabins strangers huddle together for warmth. By now there are many more women in Susannah's cabin, and somehow the bed she and Mother shared has been taken by another woman and her two young daughters, relegating them to the floor underneath. Only a smattering of straw separates them from the hard timber floor. Now Ester occasionally sleeps in the same cabin – whenever she feels threatened by the closeness of strangers in her own. It's one more body squeezed under the bed, but also more shared warmth.

One such night – where only breath is visible, caught in the beams of light that leak through the cracks in the wall, and where the only sounds are weak coughs and despairing groans – the peace is splintered by the sounds of gunfire from outside.

Everybody in the cabin is woken. Nobody speaks or moves except for parents comforting small children who have started crying. They all know it's an escape attempt.

There are more gunshots. There are shouts. The sound of dogs barking makes the prisoners tighten their curled-up frames a little more.

The dogs.

Dogs that are better fed than the prisoners. Sometimes the guards deliberately feed their dogs in front of the prisoners just to torture them that little bit more. And Susannah once saw a guard take food from a man whose only crime was to look at him, and feed it to his dog. And so Susannah wonders whether the other prisoners are thinking the same as her –

Not: *Will they escape?*

But: *How good it would be to have as much energy as those dogs, to eat as well as they do.*

Eventually the noise stops and the prisoners quietly return to an acquiescent slumber.

*

In the morning the prisoners leave their cabins, braving the searing winds to visit the toilet block, to splash their faces with ice-cold water, and then gather for roll-call. As they stand there, like an array of ice statues, three carts are hauled to the front of the formation and tipped up in front of them. Everyone takes a long look at the bodies of twenty or thirty men and women, all lank, skinny and bloodied from gunshot wounds – and all naked to shame them even in death. The faces are all familiar in one way or another, like those of neighbours or colleagues who aren't quite close enough to speak to. Everybody knows that the faces once belonged to real people who had aspirations, likes and loathings, strengths and failings, lovers and enemies.

Except that now they have none of those things. No life. No clothes. Not even dignity.

After roll-call a dozen of the younger and stronger men are picked out and told they must take the bodies out through the gates and bury them. When they return they initially say nothing, but before long reveal that the bodies that were displayed at roll-call weren't the only ones they were ordered to bury. In fact, the majority of the corpses weren't of people shot or hanged or beaten, but those with torsos overwhelmed by the scabs and dull red rashes of typhus.

Susannah is now one of the few prisoners who still work in the shoe tent. Many are ill, but more have simply given up, their weakened bodies refusing to do as they're told, making the decision for them.

But Susannah has a plan. She works slowly – not caring what leather she salvages and what she wastes – and is silent and inconspicuous while Müller is on duty.

When Keller takes over she grits her teeth and waits ten minutes. Then she closes her eyes, takes a quiet breath, and presses the knife into the palm of her hand.

She shrieks. There's blood. She squeezes her hand to force the flow of blood onto her clothing and onto the dusty earth below.

This is literally her lifeblood she's gambling with – it had better be worth it.

She looks to Keller and shows him an imploring frown, but he looks straight ahead.

'Help me!' Susannah says. 'I'm hurt.'

'You have to carry on working,' Keller says, the first words grating, the last ones in weaker tones.

'But I'm hurt!'

Keller checks for approaching guards, then steps over to her and whispers, 'What do you want me to do?' He looks at her hand and also at the dark red droplets on the ground.

'Anything,' Susannah says. 'You have to do something for me – for my family. I was sick this morning and I'm getting weaker every day. Soon I'll be too ill to work in the tent.'

'But . . . what can I do?'

'*Food.* We need *food.*'

'But I—'

'Please. Anything. And I'll do anything for you in return. People in my cabin are dying every day, and it's the same in my father's cabin. The guards try to take them out when nobody is looking, but that isn't possible because there are now so many of us. And for every one that dies three take their place. You know this is all true. I've even seen *you* taking bodies away.'

Keller rubs fingers across his forehead, then wipes the greasy sweat onto his jacket. His mouth opens to speak a couple of times but each time he swallows the words, unable to even look at Susannah.

'Please!' Susannah says again, now coughing while she speaks. 'I'll do anything for more food. Name your price. You have to help me.'

Keller says nothing.

Susannah shoves past him and runs out of the tent, towards the perimeter fence again.

CHAPTER TWENTY-SIX

At the memorial Susannah stood with leaden feet next to the cabin – the cabin that was there only in her mind – and started to hyperventilate.

She turned for help but the only thing she got was the sun blinding her, making her even more uncertain about where she was. And then her mind went back to the talk earlier that day in the Visitor Centre. The words seemed to echo out of the pine forest that formed a verdant blanket beyond the perimeter.

'The female prisoners, they had, shall we say, *other uses* to the guards.'

'Some of the younger women were very popular with the guards.'

'Those who became what you might call *good friends* with the male guards went on to become informants.'

'You see, they were on the side of the Nazis because . . . it spared them.'

Did the man in the Visitor Centre really say all of that?

How disgusting.

How dare he even suggest that the prisoners – such as Susannah – would collude with Nazis, the very people responsible for her family having to flee Berlin, having to hide out in the Netherlands, becoming incarcerated first in Westerbork and then in this very hell camp where she now stood.

There was a bench nearby, with a small rectangle of wild flowers in front of it.

She sat, and looked to the wild flowers for the answers.

As if there had been wild flowers in January 1945.

გ∿ට

Next to the barbed wire at the perimeter fence Susannah coughs again and crouches down, almost doubled up with the convulsions of sickness. This is how it started with Father. The run from the shoe tent has made her chest worse, as if glue has been poured into her lungs. But Keller isn't even out of breath when he arrives.

'I've already told you,' he says. 'If I could do anything to help you I would, but—'

'No!' Susannah says. 'We all know you have food. Look at you. Your bodies aren't thin and wasted like ours. You've got energy. You must have more food than us. You even have food for your dogs. All I'm asking for is a little more. Some bread or something with sugar. Anything.'

Keller pauses while his eyes pass up and down her body. Then he says, 'You know, if I could do anything for you that didn't get me shot, then I would.'

'Would you really?'

'I'm sure I would. But . . . it depends what you could do for me in return.'

Susannah's eyes drop to her torso. She straightens her clothing with the palm of her hand, then looks up at Keller, a scowl frozen on her face.

Keller is already shaking his head. 'No,' he says firmly. 'You don't understand. I don't mean that.'

Susannah's haggard shoulders dip very slightly as she relaxes, which brings on a short coughing fit. 'Good,' she says when she stops. 'We all know some women who do, but . . .'

'I understand,' Keller says quietly. 'I . . . I have a sister your age. I don't want that. And really, I don't want you to die.'

They are quiet for a moment as another guard passes by. He lingers, then asks if everything is all right.

Keller nods a few times and puts on a reassuring downward smile. 'Oh yes,' he says.

'Was she trying to escape?'

Keller puts on a laugh. 'Just being subordinate, nothing more.'

The other guard looks Susannah up and down, hesitates for a moment, then turns away and starts to walk briskly along an invisible line parallel to the perimeter fence.

'So?' Susannah says, once he has gone. 'What do you want me to do?'

'I'm not sure. But there are . . . there are rumours that the war isn't going well for Germany.'

'Then that's what I can do for you.'

Keller frowns, puzzled.

'If Germany loses the war I'll take you in. You can come home to Berlin with us to save you from being shot. We could say you're my older brother, yes?'

Keller laughs – at the same time almost crying – and gives his head a slow shake. 'With my name and photograph on the staff records?'

'We could get them and burn them.'

Keller gives her a pitying look and smiles glumly.

'No,' Susannah says. 'Perhaps not. Perhaps I'm going mad. I'm sorry.'

'Mad?' Keller says. He laughs again, this time a cruel cackle, but also Susannah sees the wetness in his eyes. 'Don't apologize,' he says.

'This whole thing has been mad from the start. And we get more and more prisoners every day.'

'Where from?' Susannah asks.

'Nobody knows. Even the Kommandant keeps saying, "No more." But his superiors keep saying, "Yes, more." He tells them we have thousands of prisoners sharing each toilet and pitiful amounts of food and water. They don't listen.'

At that moment Keller's name is shouted from afar. They turn to see Müller approaching.

'Really,' Keller says, now rushing out his words. 'I can't help. I'm sorry. There are thousands of you. I can't help you all.'

'Yes,' Susannah says. 'Yes, I can see that.'

Müller shouts again, this time from a few yards away. 'What's going on here?'

Keller says nothing, but holds Susannah by the arm and shoves her back towards the tent.

CHAPTER TWENTY-SEVEN

January holds her grip on Bergen-Belsen like an ice devil, yielding only when February takes over. But nobody seems to notice or care about the passing of another month.

Susannah and her family continue to work when they're well enough. It keeps them warmer than lying on the floor would, and the extra food, even though it gets less month by month, keeps them a little less skeletal than many. And, of course, her father keeps saying they should never give up hope. But as far as Keller is concerned, that's exactly how Susannah feels; they're often in the same room but eye contact is avoided.

It's a bright, dry day – but still bitterly cold – when Susannah takes her own and her mother's clothes to the washing pool. On the lonely walk she comes across a frozen puddle in the heavily rutted mud and stops for a moment; there's no rush, there's never a rush anymore; even the guards seem apathetic. She presses her toe down onto the ice layer of the puddle and watches the bubble underneath search for an escape route; there is none. She feels as helpless as the bubble.

She trudges on towards the pool and drops her clothes down on the cold concrete edge. She's alone because few prisoners now have the energy or the inclination to keep clean. Even the edges of the water are now forming crystal bonds to the concrete surround. How long before the whole pool freezes?

How long before . . . ?

How long . . . ?

Does it really matter how long before anything? It's no more than a day-by-day existence, and the concept of time has lost any meaning beyond surviving each of those wretched days.

Susannah crouches down beside the still water and feels teardrops dribble down her face. At first she makes no sound, but the tears almost give her permission to reach further, to open the door she usually manages to keep bolted. The events of the past few years run through her mind like a race through a dark and unfriendly world, and although she has cried before, this time it's different. This is no cry to get transient negative thoughts out of her system, or to make her feel better so she can last another day; this is a despair-ridden cry to God to pluck her from this living hell and take her anywhere else.

Or simply take her.

And as she prays for release of any sort, she feels the gossamer touch of a sylph-like spirit on her shoulder. She turns to see Ester, and there's no attempt to disguise the state she's in – not anymore.

Ester's eyes are even warmer than usual, and she makes no sound, just crouches down next to Susannah and puts one of those stick-like arms around her. The two girls embrace and hold each other tightly, trying to squeeze strength into their emaciated forms, until Susannah's cries burn themselves out to faint whimpers, and then to nothing.

Susannah lets go and wipes her face dry. They both turn to watch as a wagtail lands nearby and hops along to a puddle near them to drink, and then, with a fleeting song, launches itself up and away, over the perimeter fence, and into the pine forest beyond.

'Are you all right?' Ester says.

Susannah gazes out into the forest, then nods and splashes some chilly water from the pool onto her face to wash away the salty remains of her despair. There are a few minutes of silence as she sighs herself back to an acceptance of the reality of life in Bergen-Belsen. 'Ester,' she says, 'do you cry?'

Ester smiles and shows a glimpse of teeth that are now browning at the edges. 'No,' she says gently. 'No, I don't.'

'But . . . I don't understand. How can you go through all of this and not be so upset that you cry?'

'Because I believe.'

'Believe what?'

'That one day we will be like that wagtail; it might not be tomorrow or next week, but one day this will all be over and we too will fly out of here.'

Susannah says nothing, but merely bows her head.

'Don't you want to go back to Berlin one day?' Ester says.

Then Susannah's face cracks, as if she's going to relapse to tearfulness. She tightens her facial muscles to keep in control. 'Of course I do,' she says. 'I want to see my old friends, to smell the flowers in Rose Park, to . . .' She closes her eyes, holding back the memories. 'But I don't think any of that will happen, and every day I stay in here that feeling gets stronger. I feel I might die in here.'

Ester leans back and grabs her by the shoulders, giving her a shake. 'But how do you *know* that?' she says.

Susannah opens her mouth and a puff of hot air streams out, but no words.

'You have to watch the birds,' Ester says. She points over to the tangle of barbed wire near the perimeter fence, where sparrows hide in the metal maze, occasionally venturing to puddles to drink and bathe before flying back into the forest. 'I watch them and they give me inspiration. They fly in and out as they please, they have no barriers. One day we will also spread our little wings and fly away from this place. If they can fly, then so can we, Susannah, *so can we.*'

And Susannah takes a few moments to watch the birds, going where they please, then says, 'But we can't fly, Ester.'

'We can in our minds if we try hard enough. Nobody can tell us what to think. My father used to tell me that.'

'He *used to?*' Susannah says.

Ester's smile drops and her eyes show a fragility Susannah has not seen before. She looks to Susannah, then blinks rapidly a few times, but cannot stop those big eyes becoming wet and shiny. Her jawline trembles for a moment, then she bows her head and Susannah sees her shoulders quiver, almost trying to fold her body in half. Susannah, now sitting cross-legged in the mud, pulls her in and holds her tightly.

'He said he would come back for me!' Ester cries out. 'He said he would come back!' She screams as she sobs, and buries her head in Susannah's chest.

And while Ester cries on her shoulder, Susannah watches the sparrows, wagtails and blackbirds go about their business without constraint or barrier.

CHAPTER TWENTY-EIGHT

I t's now two weeks into February, and rain pelts down on the cabin roof like a hail of bullets that never ceases.

In the frozen half-darkness of morning Susannah asks Mother if she's working today. Mother momentarily opens her eyes, then says she feels too unwell to go anywhere. Susannah pats her on the shoulder and steals out of the cabin, holding a threadbare shawl over her head for shelter from the rain. She sees no guards or kapos, so runs over to the cabin where Father and Jacob are.

Their cabin is even more overcrowded than the women's. The open door throws the first grey light of dawn onto the squalid scene, and Susannah squints to pick out Father or Jacob from the curled-up bodies, which cover every inch of the floor, including under the beds. As she steps between them a guttural whisper calls her name and she spots Father. She carefully heads in that direction and hugs him.

'Are you coming to the shoe tent today?' she asks.

Father shakes his head. 'I'm sorry,' he says. 'Jacob and I, we were chopping wood until very late last night. Our backs . . . our arms . . .' And there his cracked lips give up and he holds out his limp, blistered hands.

Susannah holds them – hands once so strong but now bony

and almost lifeless – and gently caresses them. 'There's talk of the British,' she says. 'The rumour is they're advancing and they'll be here soon.'

'If you believe rumours.'

'No, Father. This is a rumour that doesn't die.'

Father scratches his head roughly, then stops and nods very slowly. 'We'll see,' he says. 'But at the moment I feel rotten. The best I can do is come over to your cabin to see Mother later today. Perhaps tomorrow I'll feel well enough to come to work with you.'

And Susannah can see in his eyes, even in this poor light, that he has almost given up, that he's hardly the Father she knows. 'Don't lose your hope,' she says.

But even as she speaks he lies down on the floor, curls up, and closes his eyes.

She wonders again whether she's right to have hope, to believe in a better world. Perhaps there's no point working in the shoe tent. But her stomach aches, and there's only one way to ease that pain: work, which will earn some extra food. She gets up, pulls the shawl over her head, and rushes out and over to the shoe tent.

Jung is on duty, so she simply ignores him, sits down and picks up a shoe from the pile. She keeps the blanket over her shoulders and takes her mind to another, better place. She remembers Rose Park in Berlin, where she used to play with friends, where she used to run free. Then Amsterdam, and a change of friends and allegiances so abrupt she felt she'd betrayed those she'd grown up with in Berlin. And, again, those feelings were forgotten when she went to the isolated farmhouse. She thinks of Maria and Erik, she thinks of Aunt Helena and Uncle Paul, and wonders whether any of them are still alive, and also whether they would want to be. Susannah's will to carry on is now paper-thin. She wonders whether those who have fallen by the wayside are the fortunate ones, because they are no longer suffering and have gone to a better place.

Surely no worse place exists than this.

Thirty minutes that numb Susannah's mind pass by, then Keller takes over guard duty from Jung and stands bolt upright, head high, while Jung departs. Susannah's weary eyes glance at him. For a split second she thinks there's something different about him, but she doesn't care enough to dwell on it. The journey in her mind, back to Berlin, is far more important.

Because *nobody can tell us what to think.*

Then her daydream is pierced as she notices Keller move. He pokes his head out of the tent entrance and looks both ways. There's something going on with his clothing, as though he's undressing. But no, he has only unbuttoned his jacket and taken out a bundle of cloth. He holds this under his arm while he quickly does his buttons back up, then turns sharply and walks up to Susannah. He does this so quietly that his actions would be dreamlike but for the din of the rain, and but for the fact she's in a living nightmare.

He takes a moment to straighten his jacket, to flatten it against his torso. 'You,' he then says to Susannah. 'I have an errand for you.'

The eyes of other prisoners now turn. Keller tells them to get on with their work. He waits for them to do so.

'Take this to the kitchen barracks,' he says, and offers her the bundle.

At first Susannah is puzzled, and just looks at what is in his hand. It appears to be a folded-up blanket. He shakes it, moves it even closer, almost prodding her with it, much as he shoved his rifle in her when they were talking at the perimeter fence. She rests her hands on it, for the first time in a year feeling the bliss of a clean blanket. The sensation of its softness on her fingertips is almost foreign.

She holds onto the blanket, but Keller doesn't let go, just gives it another, small shake.

'To the kitchen,' he says. 'You understand?'

She nods, and he lets go. It feels like there's something inside the blanket, and also something in Keller's expression of concentration. She swallows in surprise, her eyes opening fully for the first time in weeks. She leaves the tent and steps outside. The rain has eased, but still she's getting soaked very quickly. She stops and looks all around, sees only a sentry guard through the veil of drizzle, and carefully looks inside the blanket.

She lets out a gasp and tries to run to her cabin. She forgets about her weakness for a second and has to cough a few times, stumbling and muddying her knees as she does so, but not dropping the new blanket. Soon she has her feet inside the cabin door, and wipes the rain from her face, trying, in her panic, to make herself look presentable to her parents.

Then she thinks of Ester, who has been such a good friend. But Mother and Father and Jacob must come first – it's her duty. And then again, Ester has no family in the camp – nobody to take care of her. She's as good as family.

Susannah darts back out into the rain and heads for Ester's cabin. She clasps the contraband to her chest, looking left and right for guards as she picks her way over earth that has thawed slightly due to the rain. She reaches the cabin and enters.

Ester's cabin is just as crowded as her own. It feels warmer, but smells worse; faeces, urine, bodies that haven't washed in months, food utensils gathering a creeping mould. At one corner of the cabin water drips from the ceiling – still people are lying underneath because there's no choice. There are few beds here, the room is mostly a rolling sea of bodies covered in rags, with the occasional chamber pot and soup bowl scattered between them. Susannah can hardly see the wooden floor – and she can't see Ester at all. She scans the ocean of dirty cloth once more, and sees a figure smaller than the rest occupying one corner. She steps closer and whispers Ester's name through the groans and subdued chatter. Sure enough, the small figure turns and returns the whisper. Susannah makes her way across, carefully tiptoeing on the few visible spots of floor.

Ester is crouched – foetal-like – pressed into one corner, her head resting against the rough timber. There's no lighting in here, but a few strands of dreary afternoon daylight enter the cracks in the timber wall, making the cobwebs and slug trails inches from Ester's face shimmer. The gaps also let in icy jets of wind which whistle as they tingle any uncovered flesh.

And Ester is crouched – foetal-like – because to stretch out her petite frame would be to encroach on others' space. Susannah also sees another sign that order is breaking down: according to the rules men are allowed in women's cabins for family visits only during daylight hours, but rubbing against Ester's shoulder is the back of a young man half covered in a blanket, shivering himself to sleep. In a similar fashion Ester's feet are constrained by the head and shoulders of another prisoner.

Susannah has now adapted to the smell, and she knows why it seems warmer in here; the extra bodies afford everyone – including Ester – that little extra heat.

Susannah stands over Ester and asks her to sit up. As she does this it leaves enough room for Susannah to kneel down next to her. Susannah smiles but isn't sure whether Ester notices.

'I have something,' she says. Ester just gives a blank stare, so Susannah shows her the bag of sugar. And then Ester reacts – the eyes have all but lost the ability to lighten up but there's a cracked smile.

'How did you . . . ?' Ester says.

'Shh!'

'But where . . . ?'

Heads of other prisoners turn like silhouetted robots. The girls wait for them to turn back before speaking again.

'For your family, yes?' Ester says in an uncertain tone.

'A little for you,' Susannah says, knowing that a few months ago Ester would have said, 'I can't *possibly* . . .' or 'Not for *me*, surely?'

But now Ester doesn't politely refuse. This time she takes the bowl she keeps close to her belly and holds it out in front. Susannah glances around once more, then lifts the bag up. She squeezes it so that some of the precious energy crumbles off and drops into the bowl. Ester eats it as a dog might, licking up every last grain until the bowl is empty but for a layer of saliva that glistens like the slug trails that criss-cross everything around her.

The girls exchange a hug, then Susannah stands and leaves, picking her way back through the sleeping bodies, and heads outside and to her own cabin. She starts to run again in excitement but her feet slip in the mud and she's forced to slow down. By the time she reaches her own cabin the rain has mingled with tears of anxiety. She wipes her face with the blanket before entering.

Inside, she sees that Father and Jacob have come over to be with Mother as promised. Good, she thinks, one less journey, and they can eat as a family again. She hurries over to them.

'Look what I've got,' she whispers.

Her mother squints to see, and says, 'Another blanket? You have another blanket? Well done, Susannah!'

Susannah throws the blanket over her mother's shoulders, then presents the bag of sugar. Her mother touches the bag as if it's made of gold.

By now Susannah's father has got to his knees, is leaning on a bed, and shows that there's still some life left in his hollow eyes. 'Susannah, that's wonderful,' he says. But he isn't smiling, and stares at Susannah. 'Where did you get it from?'

Susannah is aware that all eyes are on her. She parts her cracked lips, but can't think of what to say.

Eventually Mother gives the bag to Father and tells him not to ask, just to eat. He shakes the thought from his head. 'No,' he says.

'Jacob and Susannah first, then you. Then me if there's any left.'

There are no more arguments. There are no more words at all. Mother reaches down and lifts the edge of the blanket, revealing a chamber pot to the left of her feet and a few eating utensils to the right. She picks up a small wooden spoon and wipes it with the clean blanket.

She hands the bag and the spoon to Jacob, who takes them without hesitation and plunges the spoon in with gusto, a single stab breaking off a chunk of sugar, which he eats. He allows a moment for the sweetness to coat his tongue, then swallows. He does the same again and again, then looks up and freezes for a second as he sees three eager and expectant faces facing him. He licks his lips, then hands the bag and the spoon to Susannah.

'Are you sure you've had enough?' she asks.

'Of course,' he says, in a voice straining to boast the first bass tone Susannah has heard from her little brother.

Susannah says she has already had some and offers the bag to her mother.

'No,' Father says. 'Have more.'

While Father pats Jacob on the back she does just that, taking three spoonfuls slowly, conscious of being watched. Then she hands over to Mother, who guides each spoonful between her lips with precision so as not to waste even one grain.

Soon it's Father's turn, and he takes two spoonfuls, leaving the remaining crystals hiding in the folds of the paper. He lifts his head back and shakes the bag, showering the remaining granules into his eager mouth. Then he tears the bag into four pieces as if dissecting a dead animal. He passes the pieces of paper around and each of them takes one. They all watch as Father starts licking the sweet side, then opens out the folds and pokes the point of his tongue into every corner so that nothing goes to waste. For a fleeting second Susannah thinks he looks like a madman doing this, before remembering the father she knew back in Berlin. Then they all do the same with their pieces of the bag.

Then Father takes back the pieces and compresses them into a pellet, which he places in the chamber pot. 'We must get rid of this without the guards seeing it,' he whispers.

For a while the electric rush of sugar makes Susannah feel drunk, all the better to ignore the jealous looks from the rest of the cabin's occupants. And then comes the nausea from a stomach that's used to nothing more than watery starch and now seems to want to take its revenge for months of neglect.

But throughout all of this there's now hope. A saviour exists, and his name is Keller.

Jacob and Mother, licking their lips, discreetly thank Susannah for the sugar, then both lie down on the floor and pull blankets up to their necks. Father looks around, then shuffles closer to Susannah. 'I need to know how you got it,' he whispers.

'I . . . I made friends with a guard.'

Father's face changes shape; it's like Jacob's used to be just before he started to cry. 'Friends?' he says. 'With a *guard*?'

'With Keller. It started when I cut my hand. He helped me, and—'

'It doesn't matter. Please. Don't tell me any more. Just tell me whether you can get some more food.'

'I . . . I . . . Yes,' Susannah says, then, in more confident tones, 'Yes. I'll try to get another tomorrow – if not, then the next day.'

'Good.' He puts his arms around her and his slender frame squeezes hers. It's the gentlest hug she has ever had from her father; he's treating her like a newborn baby.

'You're such a good daughter,' he says, his crackly voice almost breathing the words out.

Susannah tries to leave his grasp but he doesn't let her. She knows what he's thinking. She knows the tears are for her. 'It's all right, Father,' she says with the quietest of whispers into his ear. 'Don't worry about me.'

Eventually they separate, and Father takes a second to look directly into her eyes, their faces almost touching. 'Oh, Susannah, I'm so, so sorry. We had such hopes for you and Jacob.' He passes a hand along her damp hair and onto her shoulder. Then he hugs her once more, and rocks her, and Susannah feels his body pulse with the sorrow of a broken promise.

CHAPTER TWENTY-NINE

For the next few days Susannah goes to the shoe tent alone, and leaves with no package. Keller was on duty for only one of those days, and even then he didn't do anything, so Susannah accepts that perhaps he won't bring food for them *every* day.

But for the first time in months – even years – Susannah can glimpse a rainbow through the mist. Yes, every day more people die of hunger, disease and bullets, and many more flood into the camp. But some of the new prisoners say rescue is imminent – that the British, the Americans and others all continue their advance on various fronts, and that the worsening conditions are a sign of the Third Reich's increasing desperation. And Susannah thinks Keller will supply more food until then – perhaps some sugar every few days.

Also Father is in better spirits. He appears to believe Susannah when she says she hasn't given anything to Keller, or done anything for him, in return for the sugar.

The next morning Father and Jacob come to Susannah's cabin. Father says he feels well enough to go to the shoe tent, so leaves Jacob with Mother and accompanies Susannah to work. It seems his spirits are buoyed – as are hers – by the promise of better things to come, and by the prospect of more food. But today their hopes are dashed because Keller isn't on duty. However, they carry out their work and think of the next day, when he might be on duty and might have something for them.

As they walk back together, Susannah considers making a joke about Keller being their very own Zuckerman – that he is perhaps related – but she thinks better of saying this, in case it breaks the spell. Then Father stops her and turns to face her.

'Susannah, we have to tell Mother and Jacob that Keller promised us some more food tomorrow.'

'You mean we should lie?'

'We . . . we have to give them a reason to carry on.'

Susannah thinks for a moment and nods. 'That's a good idea, and I'm sure Keller will give us more food the next time he's on duty, so it's only a white lie.'

Then Father's face turns sour. 'We'll see,' he says.

'You don't believe he'll give us more food?' Susannah says, backing away slightly.

Father tries to speak, then has to gather his thoughts. 'You remember when were at the farmhouse, and in the first summer we had that beautiful honey fresh from the hive?'

'On fresh wholewheat bread.' Susannah's mind drifts away for a second. 'One of the nicest things I've ever tasted.'

'You see, we went back a week later, but it was too dangerous. Sometimes you have to accept you can only raid the honeybee nest once.'

The words upset Susannah, but she says nothing. They go back to the cabin and Father tells the white lie to Mother and Jacob. After the family have been to the kitchen to collect their ever smaller ration of bread and potato soup they return to the cabin and Susannah tries to sleep. But she's still upset by what Father said; he obviously doesn't believe Keller will help them again. It's as if he doesn't even *want* their wishes to come true, doesn't want to survive. Perhaps he's still suspicious of Keller's motives. Eventually she falls asleep wondering whether there's any substance to Father's suspicions.

But the very next day Father's white lie is proved not to be a lie after all.

Again Susannah and Father are working side by side in the shoe tent. This time Keller is on duty, and at the end of the shift he steps over to Susannah. He casually glances around, and when nobody is looking he places a small bag of sugar in her lap. He says nothing.

It looks like the honeybee has granted them another harvest.

Father looks up to Keller as if in silent worship.

'What do you want for this?' Susannah whispers.

'Shh!' Father hisses from her side. 'Please, Susannah. Let's just be grateful and leave.'

But Susannah repeats the question.

Keller looks behind him, then crouches down, so all three of their heads are inches apart. 'We've all heard the rumours,' he says. 'Of course our government denies everything and we're forbidden from talking about such things.'

'The British?' Father says.

Keller nods. 'Canadians too.'

'You want us to help you if the camp is captured, is that it?'

And for once Keller, even with his full, healthy figure and smart, clean uniform, looks every bit as haggard as the prisoners he guards. His fears and hollow spirit are etched on his cracked expression. 'I don't think it'll come to that,' he says. 'I . . . I can't do this anymore. I can't look at everything around me for much longer and do nothing.'

'Thank you,' Father says. 'Thank you so much for saying that.'

At the time Susannah is puzzled by Father's reaction. She can't understand what he means by those words.

Keller swallows. 'You people have suffered too much to owe me anything. All I ask is that you remember me – nothing more.'

'We will,' Father says. 'We will.'

Susannah doesn't speak, but knows she will remember Keller until the day she dies – whenever that day might be. As Keller stands up she points to one of his boots, the laces of which have come undone again. He hesitates, and for a moment Susannah thinks he is going to leave them undone and accept whatever scolding the other guards might give him. But he gives a weary sigh and corrects his misdemeanour.

After work Susannah and Father rush back to the cabin like school-children on their way to a party. Once there they scurry over to Mother and Jacob, and between the coughing, wheezing and asthmatic snoring Father whispers for the family to come in close. He tells Mother to get out her spoon, then opens the bag of sugar as carefully as if he is defusing a bomb.

'There's more than last time,' Jacob says, his tongue flicking out to lick his lips.

'Yes,' Fathers whispers. 'Almost half a bag. But just one spoon-ful each for now. Leave some for tomorrow.'

They start with Jacob, then Susannah, then Mother, then Father, each savouring the sweetness and passing the bag on. In silence. In celebration.

They can't resist and take two spoonfuls each and it seems like half of the sugar is gone within seconds.

'Can I save some for Ester?' Susannah says.

Father gives a solemn nod. 'Of course.'

Susannah slowly rolls up the top of the bag and places it in her pocket.

'I never thought sugar on its own could taste so good,' Mother says.

'It's the taste of hope,' Father says.

'What do you mean?' Susannah asks him.

'Well, we have sugar, of course. But it's not about that. We have something even better: we also have Keller. You know, when he gave you that bag – when he was talking to us – I didn't see a guard; I saw a scared boy. I saw someone ashamed of what's happening around him and prepared to do something to help. He's a good man, and while there are good men around – or even when there's one solitary good man – there's a future of some sort.'

Mother's face lights up as she reaches out and holds Father's hand. 'You're right,' she says, squeezing it tightly. 'Keller is a good man so there must be more.' She's more animated than Susannah has seen her for many months, like the Mother-of-old peering from beneath a shroud. Susannah looks to Jacob and they both nod in support. For the first time in months there's true optimism in their voices, as if the sugar has given their hearts and minds a boost as well as their stomachs.

Then the alarm sounds to signify that mixing time is over, and Father and Jacob leave.

Susannah holds Father's words – that there *is* a future – close to her heart as she curls up with Mother on the straw under the bed. In spite of the hard wooden boards beneath her, she falls into a deep, comforting sleep.

∾

Susannah Morgan was now sitting on a bench at the edge of the memorial taking some time to rest her legs as well as her mind. Was all of this reverie healthy? Well, that remained to be seen, but it had been a while since she last had palpitations, so perhaps she was getting used to the stress. She was stronger than her children gave her credit for. But they were well meaning. And David had problems of his own. Yes, it was time to give them an update. This time it was her daughter's turn. She took her phone out of her handbag and rang her.

'Are you sure you're okay?' were pretty much Judy's first words.

'I'm fine,' Susannah said, closing her eyes at the lie. 'It's . . . it's been worth coming.'

'So where are you now?'

'Oh, here and there.'

There was a long silence. The heavy flutter of a wood pigeon came from above Susannah's head and she watched the creature land and strut about as if it, too, thought there was something missing. Its stuttering gait added an air of authenticity to the act. It made Susannah smile.

'But . . .'

Susannah knew what Judy was going to ask; she wanted to know where her mother had been and when, and who she'd talked to and why. And what she'd been eating. And how far away the medical facilities were. Susannah knew all of this from that single 'but'. It was a legacy of her upbringing. Archie had always said she'd been obsessive and almost neurotic about the safety of their children, wanting to vet every friend and manage every hobby to ensure no harm came to them. Archie had been right, of course, but he'd also let her do it because he was someone who knew. It might have taken an almighty struggle for both of them before he fully understood – but he did know. And that was why she could read so much into her children's words.

'I'm fine, Judy. Don't worry – I've done enough worrying for the whole family. Tell me, how are things with you?'

'Don't ask me how I am, Mom. You know I'm good.'

'All right, so how's David? How's his business bearing up?'

There was more hesitation from Judy, her voice stalling at the beginning of every word.

'Not so good, huh?' Susannah said.

'Well, since you ask – no, not good at all.'

'But how is he? I mean David my son, not David the businessman.'

'I don't think he's taking it very well,' Judy said. 'And it's a part of him, he's spent twenty-five years building that operation up.'

'Judy, could you be a darling and do me a favour?'

A suspicious pause, then: 'What?'

'Tell him he's wrong. His business isn't a part of him – not to me, and not to anyone who's a friend. Tell him there's always a future – no matter what. And if he doesn't agree with that, tell him to ring me.'

'Okay,' Judy said. 'I'll tell him what you said.'

'You do that please. Now I have to go. I'll ring you again later, I promise.'

After the call, Susannah stood up and started walking to where the punishment block once stood.

And, again, she readied herself for memories of years gone by.

CHAPTER THIRTY

In the dark hours of that same night, while Susannah sleeps soundly with her mother on the straw-covered wooden floorboards, she's woken by loud noises and struggles to stir herself. She lifts her head in order to listen more eagerly. She has no idea of time, but in the back of her mind she has a fear that hangs onto her like a disease that simply will not give up the fight.

Has her hour come?

The noises settle for a while, as if they're happening further away. But they never completely stop, so Susannah is fully awake when the angry shouts and the barks come from just outside the cabin. But it still comes as a shock, and she immediately goes to shake Mother awake.

Before she manages to do that the cabin door is flung open and beams of light flash through the room, highlighting the thickness of the dust and the clouds of icebox breath coming from the mouths of the startled prisoners. There are screams and cries for mercy as the shots of light fall on face after face. But eventually the light finds its quarry, and soon Susannah feels a boot knocking her hip. She sees more flashes of light, then hears more angry talk – some from her mother – and is dragged to her feet. Blankets are pulled away sharply. A chamber pot rolls away spreading its filth. A soup bowl is tossed into the air, bouncing off huddles that flinch but determinedly stay as huddles. Before Susannah has even had time to stand up, two guards are hauling her and Mother to their feet and towards the door. Susannah hears Mother ask for an explanation; the answer is the crack of rifle butt on her skull.

The guards shout orders, and there's no time to think whether or not to obey; in a flash of panic they're both outside and breathing in the freezing air that shocks and pains their lungs. Then light falls on Jacob and Father. Each of them has a guard gripping an arm, and Father has blood pouring from his eyebrow and down the side of his face.

Now it's clear what's happening – what the four of them have in common. One of the guards searches each prisoner, and gives a cry of triumph as he comes across the bag of sugar, ripping Susannah's pocket away as premature punishment. He holds the triumph aloft and there's more shouting. Then they're all marched away – to a place Susannah hasn't been to before. The guards shove them towards a set of gates and the guard on duty there laughs and lets them through. The closest any of them gets to resistance is Father's reluctance to move as quickly as he is kicked.

Then Susannah starts to cry. There's the fear of punishment but something more: the camp she's been imprisoned in has been her home for over six months, and she's nervous because she doesn't recognize the familiar landmarks like the washing pool or the toilet block or her own filthy cabin.

They turn a corner and head for a wall. Then they go through a wooden gate in the wall and enter a square courtyard, with a curiously ornate brick building on one side and a large wooden structure on the other, with another wall straight ahead on the other side. A floodlight positioned high above on one of the watchtowers lights up the courtyard, and all Susannah sees is that the centre of the square consists of gravel rather than mud, with concrete walkways linking the buildings. That means this is somewhere important. And then, just as Susannah is rediscovering her senses, there's a commotion behind them. She turns to look but a shout and a rifle butt grinding into her shoulder-blade return her attentions to the front.

However, she's already seen the two figures staggering out of the wooden building behind her. Keller, in a grey vest and long johns, is crying like a distraught widower – one with the barrel of a gun rammed into his spine. Jung is holding the rifle, and also shouting at Keller – no, not just shouting, but screaming abuse. And that's as much as Susannah sees and hears before she's guided into the other building.

They enter a corridor – clean and nowhere near as cold as outside. The heat gives the place an air of importance – and terror. Shouted orders echo in the confined space, making Susannah's ears throb with pain, and before she has time to think they're all bundled into a large room with wooden benches, painted plaster walls and a polished tile floor. Its most telling feature is a fireplace, with glowing chunks of pine cracking and popping in the tense air. Susannah steps close to it and the strength of the heat makes her shudder.

Her thoughts are confused ones. It really does seem as if they've found a paradise of sorts, albeit one with an ominous portent.

There are six other people in the room – three prisoners, each with a guard behind them. All of the prisoners are men; one is unmarked but the other two both have blood pouring from head wounds, partially clotted to dark streaks down their faces. The one with the unmarked face appears to have a black hand, but as Susannah stares at it she sees the fingertips are dripping with treacle-like blood. All three have their heads bowed down towards the tiled floor; one has his hands together and his eyes closed and is mumbling a prayer to himself.

There's also something else Susannah hasn't seen for some time – a clock on the wall. Susannah has to think to work out the time, and think again to realize what this means – that it's an hour past midnight. Their crimes are clearly so terrible that punishment can't wait until the morning.

Somehow they all concur that talking here would not be wise.

As Susannah is thinking of her crime a single shot rings out from the courtyard. Susannah's senses are heightened for a time, there are frightened glances between the prisoners, but still no words are spoken.

For almost an hour there's silence. Although there are eleven people in the room, and although Susannah has Mother, Father and Jacob by her side, it's as if each person is alone with their thoughts. Susannah, at least, feels that way. Do the others consider their loves and regrets, their guilt and fear?

Obviously these feelings are not punishment enough.

CHAPTER THIRTY-ONE

A female SS guard enters the room, breaking the silence, breaking Susannah's train of thought on her loves, regrets and guilt. But the fear in her throat won't leave, as the guard reads out the four Zuckermans' names and the four guards behind them prod them out of the room. They cross the corridor and enter another room. This also has an open fire at one end, but is much more luxurious, with upholstered chairs at the sides and a large desk in the middle with a man behind it. There are also pictures on the walls, all of uniformed men. Susannah squints to try to make out whether the one in the middle – also the highest on the wall – is Adolf Hitler. Then the man sitting at the desk stops writing, calmly places the cap back on his pen, and looks up. He gives them all a stern glare, one by one, and Susannah feels a chill when his eyes – grey and stony – fall on her; there's no mistaking the resolve on this man's face.

'You get me out of bed for this?' he says in a gentle voice, monotone but for the final word, which is screeched.

'Not just these, Kommandant,' the guard says. 'There's also been an attempted escape.'

'And they weren't shot?'

'They surrendered, Kommandant. The guards thought it would be best to try them.'

The Kommandant sighs and gives his head a slight shake. Then he looks to the front, and again Susannah feels the steel of a stronger power in his stare. 'What's the charge?' he says.

'Breaking food distribution rules,' the female guard says, holding up the sugar bag – just as Susannah had left it, with a few spoonfuls left for Ester.

Then there's some quieter talk between the two of them, with occasional glances back to the Zuckermans.

'So where's Keller?' the Kommandant says.

'Already been dealt with, Kommandant,' the guard replies.

'Excellent.' He looks over to the Zuckermans and speaks the words as if reciting his favourite poem. 'We have food for prisoners and we have food for staff. Supplies are getting scarce and have to be carefully managed. You are charged with breaking food distribution rules, and this is treated as theft from staff. Do you all understand?'

Nobody spoke. He asked the question again, this time more loudly.

Susannah's father cleared his throat to speak. 'Please. It was only half a bag of sugar shared between the four of us. We have all—'

'Just answer the question. Do you understand the charge?'

'We understand, but we're all so hungry and weak. You don't feed us enough.'

'Mr Zuckerman, the whole of Germany is hungry. Food is scarce and we have priorities. Hence we have rules governing food distribution.'

The Kommandant starts writing again, stops briefly to think, sighing through his nose as he does so, then writes some more. There's more whispering between him and the female guard, then he sits bolt upright and pushes his shoulders back.

'Your case has been carefully considered, and you have been

found guilty of breaking food distribution rules. The penalty is half of your rations for the next two weeks.'

'Oh, no,' Susannah's mother says. 'Please no.'

'Take them out,' the Kommandant says. He takes a rubber stamp and brings it down hard on the sheet of paper he has been writing on.

Susannah's father takes a step forward and a guard grabs his arm and pulls him back. But it doesn't stop him speaking.

'But you can't,' he says. 'We were just trying to get enough to eat. We're all starving to death!'

'Mr Zuckerman. You stole from a guard.'

'But he *gave* it to us!' Father says, now raising his voice and struggling to loosen his arm from the grip of the guard, who immediately digs his rifle into his prisoner's ribs.

Then the Kommandant waves the protest away with the back of his hand and shouts out, 'Next case!'

Father huffs and puffs, but before he can force out any more words the prisoners are jostled out of the room and forced outside into the courtyard.

Susannah, Jacob and their mother and father veer towards the gate in the wall, back towards their cabin. But anger at their punishment turns to confusion as they're pulled towards the dark wooden building opposite – the building that must be the punishment block.

And as they turn they all see it – and their confusion becomes blind terror.

In the distance, near the wall, a body is slumped on the ground, its grey vest and long johns streaked with dark red splashes. Susannah gasps and starts to cry as she recognizes Keller's face, the blood still seeping from the hole in his temple. She collapses onto the floor, and is dragged the rest of the way, getting to her feet only as she reaches the door of the punishment block.

The next few minutes are lost to Susannah in a haze of sadness and resentment, but she realizes she has to think quickly or she will head for the wall too. As she's shoved into the building with the others she wipes her face and looks around. Five prisoners are already there, two of them grown men in tears. The building itself is a complete contrast to the one they've just been in.

Only a few strands of light come through splits in the wooden walls, but enough to highlight the uneven soil floor littered with dirty grey blankets. A few wooden-framed beds line the edges, two smashed and sprawled like the ends of a broken bridge. On the far side of the room is a gap leading to a corridor.

Susannah steps across, and looks along its darkness, seeing a pile of discarded clothes, and then shoes, and also a few pairs of spectacles. But then she hears the grind of boot on gritty earth and turns round sharply.

'Why are we here?' Susannah's mother asks the guards.

They don't reply.

Susannah's father tries again. 'You heard the punishment, half rations for a week. Why won't you let us go back to our cabins?'

This time the guards exchange glances. One shapes his mouth to speak but another glares at him and gives his head the briefest of shakes, silencing his colleague.

And then they're all alerted by more noises from the courtyard, and the three prisoners that were the 'next case' join them, accompanied by three guards.

Once they're in the room, Jung appears at the door as if he has been standing there all of the time. He enters and closes the door behind him, darkening the room yet more.

'What's happening?' Susannah's father asks him, his heavy breathing giving his voice a childlike quality. 'Our punishment is half rations. Nothing more.'

A few of the guards start to laugh at this, and Susannah's father turns to them, his jaw dropping, bloody saliva dribbling from one corner of his mouth.

'You're here for a delousing procedure,' Jung says with a politeness none of them has even known before.

'But . . . how can that be? There are no showers here.'

The guards laugh once more, then fall silent again when Jung glances at them.

Susannah's father drops to his knees in front of Jung. 'Please, I'm begging you. Spare our children if nothing else. Susannah is a fifteen-year-old girl. Jacob is only thirteen. What harm have they done? Please, if you do nothing else allow *them* to return to their cabins. *Please.*'

Jung steps back from him and starts shouting orders to the other guards. There's a lot of movement. It all seems so efficient, as if it's been carried out a thousand times before.

They're all shoved towards the corridor. First the five prisoners before them, then the three that have come in after them. Then it's the turn of the Zuckermans.

They hear shouts, and just about see through the dusty gloom the eight who have gone before them taking their clothes off. There are more shouts and they move out of view.

Susannah notices beams of light being broken and hears cruel laughter. But both of these halt whenever she twists and tries to home in on the source. Father, Mother and Jacob walk towards the corridor, but Susannah waits where she is.

She runs back to the entrance and pulls on the handle of the wooden door. It does nothing more than rattle in the gloom. She hears a shout from behind her and turns. Now, as dimness gives way to half-light, she cries out and falls back onto the door, feels her spine catching the rough wooden edges, but doesn't care.

Jung stands in front of her in full smartly pressed uniform. He stands a foot taller than her, with neatly trimmed hair and a cap perfectly set on top.

'You!' He grabs her arm and pulls, spinning her away from the door. 'Clothes. Shoes. *Off!*'

For a few seconds her whole body trembles, but she says and does nothing.

He shouts at her again, then points his rifle at her. 'Clothes off! Time for your delouse! In the shower!'

'Delouse?' she says. 'We all know you're lying.'

And then the sound of five gunshots makes them both freeze for a second. Susannah's throat turns dry and sticky, and she starts to cry again.

'So we're lying,' Jung says with a slow and deliberate cadence. 'Now. Take your clothes off.'

Then, slowly, from where Susannah doesn't know, a feeling of charged energy washes over her. She stops crying and wipes her face. Her shaking stops and she stands up straight, with shoulders pressed back and head held high. For the first time in months she feels some strength coursing through her body. She has nothing to lose; she realizes she has – just this once – power.

'No,' she says quietly.

Momentarily Jung drops his rifle. 'You defy the orders of an armed guard?'

She nods. 'Oh yes. And whenever I can from this moment on.'

Jung presses the rifle to her throat. 'You have one more chance, *Untermensch!*'

And his shout tells her she has won this battle, that regardless of whatever bullets and blood are to come, she knows she has now beaten him. She snarls, then spits in his face.

He runs his fingertips across his cheek, then wipes his hand on his jacket. Then he glances at the mess on his otherwise pristine uniform, and smiles as he cocks the trigger.

Susannah mumbles a prayer, then grabs the cold metal muzzle of the rifle and places it in her mouth. She grips the barrel tightly with trembling hands, closes her eyes and swallows, her throat sticky with dryness. She feels every muscle in her body go rigid with fresh, liberating energy.

The next thing she hears is a solid click. Jung takes back his rifle and pulls its bolt back and forth a few times, grunting through clenched teeth. He throws it onto the floor, then reaches for his pistol. He searches frantically, but there is no pistol. He curses a few times, then sighs and his body relaxes.

He looks her up and down, and slowly the corners of his lips start to tilt upwards.

He rasps out a laugh. 'You're lucky today, aren't you?'

She knocks past him and lunges for the door. But he flings a hand out and manages to grasp her arm. She feels his fingers digging into her shrunken muscle fibres but manages to wrench herself free. A stumble and she runs to the door. Wildly shaking hands grab the handle and pull. Now it opens, but Jung thumps his boot against it solidly and it slams shut again.

He grabs her by the throat and pins her to the door. 'From now on, you are "The Lucky One",' he says. 'Now get out!'

The door gives a screech from its hinges as it opens again. Susannah feels the shove of his boot in the small of her back and flies through the door.

'Back to your cabin!' he shouts.

She falls onto the concrete path and looks up to see Jung staring beyond her and into the distance. She jerks her head to follow his gaze, only to see Mother, Father and Jacob, together with the three bloodied men, all naked, all standing up against a wall. Her vision fades as she hears the six gunshots.

Her skull hits the rough concrete path and drags along it as she curls up and lets out a scream from her soul. She screams again and trembles, her mind flooded with echoes of the sound she's just heard. She lifts her head and looks across to her family to be sure of what she's just witnessed. She lets out another scream – one that turns to a whimper as she hits her head against the path again. She wonders what the point of the last fifteen years has been, and feels her biggest regret so far in her short life: that she isn't there with them.

෨ඏ

And then Susannah stirred, blinking in the clean sunlight, drawing one leg out from underneath her and slapping her shoe on the ground. With a struggle that brought water to her eyes she pushed down on her better knee, telling the arthritic groan in it to shut up, and slowly pushed herself to her feet. She stumbled around for a moment, the buildings in front of her appearing and disappearing like the numbers of a roulette wheel spinning past. She turned and spotted a man a few yards away, at first fearing him, then somehow confused to see no threat. Yes, he was a gardener busy raking up leaves. She staggered across the path towards him and grabbed his arm, almost pulling him over in her panic.

The man dropped the rake and held her in his arms. 'What is it?' he said. 'What's wrong?'

'It's Jung. I'm sure he's going to kill me. Please help.'

'Jung?' the man said.

'He's an SS guard. And there are others. Please. *Please* help me.'

He held her to his chest, her tears turning patches of his bib a darker shade of green.

'No, madam. That's not possible.'

'Yes, yes!' She pointed back. 'Over there, in that building.'

The gardener briefly glanced to where her wrinkled hand was cast. 'But, madam. There are no buildings left here. And definitely no guards.'

'But I . . .' She turned and gasped.

The gardener removed his gloves and put his hand behind her, gently stroking the top of her back. 'I take it you've been here before – a long, long time ago – yes?'

Susannah looked again as a solitary wood pigeon landed in the emptiness – the beautiful, natural emptiness. She took a moment to catch her breath.

'Yes,' she said. 'I was one of the lucky ones.'

PART FOUR
The Lucky One

CHAPTER THIRTY-TWO

I n the weeks that follow the loss of her mother, father and brother, Susannah's only consolation is Ester. She's too upset to even enter her own cabin and sleeps next to Ester at night. She also stays there during the day, retreating into her mind, to the happy times in Berlin with her family, before all this madness started. She reconsiders the reservations she had about moving to Amsterdam, now long gone, the times she spent getting to know new friends and enjoying the thrill of being in a new city. Yes, for a while it even felt like an extended vacation.

Even the stay at the remote farmhouse didn't feel dangerous or depressing. In spite of the cold, cramped conditions and the arguments, she still held sweet, dear memories of her time with Uncle Paul and Aunt Helena, and of learning to play what seemed like every card game ever invented.

Westerbork was worse but just bearable, still a pleasant life of sorts, with warmth, edible food and the constant company of her family.

Of course, falling off a cliff can hold some pleasures until you reach the bottom.

So she spends the days lost in her own world, thinking of the good times, and crying for the family she knows she will never see again. She cries for Keller too and knows that if it wasn't for her stupid mistake they would all be alive. She knows there is blood on her hands that she can't simply wash off. And she knows there is only one way she can be with them all again and ask for their forgiveness.

And so, in her confused state, she also tries to forget the good times – because when she doesn't think of these, the pain is merely a dull ache in her heart that she can cope with – and she yearns for the time when she will see them all again.

For weeks she relies on Ester to tell her what's been happening in the camp, but in truth doesn't care – she might as well be listening to a news report:

The small crematorium used for burning bodies has quickly become overwhelmed.

Even the mass burnings and burials have stopped because too many people have been dying.

The prisoners have resorted to dragging the corpses as far away from the buildings as possible and simply leaving them there.

Now the prisoners are too weak and the sheer volume of dead flesh too much, so all they have energy for is making sure the bodies are taken out of the cabins.

And the cabins are so disgusting even the guards no longer visit.

End of news report.

On the few occasions Susannah leaves the cabin she sees the piles of bodies for herself – and realizes Ester isn't exaggerating. Conditions have spiralled into the animalistic, making life at Westerbork seem luxurious.

For weeks Susannah does no more than exist, getting up only to eat the twice-daily meal – the thin soup and chunk of stale bread – that Ester brings her. She doesn't turn up for roll-call and the guards don't come and tell her to – perhaps they too have given up.

She doesn't wash or change her clothes; she hardly ever leaves the cabin, but mainly stays on the floor with her eyes closed, imagining a bright light – a strong sun of the purest white – concentrating her mind on absorbing its motherly warmth, bathing in its healing light. Think of that, not reality, and the pain stays still. Think of the fantastic and her mind has no room for the thoughts of reality that hurt.

Yes, if she concentrates on the light in her mind, then perhaps she can make whatever world she wants there and she can choose whoever she wants to be in it. And then the horrible other world will be all over and she will be released from this misery.

Occasionally she feels her shoulder being gently shaken; it's Ester taking her pure white dreams away by bringing food. Although younger in years than her, Ester talks to her, comforts her like Mother used to, and tells her to hold on, that the rumours of the advancing British army become stronger every day with each new set of prisoners.

Susannah has heard that too many times before and prefers the reality in her mind.

Only in early April do Susannah's thoughts of wretchedness start to wane just a little, and she feels well enough to go out and experience some real sun. Perhaps there's some water too. Her weakened legs are barely able to carry her, but she goes – something, somewhere, guiding her to the door, to a freedom of sorts. Her pale skin isn't used to the sunlight and, although it's only early spring, it feels as if her skin is being burnt. Even if she faces away from the sun she can't bear to open her eyes to anything more than slits. But she stumbles over ruts in the mud tracks, then glances down to see the ruts are not made of mud but are bodies – not fresh ones but rotting ones, the skin diseased and spotted with areas of squirming maggots.

And yet there's more to see. The mud that's everywhere is

splattered in parts with faeces, blood and vomit. There's the occasional body that has had its internal organs raided – because in these desperate times any common, decent humanity has long since expired, along with hope.

The images before Susannah shock her awake and she looks further, now ignoring the headache caused by the pain of the light in her eyes. What's a headache when you're living in hell?

The things that move most – apart from the creatures that have started to crawl and feast on the carcasses of the prisoners – are birds that flutter and gaily swoop along. Sparrows twitch, thrushes and blackbirds hop, wagtails bob their back ends merrily up and down. All are oblivious to the sorry scene before them. In contrast, any human that moves does so as slowly as a slug.

But there's more to see. The gates are still shut, the barbed wire still threatens to release what little blood is left in any bodies that venture near it.

Susannah soon feels too weak and tired. She's scared that if she moves any further away from the cabin she won't have the energy to return, so retreats into the stinking cave she now thinks of as her home.

Over the next few days Ester tries to keep Susannah's spirits up, but it's a hopeless case. She, like Susannah, is covered in itchy scabs and rashes – the legacy of the lice and fleas that celebrate the squalor.

And then the food stops completely.

And then the water supply gets turned off.

They've been locked in the camp and left to rot.

This is nothing more than a mass oubliette some distance beyond the ragged edges of a twisted civilization.

And in that mass oubliette Susannah would lie still and let herself die if it weren't for those damned lice and fleas, constantly itching one area of skin or another. They're everywhere, but congregate mostly around armpits, the pubic area, and on heads that once again have hair because there's nothing to cut it with. Now her sole activities are resting, scratching herself until she bleeds, and picking off and crushing the lice. On one occasion she picks one of the creatures out of her hair, rolls it between her fingernail and the palm of her hand to crush it, then tries to look more closely. She holds it up to the light and squints her lazy eyes to focus on its broken body, which looks like a tiny fragment of brown glass covered in brown liquid. She closes her eyes, opens her mouth, and places the tiny speck of meat on her tongue. Sickness spreads across her face like black cloud spreading darkness. She knows the grimace costs her more energy than would be gained by eating the louse, and spits it out – or rather she forces it off her tongue and out of her mouth with her front teeth, leaving it to dribble in its saliva cocoon down her chin.

Her clothes are baggy on her shrunken frame. She's dehydrated, riddled with fleas, lice and their eggs, and diseased with the rash of typhus. She knows that if she had the energy to inhale through her nose she would smell just like the rest of the prisoners – of stale sweat, urine, faeces and dried blood. Of creeping death.

How on God's earth did she get from life in Berlin – and being protected by loving parents – to this?

Is she really 'The Lucky One'?

And soon she doesn't even have the energy to scratch. She curls up, covers her head with the crusty blanket, and begs God to take her.

Now she doesn't dream or reminisce, she doesn't sleep but drifts in and out of consciousness, visiting the other side. The better side. The pure white side. As she connects to this better world her thoughts flutter back and forth like the birds that criss-cross between the pine forest and this hell on earth.

At least Mother, Father and Jacob have avoided this torture.

Perhaps it's they who are the lucky ones.

There are no more tears. There's no more scratching and scraping of skin. There are only barely noticeable movements of Susannah's chest, and gasping breaths from a dry, sticky mouth held agape.

Susannah curls up a little more. She waits to die.

And then, between the bouts of delirium that make the whole room sway, she feels her shoulder being rocked, as though someone or something is trying to wake her from her sleeping death. Her eyes slowly open but can't focus and see only blurry movement. Then she hears Ester talking – because hearing takes no energy. Even Ester has little spirit left in her, but still manages to talk to Susannah, to tell her in some dull shadow of those excited tones that something is happening outside, that the gates are open, and that soldiers in different uniforms, who don't speak German, are all around them.

But Ester is wasting her breath.

Susannah curls up yet more. She *wants* to die – to slip into her pure white world and stay there for ever.

CHAPTER THIRTY-THREE

With help and warmth from the memorial gardener, Susannah eventually calmed down enough to see that she was back in 2009 – that there were no old buildings left, and that there were no SS guards.

'Here,' he said to her. 'Let me help you walk back to the Visitor Centre.'

She drew herself away from the man's strong arms. 'Yes,' she said, nodding. 'Thank you. That would be nice.'

And then, as they started walking, she looked across to him. 'You must think I'm an old fool, making such a fuss about something that happened years before you were even born.'

The man swiftly shook his head, then said, 'Forgive me for asking, but were you a prisoner here?'

'A prisoner?' She cast a glance around her. 'This was once my home. I remember the wooden cabins, the barbed wire, the electric fencing, the mud that was absolutely everywhere. But, you know, most of all I remember the voices; they seem to linger in my mind more than anything else.'

They walked in silence for a while longer, then Susannah stopped to catch her breath and looked towards the surrounding forest. 'No,' she said. 'Actually I'm wrong. What I remember most of all are the birds flying back and forth between here and the forest just as they used to all those years ago. Nothing seems to have changed as far as they're concerned.'

As they approached the Visitor Centre Susannah stopped still. 'I . . . I don't want to go into the cafeteria again.'

'You don't have to eat in there; you can just rest.'

'It's not that,' she said. 'I can't face . . . I know it sounds stupid, but it's the noise, and the people.'

The gardener thought for a moment. 'There's always the multimedia room.'

'The what?'

He pointed to a newish building at the far end of the Visitor Centre. 'The multimedia room. It plays documentary video films.' He shrugged. 'It's usually very quiet there, with comfortable seats. Like being at the movies, yes?'

Susannah nodded. 'Quiet and peaceful with comfortable seats. You know, young man, that sounds exactly what I need.'

He showed her to the door, which opened without a sound, and led her inside.

'Are you sure you're okay now?' he said. 'I have work to do.' He edged to the door.

'You're a very kind man,' she said. 'I think I'll be fine now, thank you.'

Only when the gardener left did she take a look around and realize she had the place all to herself. And he was right; it was, indeed, just like a small movie theatre. And, yes, the seats were large, well-padded affairs. In fact, the place resembled one of those home movie theatres that one or two of her better-off neighbours back in North Carolina had in their basements or in shacks in their back yards.

And it was dark. But it wasn't quiet.

She settled herself down into one of those big, comfortable seats with a relaxing gasp and closed her eyes.

No. It wasn't quiet.

On the display screen that dominated the front of the room a man was talking. There was something about him Susannah warmed to. It was partly because he was such a sweet old thing, and partly because she felt an immediate empathy with him. What was it about him? Of course, it was only because, just like her, he was one of those dewy-eyed old fools who obviously couldn't forget what had happened all those years ago, someone else still quite obviously suffering over sixty years later. He stuttered and almost broke down as he talked about how he worked around the clock and catnapped here and there to get sleep, and described how he buried bodies and couldn't get someone or other out of his mind.

And then he stopped talking, and there was peace and quiet. Good. As cute as the old guy was, Susannah had herself to think of. She was exhausted – physically and especially emotionally – and perhaps Judy and David had been right: perhaps dragging her weak and decrepit old body all this way hadn't been such a clever move after all.

Sure, she had her answer – sort of. But at what price?

Seduced by the silence and the dark, warm comforts, she closed her eyes and her mind wandered off to a better place – the place she'd always thought of as the start of her new life, after she'd recovered from the horrors of Bergen-Belsen.

༄

After she'd got married to Archie, Susannah had wanted to stay in Wilmington to be close to Paul, Helena and Reuben. They'd all settled there because of a farm specifically set up for Jews fleeing

Europe, and because the coastal plain most resembled the landscape of the Netherlands, which was where Paul and Helena occasionally said they were from, because sometimes – just sometimes – it wasn't exactly helpful to your social life to say you were German.

Now Susannah and Archie had been married for two years and, although neither of them could bring themselves to admit it, they'd been two pretty horrible years.

Archie had been trying to control her. Telling her how much drink she was pouring down her neck. And he kept on telling her not to buy so much food, that there was no shortage in the stores and she didn't need fifteen tins of this and twenty boxes of that, and especially bottles and bottles of *you know what.*

She'd confessed to Aunt Helena that they were having difficulties, that Archie was trying to control her, and although Helena hadn't exactly taken his side, she didn't seem to be much help either, saying she should try to see things from his point of view. It was about then that Susannah and Archie had had their first major argument – the one where Archie had told her she had to see the doctor again.

And that hadn't helped. She just wanted them all to butt out and let her sort out her own problems – *her way.*

And her way meant drinking as much as she wanted, whenever she wanted.

The housework piled up, the only time she seemed to leave the house was to buy more groceries she didn't need but somehow had to buy 'just in case they ran out', and she felt like Archie was hardly speaking to her. Of course, years later she realized that he was talking, just not saying what she wanted to hear.

It was about then that she had the car accident. She reversed the car straight out of the drive, then her foot slipped off the brake pedal and she carried straight on across the street into Mr Carlton's new Buick.

At first Mr Carlton accepted the accident as exactly that. He asked whether she was all right, and told her not to worry, that these things happen. Then, when she got out of the car he started sniffing the air around her like a wild bear. At that point he changed. He went very red in the face and became short with her, saying he would sort things out with Mr Morgan later on – after he had put her car back onto her drive because she was in no fit state to do it herself.

It was to be another two years before Mr Carlton said another word to her.

However, the real problems started when Archie came home and saw the damage to the car.

'So which came first?' he said. 'Did you get drunk because you smashed the car or did you smash the car because you were drunk?'

It was a fair, if sarcastic, question.

But Susannah matched it. 'You know, honey,' she said, 'to tell you the truth, I'm too sozzled to remember.'

'I can believe that,' he said. 'Perhaps you're too sozzled for anything. As always.'

'Perhaps I like being too sozzled,' she said with a laugh.

'Like or love?'

She shrugged but didn't answer.

'Whatever,' he said. 'I can't handle this.'

Then he started swearing, saying he'd been good to her and given her what she wanted, and didn't understand what her problem was or what he'd done wrong. Then he stopped himself, thought for a moment and just said quietly, 'For God's sake, Susannah, I know what you've . . . I mean, I have some idea of what you've been through, but if you want to kill yourself there are quicker ways of doing it.'

He turned towards the door and started walking.

'Isn't that what you want?' she said, spitting the words out.

Then he just gave her a pitying look and shook his head.

As he reached the door she shouted out for him to stop.

'Why should I?' he asked.

'You . . . you haven't eaten, and you've still got your work clothes on.'

'I'll be fine.'

And he said it with that annoying calmness again, the air of normality he must have known wound her up like a toy racing car.

'Please stay,' she said, her face now cracking.

'I just need a break from it.'

'From me?'

He ignored that and reached for the door handle. She ran to him, her hands mauling him.

'Archie, please don't leave me.'

He brushed her hands aside and sighed. 'I'm not leaving you, Susannah. I just can't cope with this – with you like this.'

But, then again, he always said that – always denied he was leaving her.

'Please, Archie. Tell me the truth. I can take it.'

'I always tell you the truth.'

'I can give up the drink if I have to. Just tell me you're not going to leave me.'

He looked her up and down.

Like she was a whore.

'I'm not going to leave you,' he said.

Sure, he looked her in the eye when he said it, but he paused, he definitely paused.

'I love you, and I want to spend the rest of my life with you. It's just . . . when you . . .'

Yes, he definitely paused, like he had to give the matter some consideration rather than let the instinctive answer fall out.

Then she stood in front of the door. He sighed and shook his head, this time giving his brow a wipe for good measure.

'I can't talk when you're like this,' he said, pushing her to the side.

'Please don't leave me.'

'I am NOT . . .' He took a moment to calm himself down a little, then, seeing the tears streaming down her face, lowered his voice. 'I'm not leaving you, Susannah. I just . . . I need some fresh air. I'm going for a walk, that's all.'

And with that, he left.

I'm not leaving you, and then he left.

Susannah spent a few minutes – no, it was probably only a few seconds – staring at the door, then she went into the kitchen to open a bottle.

And after the first glug she knew why Archie had hesitated. It was guilt over his other woman. Yes, that was it, guilt over the woman he was planning to leave her for.

Some time later – there was no way of telling how long except by fingers of gin – she stumbled out onto the front lawn, bottle in hand, and prepared to address the scary and unwelcoming neighbours – those anti-Semitic sons of bitches who had ignored her, had twitched those drapes whenever she'd left the house, and who she knew for certain were talking about her behind her back. Well, she was just going to have to tell them she couldn't give two green figs for what they thought about her, that if it was true that America was a free country, then she was free to drink however much she damn well wanted to, and they could gossip about her and give her disapproving looks as much as they wanted. She simply didn't care for them and their like. In fact, they could all rot in hell – not that any of them had the slightest notion of what hell was really like.

Back in the real world, however, she spoke no words at all.

In her stupor she tripped on the edge of the driveway and felt her feet pull away from underneath her. She twisted her torso – because the only important thing right now was trying to keep the bottle she was holding upright. After all, losing any of that precious juice was hardly likely to make life better, was it?

And because she was unable – or unwilling – to use both hands to break her fall, her ribcage took the brunt of the fall. The pain, although dulled by drink, made her pass out.

When she came to, prostrate on the lawn, she could feel something slight and delicate resting on her outstretched hand. She didn't move, but slowly opened those bleary eyes to see a wagtail perched on her thumb.

The bird was small, plumper than it had any right to be, but with warm dark eyes and skinny legs. It started chirping, and for a second Susannah saw Ester in feathered form, singing to her, and heard her giving that old pep talk. 'You must keep hoping,' Ester says. 'You have to do your best to survive and hope that things will get better. Otherwise there's nothing – no point in living.'

And, while her head was spinning like a fairground ride, she wondered what Ester would have told her to do had she really been there. Would she have told her to stop drinking, or to try to forget what had happened?

And what if Susannah were to say she couldn't imagine a life without drink – could see no escape, no way of living without her unquestioning liquid friend? What would Ester have said to that? Of course, she would have told her that nothing is impossible if you think hard enough, that there's always a way out, that you're never a prisoner in your own mind.

And that was more or less what Susannah heard the little wagtail say. Then she watched it stretch its wings out one at a time, then crouch down and leap into the air. Its wings took care of the rest, and it circled Susannah a few times before swooping away, over the fence and into the small wood beyond.

Susannah closed her eyes again and stilled herself to think on.

That didn't take long, and a few minutes later she lifted herself up, wincing at the pain in her side, and turned her attentions to the bottle still in her hand. She stared at it for a moment, then slowly turned it upside down. Then she watched until every last drop of the liquid had drained out and been sucked into the parched lawn. And, as those last drops fell, she thought she heard a final encouraging chirrup from the small wood beyond the fence. She struggled to pick her disorderly body up onto its feet and took her old friend, the bottle, back inside the house.

The next few weeks turned out to be a lot easier than Susannah thought they would be, because whenever those three cracked ribs made her wince in pain it reminded her of Ester's words.

And she never touched a drop of alcohol for the rest of her days.

CHAPTER THIRTY-FOUR

Susannah felt refreshed enough to open her eyes. The audio-visual presentation had seen fit to stop – or, at least, to stop the old fellow talking about his wartime experiences – a few minutes ago. It was as if it knew she took a side salad of quiet with her solitude. How understanding.

She looked around to find out she was still the only person in the room. Good. Those seats were mighty comfortable. Having a rest had made her feel sleepy – and that wasn't a contradiction but a self-indulgent advantage that came with age. She took some slow, deep breaths through her nose and closed her eyes again.

❧

Susannah hears a voice – a foreign one – and she feels simultaneously shocked and desperate to find out what is happening to her. She tries to wake herself up but can't; her body refuses to obey orders and does nothing. But she can feel her body even if she can't move it – and it feels slim and young, but at the same time fragile. Although she can't open her eyelids there's now a light forcing its way through them, warming her.

She feels her shoulder being nudged again – this time not by Ester's delicate hand. She hears gentle talk in a language she doesn't understand. Could it be English? She feels warmth pressing on her shoulder, and tries to open her eyes. But they're like sticky, cobwebbed doors. Then she sees only a blur and language is irrelevant. She looks up and the blur moves. Her eyes follow it. She hears more words, and even though it's in that foreign tongue again she senses the anger, a controlled anger but, nonetheless, one that contrasts with the gentle touch that woke her up.

There's more touching – her hair, her shoulders, her legs. Then she hears the sound of a grown man crying, which is the same in every language. She's left alone while this happens, and she senses the moment has gone. There isn't even a jot of worry at being left alone again.

Because she doesn't want to live.

She strains to lift her eyelids fully open, then moves her lower jaw up and down. It's an effort, and she knows her lower lip moves only a fraction of an inch. Her tongue is stuck to the arid interior of her mouth. The vague figure, now a few feet away, starts to move closer again. He starts talking. It's English – definitely English – so the words could be anything, but there's a special comfort in the voice that gives meaning beyond words. It makes her feel calm and safe in a way she hasn't felt for months or years.

She feels something wet touching her lips, and then again. It's water, and it trickles into her mouth and feels like a monsoon giving life to a desert. Her tongue can now move. Some water gets to the back of her throat and she gives a gentle swallow. More water follows, then more. It's like an electric current flowing through her, enough to make her open and close her mouth.

Yet more water dribbles into her mouth, and then it stops. Next she feels a harsh graininess on her lips, almost cutting them. Her tongue slips out and touches the substance. It tastes of ecstasy, of life and of every good memory she ever had.

Sugar.

Soon her mouth is alive and singing with the nectar.

Then she starts to move a little more, but slowly, grabbing for more sugar. And her eyes start to function. In front of her, crouching down, is the man. He's young and wearing a smart uniform. A metal bottle and a paper bag rest on his lap, and in one hand is a spoon. When he sees Susannah moving he puts them all away and starts touching her – her face and her shoulder. He takes a blanket out of his bag and puts it over her; it's as soft as a crying baby's first blanket. Then the man feels her feet, and she hears a disappointed groan, followed by what sounds like a curse under his breath. She glances across. He's taking his shoes and socks off, and soon her feet feel warm for the first time in months.

But then, mysteriously, the man walks away, turning his back on her. Susannah hears more crying.

She starts to cry too, but silently and inwardly, and she doesn't know why.

A minute later she feels her body being hoisted up and her head is spinning. And although she makes no sound she's still crying inside. However, with the warmth of another human being, and another glimpse of that rainbow, she feels better. She feels like this man will hold her until her sadness flies away.

Then she passes out.

She's woken only by the rage of daylight and immediately shuts her eyes to its harshness. But in that instant she sees enough; she sees she's still in the man's arms, and she sees the cabin door pass her by. The cool fresh air hits her like the rush of smelling salts, and then she hears a shout and a scuffle of some sort.

Then she hears the shout again, this time the words are clearer: 'The Lucky One!'

Unlike the voice from the man carrying her, the mocking shout is in German. She hears more blows and angry words and then she feels her body being sharply twisted away from whatever is going on. She grips the arm that holds her, and then, as though the exertion is too much, she relaxes and passes out again.

CHAPTER THIRTY-FIVE

Susannah is now conscious of feeling weak and hardly being able to move – but also conscious of a voice – a friendly, recognizable one this time – a piece of the jigsaw of who she once was.

But no – there are two voices, two jigsaw pieces. That means she has twice the chance of working out what's happening to her.

They are German voices, and as she starts to move her head, feeling giddy as she does so, the voices get louder, more agitated. She feels threatened by the emotion in the voices, but cannot understand. Through her eyelids there's a pink brightness, a painful light.

Then there's nothing.

Susannah wakes again, and the voices are no longer there. She feels it's safe to listen, but there's nothing except a drone. Then she hears cracks in the distance – at once sharp yet faint – one every second. She opens her eyes. There's nothing more than dimness. Good. No pain. But a faint yellow light glows in the distance.

Is this heaven?

She strains to focus, sees a shape drifting from left to right towards the yellow glow. The shape stops moving and with it the sharp cracking noise stops. Susannah starts to focus properly, on a human figure in blue. The figure starts to move and the regular tick-tocking cracks start up again.

Her eyes explore more. At the yellow glow there's another human figure. It's at a desk of some sort, one with a lamp on it. Her head moves to allow her eyes a wider view, and she sees beds with huddles on them. But here there's just one huddle per bed. The beds are spaced out. The sheets are white. There are no huddles covering the floor. She strains more to focus, and sees clear tubes leading to her arm.

No, this is not heaven – only a heaven of sorts.

When Susannah wakes again she almost feels human. The brightness is now not so painful to her eyes, and after blinking a few times she can see quite clearly. She turns her head to the side, and in front of her she sees a man with hair instead of a face. No, silly. It's the top of the man's head. It's a sight she has seen before somewhere. *But where?* The man is sitting in front of her with his head down, reading a book.

Susannah stares for a few seconds, but he doesn't move. Then he turns a page of the book and looks up. Now she sees his face, and it's a familiar one.

And a shocked one.

The book drops to the floor and so does the man, onto his knees. He leans forward, his face moving closer to Susannah's.

For a moment her heart jumps with fear at the sudden movement.

The man turns away from her and shouts a few words in German. 'Helena!' he says. 'Helena! Come here!'

Another face from Susannah's past appears next to the man's. And then she knows. It's Uncle Paul and Aunt Helena. They both look well – thin, but not thin like the ghosts in her nightmares. So is she in heaven after all? Perhaps that's it, Uncle Paul and Aunt

Helena went to heaven and now she has joined them. Susannah feels tears tickle the side of her nose and twitches it.

'Look,' Paul says, gasping with excitement. 'She's moving!'

'And is that a smile?' Helena says. She makes a spitting noise, gasps a couple of times, and starts to cry too.

'Nurse!' Paul shouts out, this time without taking his eyes off Susannah, and then he stammers and says a few words in what Susannah recognizes as broken English.

A nurse comes, says she speaks German, and there's more talk between the three of them. The nurse says they have to leave now, that this is too much excitement and the patient must rest. Paul agrees and says that they'll return tomorrow. Helena wipes tears from her cheeks and holds her face close to Susannah's, putting a supporting hand behind her head and kissing the top of it. She tells her to fight.

Fight?

That is funny.

Then Paul squeezes her hand, they both look at her for a few seconds, then turn and leave.

For a second Susannah wants to cry out, to beg them not to go, but the nurse talks to her instead, saying a few words in German: 'Rest' – 'Tomorrow' – 'You will see them.' Then there are more words in English. Susannah understands a little English and concentrates to understand, but fails because her mind is fuzzy. However, she knows by the tone of the words that they're helpful and comforting. The nurse takes her temperature, nods, then closes the slatted blinds at the top of the bed.

Yes, the nurse is right. The excitement has taken its toll; Susannah closes her eyes and is soon asleep again.

It's early in the morning when Susannah wakes again, and she has the energy to sit up in bed.

With a clean nightdress and starchy white bed sheets the whole scene has a synthetic feel to it. Like the birdsong at the edge of the camp, there's a heavenly, ethereal quality to everything here.

Wherever here is.

Within half an hour a nurse arrives with a small bowl of warm porridge and places it in front of her. *But what should she do with it?* She sniffs it and retches, making the nurse pull it away from her. The nurse waits a few moments, then lifts a spoonful of it up to Susannah's face. She tells her to open her mouth and close her eyes, which she does. And then the nurse is telling her to swallow, but she takes no notice, almost choking on the porridge before spitting it all back out. She wipes her mouth and looks up to the nurse, who tells her it's all right, and that they can try again tomorrow. Then she gives Susannah an artificial smile – the sort of flat smile Mother gave her on their last day in Berlin. Susannah starts to apologize for spitting the food out, but needs three attempts to get her vocal cords working. The nurse shakes her head, gives her a proper smile, then leaves.

Susannah spends a few seconds looking all around the room. Then she thinks of Mother's smile again.

Mother? Where's Mother?

She must be somewhere.

She tries to swallow the residual taste of porridge in her mouth, but it hurts her throat, and she lies back and closes her eyes.

Then she hears six shots ring out and it jolts her eyes open.

Then she hears nothing, thinks she must have imagined the six shots, and closes her eyes again.

Within seconds she's asleep.

CHAPTER THIRTY-SIX

Another day – perhaps the next day – Susannah wakes again and the nurse brings more porridge. It still tastes horrible and she still can't swallow properly, but she forces down a few mouthfuls before retching and almost bringing it back up. The nurse tells her it's all right, that she's doing well, and gives her another smile. Is this Mother?

No.

So where's Mother?

She looks around the room again, beyond the other beds, while the nurse says they'll try again tomorrow, and also says a few more words Susannah doesn't understand.

When the nurse has gone Susannah starts to feel sick and nauseous. She leans back on the pillow and tries to keep still and calm to keep the food down. It feels horrible and she feels the urge to expel the substance, but somewhere in the back of her mind she knows she has to eat.

But where's Mother?

And Father and Jacob too. Where are they?

The next time Paul and Helena visit, Susannah is able to greet them properly, which lights up their faces. They talk over one another in their excitement to speak first, and now Susannah can make sense of the words.

'You look so much better than yesterday,' Paul says. 'How are you feeling?'

Susannah goes to speak. Again her voice is weak; she speaks slowly and needs to rest after every few words. 'Not very well,' she says.

Paul frowns in sympathy and tells her it's understandable.

'We couldn't believe it when we saw you,' Helena says. 'There was so little left of you.'

'Where's Mother?'

Paul and Helena freeze.

But it's a simple question, isn't it?

'And Father and Jacob too. Where are they all?'

Paul looks away. Still there's no answer.

'Are their beds nearby?'

Paul and Helena look to each other, then to Susannah.

'Are we all back in Berlin?'

'Susannah,' Paul says. 'There's no easy way to tell you this. You were in the concentration camp, in Bergen-Belsen. The British found you when they liberated it. You were close to death, but you've survived. And that's nothing short of a miracle.'

'Yes,' Helena adds. 'So many people died there. And still, even now, they keep dying.'

And then Susannah realizes just why the room, the bed, the food and the people seem so heavenly. She struggles to comprehend that this isn't heaven after all, but she knows. Her jaw drops and she lets a few gasps in and out of her mouth.

Paul holds her hand tightly. 'Your mother and father and Jacob . . .'

'No,' Susannah says. 'Please don't say it. Please!'

Paul, himself breathing heavily and starting to cry, says, 'They didn't survive. They were . . .' His face cracks and he splutters the last few words out: 'They were shot by the guards.' Then he starts to cry.

Susannah hears nothing else, but bursts into a tearful, knowing anguish.

It may be because she knows the memories she has been having of those six shots are there for a reason.

Six shots?

And then she starts screaming. 'The guards! The guards!'

Paul is talking but the volume of her screams drowns out his voice.

Paul and Helena try their best to comfort her, but their attempts are worthless. Nurses and doctors are called. In one or two words of German they tell Paul and Helena to leave, that Susannah needs rest. She feels a sharp jab in the top of her arm and then nothing.

She feels a sense of the passive, calming her and soothing her worries. Far and near blur to the same. The only colour she senses is white. No, not white, but every colour. Her feet are bathed in warm water, and then she notices the figures appearing in the distance, all in dazzling white robes. There are three of them. They approach, almost floating, and, yes, Mother and Father and Jacob are waiting for her, all bright and pure and clean and content. Beyond the world of suffering.

They are so bright they *are* the light. Then Susannah's heart feels heavy because something isn't right. The figures don't speak, yet she hears them all mention her name as they smile astral smiles. She wills them to come closer – to where they belong.

But something is wrong.

The robes are no longer brilliant white, but have red marks, which grow and consume the whole, dripping onto the earth. Then

Susannah sees marks on their faces – marks that weren't there before – and their smiles turn to fear and panic. One of them screams and now has a pale and gaunt face. They all scream, and now they are little more than cadavers, covered in scabs and pockmarks.

The first figure, his face now filthy and purulent, pulls apart the top of his robe to expose a torso engulfed in yet more scabs and rashes, the skin pulled taut over bones.

Still Susannah wants them to come closer, begs them. But they float away, back into the distance.

When Susannah wakes again she knows within seconds that in spite of the starchy sheets, clean floors and nice people this is no heaven – not without Mother, Father and Jacob. But now she doesn't have the energy to scream.

As she lies on the bed, woozy from too much sleep and chemicals that numb her emotions, she runs through the events in her mind, wondering how they all came to be shot. Was it something to do with her? There was sugar involved, and a guard – a guard with a crooked tie and a kindly face.

When Paul and Helena next visit the talk is subdued and kept to an efficient transfer of information. For Susannah it's like listening to a news report on the radio, where the facts are stated as if people – real people with feelings and loves and loved ones – don't come into the equation.

But Susannah has no choice but to listen to the information. She learns that the Allied forces marched deep into Germany. The Führer committed suicide and what was left of the Third Reich surrendered. The war in Europe is over. The German officials – including most of those from Bergen-Belsen – have been imprisoned and are awaiting trial. The scenes inside the camp were filmed by the British and have been broadcast all around the world so that there can be no denials, no doubt, no accusations of exaggeration. And, like everyone else, Paul and Helena watched the footage with incredulity and disgust.

'But I don't understand,' Susannah says after thinking the information through. 'Where am I?'

Paul speaks slowly, as if it's complicated. 'You aren't far from the camp,' he says. 'This place is a makeshift hospital unit set up near Bergen-Belsen.'

'Am I alone?'

Paul's jaw quivers and he gives a few very hurried nods. He goes to talk but stops to wipe away a tear. 'I'm afraid so,' he says. 'And I know it's terrible, but your mother and father . . . and Jacob . . .'

Susannah starts crying again and doesn't hear the rest. But Paul and Helena stay and comfort her. Eventually she calms down, this time without the help of an injection.

'But you're here, Susannah,' Helena says. 'That's a good thing. You have to look to the future.'

'Future?' Susannah shakes her head. 'I don't want the future.'

'I know it's hard,' Paul says. 'But it's like the authorities here say. Although we have to respect the victims who perished, above all we must concentrate our efforts on helping those who survived, people like you.'

'And we almost feel like your parents,' Helena says. 'I know it's not the same, I really do, but after our time together in Amsterdam and the farmhouse I almost feel like you could be my daughter.'

Susannah thinks for a moment. *The farmhouse?* Yes, that came after Berlin and Amsterdam, but before Westerbork and Bergen-Belsen.

'I enjoyed the farmhouse,' Susannah says.

'So you remember it?'

'I remember the warm milk, the honey, playing in the stream with Jacob. It was the last time I felt free.'

214

Paul leans in, his face inches from hers, a look of resolve on his face. 'You're free now, Susannah. Whatever happened to you in the past, you're free now.'

That's difficult to believe.

In the camp Susannah felt free in her mind. Now she might be free in body but she feels imprisoned in her mind. She can't escape from the bad thoughts.

But she can try.

'What happened to you?' she says.

'We stayed at Westerbork,' Paul says. 'I've no idea why. We knew you all had been taken away but didn't know whether you'd gone to Bergen-Belsen or Auschwitz-Birkenau.'

'We heard terrible things about both places,' Helena says. 'We prayed for you every day.'

'Yes,' Paul adds. 'The rumours of what was happening were unspeakable.' He shakes his head. 'But, as it turned out, they actually underestimated the horror of it all. And when we were liberated by the Canadian forces we started getting some information. We got access to the records showing where you'd been taken.'

Helena continues, 'It was only a few days after we were freed that Bergen-Belsen was liberated too. When we heard about it we asked to visit.'

'It was awful,' Paul says. 'When we discovered what had happened to . . .' He swallows and takes a deep breath. 'We found out what had happened to the others at the punishment block, but there was no trace of you. It was only by chance we found another girl who told us she knew a Susannah Zuckerman who was still alive. We spent hours searching, and eventually found you; the British had got your name wrong.'

'Not that we blamed them, of course,' Helena says. 'What mattered to us was that somehow you had survived, even though doctors told us you might not live for long.'

'You know, so many people are still dying,' Paul says. 'Their bodies are so weak.'

At that moment a nurse arrives and tells Paul and Helena they must now leave, that Susannah needs her rest.

As they get up to go Susannah stops them, holding onto Helena's hand after they have embraced each other. 'I have a friend,' she says. 'A friend called Ester. Was that the friend you talked to? Was she the one who told you about me?'

On hearing the words Helena turns and covers her face. She whimpers and walks away, her heels causing more of that regular cracking on the floor.

Paul kneels down at the bedside. 'Tomorrow. I'll tell you tomorrow. You've got to get some rest.'

'No, Uncle Paul. I want to know *now*. What's happened to Ester?'

Paul closes his eyes and struggles to hold the tears back. 'She was a good friend to you, wasn't she?' he says, then sniffs.

The words make Susannah's ears tingle red with fear. 'But you've spoken to her?' she says. 'So she survived. She must have survived. She must have been the one who told you about me. I remember now, she came to tell me the camp was being liberated. Was it her?'

Paul nods. 'You're right; she was the one who . . .' He paused and swallowed deeply. 'It was purely by chance, because she heard that we were Zuckermans too. She came over to us and said her best friend was a Susannah Zuckerman, that you definitely had survived.'

'She's very talkative, isn't she?' Susannah says.

Paul covers his forehead with the palm of his hand and gives a deep sigh.

Susannah sits up, giving him a suspicious sideways look. 'She *is* well, isn't she? She was strong for me when I'd given up hope. I don't think I could have survived without dear Ester.'

'Listen, Susannah. Yes, she . . . she survived the camp, but you see . . . she was very sick. Her body was . . . was just too weak.'

'What do you mean?'

'I'm so sorry, Susannah. But . . . Ester's heart gave up two days after the liberation.'

As Susannah's head starts to spin, Helena reappears, and she and Paul both hold tightly onto her again. *Because it's like hearing about Mother, Father and Jacob all over again.* At least somewhere in the dark corners of her mind she knew what had happened to them, and could comprehend it. But Ester? Playful, energetic Ester with the large warm eyes? Ester, who fed Susannah during those final weeks in the camp? The Ester who kept her alive?

Susannah screams out to anyone listening, she screams that she can't live like this; that she wants to die; that she wishes she had died.

Helena holds her tightly and rocks her as she would a baby.

But it doesn't help. Nothing helps.

Again, a doctor arrives with a sedative, and as it takes effect Susannah feels a welcome relaxation that blanks out all feeling. The last thing she hears is Helena telling her twice not to give up, and that they'll see her again tomorrow.

Then she dreams again of the bright world where she can be with the people she misses and they can all comfort one another.

CHAPTER THIRTY-SEVEN

When Susannah wakes up from the sedative it's the middle of the night. She feels woozy but her head has had its fill of sleep. Aunt Helena's words run around in her head, and she wonders whether she ever wants to eat again, or whether she really would prefer to give up. *Or whether she has any choice in the matter.* All she wants to do is dream of her eleventh birthday – the last one she celebrated in Berlin – at her home. She still has those precious memories. Ester told her that in your mind there's no prison, and she was right. Nobody can ever take away those memories of playing in Rose Park with her friends on her eleventh birthday, or of the meal Mother had spent most of the previous night preparing, of the home-made cakes and pfannkuchen. After all she'd been through she still had all of those memories.

But what should she do with those memories? And what would Mother and Father have wanted her to do now? She takes some time to think about these questions, and also about the strange dream of the white world.

Gradually the answer becomes clear. They would want her to be strong, to survive.

To give up would be betraying them.

*

The next day, when Susannah talks with Paul and Helena again, there are no tears. And the sad thoughts they all have merely bubble underneath talk of Susannah putting on weight, of Reuben doing well at school in America but also desperate to meet the parents he hasn't seen for four years, and of the plans they have for Susannah to continue her education once she recovers fully, which she will.

She thinks for a moment about the last of these, then nods in agreement.

After that there's a lull in the conversation. There are heartfelt smiles, there are hands holding hands, and there are fond glances between all three.

'And to think,' Helena says, 'we were led to believe we'd lost you too.'

Paul sighs. 'I still don't see how they could have got your name wrong.'

'Who did they say I was?' Susannah says.

'We kept asking the British about the Zuckermans,' Helena says. 'All they would say was that records kept by the guards said you'd been found guilty of stealing food and had all been shot.'

Paul leans forward. 'But that was when we met your friend Ester. She heard us talking and told us you were still alive. She was certain you'd survived even though your father, mother and brother had all been shot. I still can't believe what happened to that girl . . . such a sweet little thing.' He bowed his head for a moment and gathered a few thoughts before continuing. 'So when we asked to see her again the next day, to ask more questions . . . It was all a bit chaotic, but we were told she'd had a heart attack.'

'But because of her we knew you were alive,' Helena says. 'We had to look at hundreds of young girls – all as sick as you – but eventually we found you.'

Paul leans over to the end of the bed and picks up the board that hangs over the bedframe.

'See,' he says. 'The British gave you a different name.' He points to the board and Susannah holds it and reads it. The words 'Dee Glucklisher' were crossed out and 'Susannah Zuckerman' written in above.

'"Dee Glucklisher"?' Susannah says.

'I thought it was some sort of joke at first,' Paul says. 'In very poor taste. I was going to complain.'

'In the end,' Helena says, holding his arm, 'I persuaded him to just ask about it.'

Paul nods. 'They said the SS guards called you that name on the day of liberation. It must have been *Die Glückliche*, but I can see how the British would have thought it was "Dee Glucklisher".'

'It sounds stupid,' Helena says. 'I can't see why the SS guards would call you "The Lucky One". What was lucky about what happened to you?'

A short laugh escapes from Paul's mouth. '"The Lucky One",' he says. 'It would be funny if not for . . .'

'Why would they call you that?' Helena says to Susannah. 'Have you any idea?'

Susannah feels that nausea welling up inside her again and her mind goes into a tailspin. She starts to feel the searing heat of guilt. Should she air her thoughts as she tries to piece together her memories of why she's been christened 'The Lucky One'? Her mind swirls with thoughts of bags of sugar and Keller and her family devouring the sugar as if it were the last food on earth. Did she persuade Keller to give them food? And if so what did she do in return? More importantly, would Paul and Helena believe her? Or would they blame her for the deaths of her mother, father and brother?

And then a spark hits her all the way from Berlin.

'What day was it?' she finally says. 'What date was the day of liberation?'

'April the fifteenth,' Helena says.

'Oh, yes. That's my birthday,' Susannah says. 'The guards were probably mocking me – saying how lucky I was to be rescued on my birthday.'

Paul pauses for thought, then says, 'But why would the guards be interested in your birthday?'

'I don't know, but—'

'Your birthday?' Helena says. She leans back and takes a moment to think, squinting into space. 'But your birthday is in early May.'

Susannah shakes her head. 'It's April the fifteenth.'

'No, no,' Helena says, now laughing. 'I remember it from when we lived together. We celebrated it in May. I don't understand—'

'Please!' Susannah's hand starts shaking, and she presses it to her forehead. 'Please. I . . . I don't know. I feel so tired. Why are you arguing about it?'

Helena opens her mouth to speak but Paul gets there first.

'Leave the girl alone. You think she doesn't know her own birthday?'

'But I was only—'

'And anyway,' he continues, 'I like it – "The Lucky One" – it has a nice ring to it. And after all, it's true. It's not a question of gloating over the misfortune of others, but celebrating good fortune.' He leans forward and holds Susannah's hand. 'You'll always be "The Lucky One" to us, Susannah.'

'Yes,' Helena says, 'I know that but—'

'Well, if you know it, then just accept it,' Paul says.

Helena nods. 'Yes, of course. You must know the date of your own birthday. I'm sorry, Susannah.'

Susannah smiles, thanks them, and rests her head back on the pillow. She sees her aunt shrug acceptance before she closes her eyes.

'Come on,' Paul says. 'Let's leave and let her rest.'

Susannah feels two kisses on her forehead, then there's quiet.

When they're gone Susannah steps out of bed and steadies herself on her feet. She feels dizzy and has to hold onto the bedframe for support. She picks up the board and reads it once more.

'"Dee Glucklisher",' she mutters to herself, almost breaking into a laugh.

With slow, weary footsteps she edges her way to the end of the bed and hangs the board up where it belongs. On the way back she sees something in the small cabinet next to the bed.

She stares for a few seconds, and soon a nurse comes over and asks her in broken German whether she needs anything.

'Whose are those?' Susannah says, pointing to the green woollen socks in the cabinet.

The nurse shrugs, and calls over another nurse – one who speaks German.

'Whose are these socks?' Susannah says again.

'They're yours,' the nurse says. 'They were on your feet when you came in here. They were the only pieces of clothing that were worth washing, everything else was just rags so got destroyed.'

Susannah picks them up, then nods to the nurses, who leave.

She sits back on her bed and holds the socks close to her chest. Even now their softness and warmth bring her comfort.

In fact, they remind her of the special comfort of a voice.

PART FIVE
The Wretched Legacy

CHAPTER THIRTY-EIGHT

Susannah woke up in the multimedia room of the Bergen-Belsen Memorial.

She must have dozed off. *Again.*

Why was she here? Oh, yes, she'd had a funny turn, and the gardener had consoled her outside the open space that had once been the punishment block. He was such a kind man, holding her in his arms and bringing her here because it was so quiet and cosy. He seemed to understand that she wasn't just being a silly old woman – that she was here for a purpose. And he made his excuses and left only when he was sure she was okay.

He was a kind, gentle man. Such a kind, gentle German man.

And a clever one too. He was right when he said the seats were comfortable. She felt like she could have stayed here for ever – or, at least, as much 'for ever' as she had left. She really had to leave, but the fact that the room was dark and quiet and just the right temperature didn't exactly make her feel like rushing out.

But no, she had to leave the place – the memorial, that is. She'd found her truth. The memories brought back by her visit had clarified things she'd fussed about and lost sleep over for more than sixty years. So from that angle it had been a worthwhile trip. However, the trip was now over.

She pulled the handles of her handbag over her wrist and placed the palms of her hand on the sides of the chair, then steadied herself to push and get to her feet. It was the sort of planning that an eighty-year-old body demanded – otherwise it would be *You didn't tell me you were going to do that* or *That's way too much weight for these old joints.*

But, as she braced herself, the darkness and the silence were broken as the screen at the front flickered back into life. She heard footsteps behind her, and turned to see a young couple walking through the door behind her. There was obviously one of those new-fangled sensors that detected someone entering the room – something Susannah found just too helpful and not a little creepy. The couple who had just entered, however, patently didn't find it creepy and settled down on the opposite side of the room to watch the main feature from the start.

Well, she *was* comfortable. Perhaps she should watch it properly, from the start.

Twenty minutes later Susannah was even more dazed than before, as though her blood had stopped flowing.

The piece of film she'd just seen had been horrific, sad, funny, touching and just plain strange all thrown into one big mixing bowl and given a whirl.

In those twenty minutes her trip to Europe had taken on a whole new perspective, so much so that she had to take a little time out to recover before she could even consider leaving.

But leave she had to, so ten minutes later, and with the heaviest of hearts, she left the multimedia room and walked back out of those gates for good.

There she turned and saw no barbed wire or lookout towers.

She smelt nothing but fresh sharp pine, and heard nothing but the polite chatter of tourists cutting across the backdrop of a calm breeze whistling through the forest. She looked again and again, and kept her eyes on the place, even when the coach pulled her away and onwards back to Hamburg.

She kept her eyes on the place for as long as she could, because she knew she would never see it again. But then, the same could be said of so many things – beautiful things. Not seeing this wretched place ever again would be no great loss.

And it was on the coach back to Hamburg that she made up her mind about something she'd been struggling with for a few days: whether or not to visit her birthplace.

She'd spent the first eleven years of her life in Berlin, and then the next few years dreaming of going back to the street where she grew up. But she never had returned in all of those intervening decades – not once. During all those years in North Carolina it hardly seemed relevant, and going there would have been going backwards, not looking forwards. And, of course, for many years there had been that abominable wall too. Yes, there had been no shortage of excuses to choose from.

But the actual *reason*?

Only now did she realize that the reason for not returning had been fear. Throughout her time in America she'd been anxious about reliving that part of her life and terrified of what it might do to her. Would it bring back even more bad memories of that sunny morning in 1940 when the family had gone on their 'long vacation' – or of the years that followed? And could those memories lurch up and destroy her settled life? They were certainly capable of such a thing.

Of course, none of that mattered now, because those memories were back with her anyway and as large as life.

So could Berlin harm her now? After all, it was only a big German city, and, like Hamburg, probably resembled any modern

US city more than it did the Berlin of 1940 she remembered. There was nothing to be scared of.

She'd tossed the dilemma around the barren edges of her mind for days, but on the coach trip back from the memorial to Hamburg she made up her mind.

No. She wasn't going back there. Her memories of the place were happy ones and didn't need fixing in any way.

But she did have to leave Hamburg; she'd been in pretty much every shop in town so there were no excuses there.

Tomorrow she would fly out.

Over her evening meal in the hotel, more recollections came back to Susannah. She'd always known the basic details of how she'd ended up in North Carolina, but now she thought about those experiences – the months after liberation – in a new, warmer light.

ᐯ

Within days of being rescued she was well enough to leave the makeshift medical centre and had been moved to a house a few miles away. There was food, rest and warmth. But most of all there was Uncle Paul and there was Aunt Helena, who both visited every day and gave her a reason to try to eat and drink properly, which her body took some getting used to.

Then there was some walking, trying to regain her sense of balance and get some muscle strength back into her feeble body. They told her that her heart could give out at any moment, that it was affected more than she could know, and that it would take years to repair the damage.

She thought of Ester and took those warnings seriously. And it wasn't just Ester; it seemed crazy that within weeks of liberation so many prisoners had died through the effects of illness and malnutrition. Susannah's body felt wrecked and old, and night-mares made her wake up soaked in perspiration, so she really did sometimes wonder whether she was one of the lucky ones.

Within months that part of Germany was being administered by French forces, and Paul and Helena persuaded Susannah that living so close to the concentration camp wasn't appropriate now she'd made a basic physical recovery and her life wasn't in immedi-ate danger.

Susannah remembered thinking, again, that perhaps she was going back to Berlin, to finally meet her old friends, the ones she used to play with. But Paul and Helena insisted that even when she was fully recovered Berlin was still not a safe place for them to go to. Not yet.

So Susannah embarked on yet another long journey, this time to Sweden, to convalesce with other survivors. In that establish-ment there was more exercise to build up her wasted muscles, and there were interviews to assess her mental state. Paul and Helena followed, staying nearby, and visiting every day.

However, soon there came that day when they said they had something important to explain to her, and took her to the local park to talk.

It was July, and roses that were trailed up walls surrounding the park left their faint sherbet scent lingering in the air.

For Susannah it was another reminder of better times – of where she yearned to be.

'You remember Reuben?' Paul said as they sat together on a bench.

'Of course I do,' Susannah said, maybe a little too quickly.

'I'm sorry. Of course you do. Well, the fact is, he's settled in school now – in America – and we think it's best for him to stay there.'

'That's a shame,' Susannah said. 'I'd like to see him again.'

There Paul took a moment to find the right words, eventually saying, 'It's a difficult situation back in Berlin.'

'The Jewish leaders are saying we're, in effect, homeless,' Helena said. 'A lot of people in our position have simply lost faith in the countries they were born in.'

'And you?' Susannah said.

Paul glanced at Helena, then nodded. 'I honestly can't see how we can feel safe back there.'

'So . . . ?'

'The thing is,' Paul said, 'we're welcome in lots of new countries.'

'Including America,' Helena added. 'Where Reuben is.'

Paul leaned forward, his face brightening up. 'And . . . well . . . we've obtained permission to be with him, to live there permanently.'

As Susannah's face started to crack, Helena held her hand. 'There are projects set up for us,' she said. 'Farms and businesses that will give us work.'

Then Susannah started to cry, saying she couldn't live without them now she'd been reunited with them, that she had no one else.

And then, in the middle of the park, Paul knelt down in front of her and held her hand. 'We agree with you, Susannah.' He looked to his wife.

'Susannah,' she said. 'We want to take you over to America with us; we can call it adoption if you like.'

'We know we can never be proper parents to you,' Paul said. 'And anyway you're not a child anymore; you're a young woman.' Then he held her hands more tightly. 'Susannah, you have the freedom to go wherever you want to. But we want you to come with us.'

Helena put a hand around her shoulder. 'Please, say you'll come with us. We can start a new life together, away from Europe.'

Susannah thought for a moment. First she gets shunted around Europe, now to a new continent. 'But we're from Berlin,' she said. 'We're German.'

Paul smiled at her. 'And look what that's done to us.'

Susannah did. She looked down at her body – the front of her torso almost concave, her hands still weak and bony in spite of the good diet she was now enjoying. And she was still having the bad thoughts. Perhaps if she went to America the bad thoughts would stay behind.

'It will be good to see Reuben again,' she said, showing a delicate smile to Paul and Helena.

Paul's face creased up and he threw his arms around her. Helena was smiling and crying at the same time.

So, by late 1945, Susannah hadn't merely seen Reuben again, but was living with him and Paul and Helena on a farm on the outskirts of Wilmington. Meeting him was awkward; it had been seven years since they'd played together in Berlin, and now he was a grown man who had progressed so much in life. But in time they became something like a family unit, Paul and Reuben supporting Susannah while she went back to school. Uncle Paul made it clear that nothing could replace Susannah's real family, but they were never lacking in food and warmth, and so her body fully recovered.

Her mind was a bigger problem; the nightmares did not, as she had hoped, stay in Europe, but were a constant reminder of her other life. And, just occasionally, she also dreamed of the pure white world where all the people she missed lived, but where she couldn't be.

⁊ↄ

Throughout that evening, spent alone in her hotel room, Susannah's mind churned over those post-war years. They should have been joyous ones, what with a new beginning in a safe and welcoming country. The truth was that for her they were turbulent times. It seemed so many people around her had only a superficial understanding of the struggles they had undergone in Europe – or had soon forgotten them. And then there had been the joy of meeting Archie, getting married, and having a family. Archie had truly been the love of her life and she missed him and wanted desperately to talk to him and hear his voice every single morning. But in these dark years, when her tribulations should have been about dealing with being widowed, she was troubled by something else. It almost stopped her grieving properly for Archie, and she didn't want that.

That night, as she lay alone in her bed with the distant city hubbub her only companion, her sleep didn't come as well as it should have done. There was something missing. There was, perhaps, something else she needed to do. Something to give her some more of that 'closure'.

The next day Susannah gathered her possessions and left for the airport. She bought the ticket and considered phoning David or Judy to tell one of them what her plans were.

But David would have got himself all upset and she didn't want that – not now he was at what Archie used to call 'that high-blood-pressure age'. And Judy might not have got quite so upset, but still would have tried to talk her out of it – to tell her she missed her and wanted her to come home.

She ummed and aahed for half an hour and eventually decided against telling them. Better to just do it.

Two hours later she was waiting at yet another of those damned luggage carousels.

Still, at least now she was starting to get the hang of setting her suitcase up. She turned to leave, but realized she was in a city where nobody knew her and she knew nobody. She found a quiet corner of the airport lounge – because there just might be some shouting – and rang Judy.

'Are you at the airport?' Judy said.

'Umm . . . kind of.'

'Kind of?'

'I've just got off my flight.'

'You're back? Are you going to get a cab home or do you want me to drive out?'

'Are you sitting down, Judy?'

There was a short silence, followed by, 'What? What is it? Tell me, Mom.'

Susannah spoke the words slowly. 'I'm still in Europe.'

'Oh really? Whereabouts?'

'Now don't get upset, Judy.'

'Just tell me exactly where you are.'

Exactly? Susannah looked up at the sign above her head and said, 'Heathrow.'

'What the . . . ? You mean Hanover? Is that it?'

'Very good,' Susannah said. 'Top marks for geography but Judy must listen more in class.'

Susannah heard a little heavy breathing down the line before Judy spoke again. 'Okay. So I'm worried. Mother, tell me where you are – where you really are.'

'Why don't you listen to me sometimes? My body's as clapped out as that old Toyota your father wouldn't get rid of, but my mind's still working. I told you, I'm in *Heathrow*.'

'*Heathrow?* As in *London?*'

'I sure hope it is.'

'Oh, well, as long you have some vague idea what country you might be in, then I guess everything's fine and dandy.'

Susannah aimed a laugh at the mouthpiece. 'I have no idea where you get your sarcasm from, my girl, but it suits you down to the ground.'

'Mother. I'm serious and I'm worried.'

'That sounds seriously worried.'

'Mother!'

A shout. A shout from Judy was rare. Perhaps she'd gone too far.

'Listen. Stop with the anxiety attack. I know what I'm doing and I'm fine.'

'So, are you going to tell me what possible reason there could be for visiting London?'

Susannah took a breath and started to speak, hiding the tremble behind a stronger volume. 'I'm looking for someone . . . I . . . I'll tell you about it some other time, all right?'

There was no answer.

'I thought so. I have to go now. I'll ring you again when I've found a hotel.'

CHAPTER THIRTY-NINE

In the library Susannah found the address of the government office she needed to visit, and found a quiet but comfortable hotel just around the corner. As it happened it was a short tube ride from Buckingham Palace, and she read the courtesy tourist information left in her hotel room with a casual lack of interest.

She had someone much more important to see.

At the evening meal the waiter studied her face for a moment, then asked whether she was feeling well, and she gave him an indignant, suitably offended expression. However, she made a point of looking at herself in the mirror when she got back to her room.

And, to be fair, the man had been right; she looked pale and drawn. Was it the illness or the memories she'd hidden away for so long finally taking their toll? She lifted the phone, phrasing, in her mind, a query about the nearest medical facilities, but when the woman answered she politely said she'd made a mistake and put the phone down. She didn't want to talk herself into illness.

In spite of her tiredness, sleep didn't come easily that night. She switched the TV on, read some more tourist information, but eventually simply lay in the darkness resting.

*

The next day she walked the short distance to the British Forces War Records Office. The man at the counter said it was all available online, but Susannah said she wanted to talk to a human being, not a pane of glass.

The man sighed, took the piece of paper Susannah was thrusting towards him, and read it aloud. 'Teddy Cooper. The 63rd Anti-Tank Regiment.'

After tapping his keyboard a few times he jerked his head up and a smile appeared on his face as if it had just been stuck on. 'Yes,' he said.

'Yes, what?' Susannah asked.

'Edward Philip Cooper. Yes, he did serve in the 63rd Anti-Tank Regiment.'

'It's *Teddy*, not Edward. And I know which regiment he served in. I want to know if he's still alive.'

The man harrumphed and took a moment to calm himself. 'Well, he's still alive as of the first of this month.'

'So where does he live?'

'Oh, I couldn't possibly tell you that, madam.'

Susannah opened her arms, drawing attention to her meagre, sagging frame. 'Why the heck not? What d'you think I'm gonna do, go and beat the guy up?'

'That's not the point. We can tell you everything about him, where he came from, what outfits he served with, what countries he fought in, any medals he—'

'That's no use to me,' Susannah said with the angriest frown she had the energy for. 'I don't care about his war records; I just need to meet him.'

'You . . . you can't.'

'Why not?'

'We just don't give that sort of information out.'

Susannah spent a moment trying to put on a pleading expression but it simply didn't fit today. 'Look, mister. I really need to find this man. I don't expect you to understand, but it's really important to me.'

She could tell him she was dying of cancer. That might help, but would it be cruel and manipulative? She swallowed the idea. For now.

'Important?' the man said.

'Do I sound like I've just come here from around the corner?' She squeezed a tear from her eye and made a meal of wiping it away.

The man pursed his lips in thought, then said, 'The best I can do is take your details and pass them on to him.'

'I'm . . . I'm not too well. How long's that going to take?'

'I don't know. We have a backlog of requests, and . . .' His words trailed off as he noticed Susannah opening her purse onto the counter.

'Look here, mister. I'm desperate. You can have everything in here, all of your pounds, every last one I have. I just need to see this old friend, please.'

'Oh no, madam,' the man said. 'I'm afraid it doesn't work like that.' He shoved the money away from him, drawing his head back at the same time as if the crumpled notes were giving off a bad smell.

'Why not?' she said.

'Well . . .' The man looked confused for a moment. 'It just doesn't. It's not allowed.'

'Mister, sometimes you absolutely *should* break the rules – especially when time is short. And I promise you it is for me.' She grabbed a pen from the counter and scribbled on a nearby leaflet. 'Please. Give him my name and phone number. Tell him to ring me.'

'Okay,' the man said, through a sigh. 'Please take a seat and I'll see what I can do.'

*

She'd been in the seat for no more than two minutes when the man called her back to the counter.

'I've called your Edward Cooper.'

'Teddy. Call him *Teddy*, please.'

'Okay, *Teddy*. But I'm afraid he doesn't want any war-related visitors.'

'You spoke to him?'

'I spoke to his son.'

'Did you tell him I really wanted to meet Teddy?'

'Yes, but—'

'Did you tell him I knew Teddy from long ago?'

'Well, no. You didn't say—'

'Did you tell him I only have a few months to live?'

The man's voice stuttered, then coasted an octave higher. 'Oh, I didn't . . . umm . . .'

'Now you ring the man again and tell him I need to see his father.'

The man cleared his throat as if to speak, then clamped his mouth shut and left the counter to go into the small office.

When he returned he jumped very slightly as he found Susannah still waiting at the counter. She raised her eyebrows expectantly but there was a long pause before he spoke.

'Well,' he said. 'He took your details.'

'He's going to ring me?'

'That's out of my control, I'm afraid. But it sounded like he wrote down your phone number.'

She reached across and grabbed the man's hand. 'Thank you, sonny,' she said with a flash of yellowing teeth.

The next few hours felt like a week for Susannah.

As she wandered through the streets around her hotel – merely to keep her mind occupied – she kept checking her phone; first every ten minutes, then every five, then keeping it in her hand as she walked on, eventually returning to the hotel for a rest.

She spent half an hour in her room, mostly just staring at her phone, willing it to ring.

When it did go off she nearly exploded into action, struggling to get to her feet and walking to the window for a better signal as she answered it. 'Yes, yes, hello?'

'Mom?'

She let out a groan. 'Oh, David, it's you.'

There was a long pause from him. Too long.

'What do you want?' she asked.

'Judy told me you were in London.'

'And?'

Again, David flustered for a few seconds before replying. 'What in God's name are you doing in London?'

He was worried.

Of course he was. And he had every right to be. And she had no right to fob him off. She thought about what he'd said for a moment. What, indeed, was she doing on this wild-goose chase while her family were missing her?

'Mom? Are you having . . . problems?'

And as he said that, her resolve returned. This wasn't a problem – it was duty. There was no way she was going to get back on a plane just yet.

'No, David. I'm fine. I'll explain later, but I'm expecting a call from someone. I have to go.'

'Okay.'

'And David?'

'What?'

'It's good to hear your voice again. I miss you.'

There was a long pause before David said, 'Hurry home, Mom.'

A few seconds later she closed the call and eased herself onto the armchair. It felt like that explosion of hers when her phone had gone off had pulled a hundred muscles.

The phone went off again; this time she tried not to race.

But she couldn't stop her heart racing – it was him.

Yes. Teddy's son had thought fit to call her after all. His name was Dennis, and he sounded guttural, as though angry about something.

And at first Dennis asked Susannah short, defensive questions. Who was she? What did she want? Susannah didn't say too much, only that she was eighty years old (she said that three times to stress the unthreatening nature of her enquiry), that she was over from the States (an ally) and that she knew Teddy from a long time ago.

'He's never mentioned any *Susannah*,' Dennis said.

'Oh, he doesn't actually know my name,' Susannah said, and then groaned at her own stupidity. *Did that sound like they were 'old friends'?*

'So how does he know you if he doesn't know your name?'

Susannah sighed. 'It's a long story. But we definitely *have* met, believe me. And we *are* friends.'

Then there was a long pause before Dennis said, 'Are you sure you're American?'

Yes, the question, taken literally, was a stupid one, and she had every right to point that out. But she didn't. And yes, even after all these years there was still a Teutonic cut to her accent, but she was a US citizen and considered herself to be fully American – not half or three-quarters. So she answered in a very confident affirmative.

'I'm sorry,' he said, now with a nervous tremble to his voice. 'It's just that . . . my dad has a problem with Germans. And to be honest I don't blame him.'

'No,' Susannah said between bites of her lip. 'I can understand that.'

Then she waited, saying nothing.

'Mmm . . .' he eventually said. 'I'm not sure.'

'I think he'd like to meet me,' Susannah said, trying to sing the words in a bright manner.

'Where are you now?' he said.

Susannah told him and to her surprise he said he'd be there within thirty minutes. Apparently he lived in a place called Essex, and took the train into London every day to work. And he was just about to leave the office.

He made it crystal clear he wanted to check her out. That sounded promising. And if he cared enough about his father to do that, then he would surely be a fair and open-minded man.

When Susannah put the phone down the room started spinning and only stopped when she lay down on the bed. The dull ache in her belly was making her feel weak and tired, so she took a couple of painkillers and closed her eyes for a few minutes.

When she opened them she still felt weak and queasy, but also felt that this was no time to let her illness get the better of her. She sat up on the side of the bed and took a few deep breaths.

She had twenty minutes before he was due, so there was no time for self-pity.

A quick wash of her face.

Fifteen minutes left.

Touch up her make-up.

Ten minutes left.

What to wear?

Five minutes left.

Where would he meet her? Would he ask for her at the lobby? Would he expect her to be waiting there for him?

Then those twenty minutes were up.

And after that another ten minutes flew past while she went down to the lobby, told them she was expecting a visitor, and had a quick look around the area.

She returned to her room and another fifteen lonely minutes went by.

She looked at her sagging features in the mirror. Perhaps the man had chickened out. Or he'd been stringing her along to make fun of her, and she'd been a fool to expect anything more.

And then her phone started ringing.

CHAPTER FORTY

Susannah was a little disappointed at first.

She'd had an image at the blurry edges of her mind of what Teddy looked like in his younger days, and hence what his son might look like now.

But no.

When she went down to the lobby to meet him there was no bond or magical memory or instant chemistry. He was bald, stout and flushed in the face as though he'd been running.

However, he was polite, offering her a gentle handshake and a smile that got friendlier as it unfolded, and his face seemed to melt a little as his eyes ran over her frame. Perhaps, Susannah thought, he now realized he'd been stupid to doubt her intentions.

After stilted introductions they went into the hotel bar and ordered drinks.

'Tell me,' Susannah said as they sat down together in a quiet corner, 'how is Teddy?'

Dennis paused, and looked at her out of the corners of his eyes. 'You didn't tell me exactly how you met my father.'

'No, I didn't. It's . . . awkward to explain.'

'I'd still like to know. I'm his son after all, and he's a bit fragile.'

'Dennis, can I be blunt with you?'

'I'd prefer *Mr Cooper*,' he said. 'And, yeah, be as blunt as you like.'

Susannah took a long sip of drink and paused. 'Do you consider yourself a good son, Mr Cooper?'

'What sort of a question's that?'

'I'll take that as a *yes*. Then please. Just trust me. Your father and I know each other. I don't . . . I don't really want to go into details, but I know he'd like to see me again.'

The man's phone went off. He took a moment to check the caller, then switched it off.

'So how is he?' Susannah said.

'I take it you were in the war with him?'

Susannah nodded, but kept her mouth shut.

'In that case I'm not sure I want you to meet him.'

Susannah felt her heart weaken. 'Why not?'

'It might . . .'

There was a long pause, as if the words were stuck in Dennis's mouth and he was having difficulty dragging them out.

'He isn't ill, is he?' Susannah said. 'Please tell me.'

'Mrs Morgan—'

'Call me *Susannah*. Please.'

'My father was a happy bloke for most of his life. I know he suffered in the war – I mean, he never talked much about it, must have kept it inside. But he was a great dad to me – if he was having problems while he was bringing up me and my brother and sister, then he hid it well.'

Susannah struggled to keep quiet. She was bursting to say she could understand that a thousand times more than he could. *Been there, done that, got the floral blouse*, as she said to her grandchildren all the time. But Dennis was opening up and it was best she zipped her mouth.

'But four years ago Mother passed on.'

'Oh, dear. I'm so sorry, Mr Cooper.'

'Thanks,' he said, twitching his mouth downwards at the corners like a ten-year-old about to cry.

'My Archie passed on only three years ago – it was heart disease. He was Scottish, with a little of that red hair, and I swear he was the kindest man that ever walked this earth. I've got a son and daughter who would do anything for me, but I miss Archie so much it physically hurts. Even now, when I wake up, I think for a second it might all have been a dream and maybe he's lying right beside me. Then I turn and I'm all alone in bed, even the dip where he slept isn't there anymore.'

Then she looked straight towards Dennis, but looked through him. 'And the bad thoughts – the nightmares I used to get when I was younger – I feel them threatening me, and there's nobody there to protect me from them.'

Dennis drew back and folded his arms at this. 'Nightmares?' he said, his frown squeezing his eyes almost completely shut. 'What sort of nightmares?'

'Really, Mr Cooper, I think I understand how your father feels. I can assure you there's no way I'd want to upset him in any way.'

Dennis took a moment to think, then unfolded his arms. 'Look,' he said eventually. 'Call me Dennis. And I'm sorry about your husband.'

'That's quite all right, son.'

'But . . . well, I'm not saying you'd deliberately upset him, it's just . . .' He rolled around on his seat for a few seconds to buy some time to think. 'It's just . . . it's difficult to talk about it.'

Susannah waited, then said quietly, 'Go on, please try.'

'You see, after Mum died he spent a couple of years on his own, and obviously hated it, so he moved in with us – me and the wife and our two girls. And I don't know whether it only started when

Mum died, or whether he's been hiding it all these years – he won't say – but he's been . . . well . . .'

There Dennis stopped and filled his lungs, his chest getting even bigger, then exhaled slowly.

'Is it nightmares?' Susannah said.

He nodded.

'And flashbacks?'

And then his face showed some creases that hadn't been there a few moments before. Susannah read his face perfectly; it was as if he had *You know, don't you?* stamped on his forehead.

And then Dennis's motor kicked into action, and the words didn't stop for some time.

'I don't understand. It all happened so long ago. He's been getting headaches, not sleeping much, and talking in his sleep whenever he does – almost shouting. Getting all agitated – really frightened – at the slightest things. Doctors say it's post-traumatic stress, but it . . . it all happened over sixty years ago. I just don't get it. I thought he'd be over all that by now. I mean . . . why now? He even went back to the place a couple of years ago – to Bergen-Belsen – and did a little talk on his experiences. He thought it might help.'

'And did it?'

'Tell you the truth, I don't think it made him better or worse. And that worried me. I mean, it would have been good if bringing the memories back had helped, or even if it had made him worse. Then at least I'd know how to help. Trouble is, nothing seems to make any difference. He still has these . . . sort of . . . episodes. And I can't do anything to help him.'

'Oh, Dennis.' Susannah shook her head. 'Don't upset yourself. Just be there for him.'

Dennis had a furtive glance around the bar before wiping a tear from his cheek and sniffling. 'Why's this all happening to him now, though?'

'Because what happened there – what your father witnessed – was so unimaginably horrible.'

'I know all that. I read up on it.'

Susannah tutted a laugh and shook her head. 'I'm sorry, Dennis. That's simply not the same as being there.'

Dennis nodded and took a few deep breaths. 'No. I'm sure.'

'Oh, poor Teddy,' Susannah said. Then she felt her chest convulse, her neck tighten, and she squeezed her face right up tight to try to hold back her emotions.

Dennis got up out of his seat and stepped over to her. Then a member of staff even came over and asked if everything was all right. Dennis said it was, thank you, and sat down beside her.

'I'm sorry, love,' he said. 'I didn't mean to . . .'

Susannah nodded and tried to gulp her sadness back inside. 'No, I'll . . . I'll be fine, really.'

Dennis placed a hand over hers, and for a few minutes all they did was sit in silence.

'You've got a lot in common with my old man,' Dennis said eventually. 'I can see that now. But . . . I'm still not sure about meeting up, about what it'll do to him. It could, like, stir things up, make him worse.'

'That's all right,' Susannah said. 'I can understand. Really, I can.'

'So can you understand now why I didn't want you to meet him?'

'And perhaps you can understand why I *do* want to.'

He stared her out for a moment, then nodded. 'I'll give you that.'

'Dennis. I said I'd be blunt with you, and the truth is that I just don't know how it might affect him – for better or worse.' Her eyes glazed as she looked over Dennis's shoulder and into the distance. 'Perhaps I'm just being selfish.'

'"For better", you say?' Dennis said. 'You think it could even . . . help him?'

'I'm just being honest with you, that's all,' Susannah said. Then she turned and looked out of the window, at the sun streaming down onto the street. 'The thing is, this is the last summer I'll see.'

'What do you mean?'

'I have a terminal illness. Didn't the man at the war office tell you?'

Dennis's face dropped. 'Oh, blimey . . . I'm sorry. He just said you didn't have long left. I thought he meant you were about to leave London. If I'd known . . .'

'Don't, please,' Susannah said, waving a hand towards him. 'Just forget that. Let's cut to the chase. And the chase is that I really, really want to meet up with Teddy again. It's for myself, not for him, but if you really don't want me to, I'll get on a plane and you'll never see me or hear from me again.'

Dennis pursed his lips in thought, then took a sip of his drink. 'Just one thing,' he said. 'Your accent.'

'Is it that bad?'

'You're German, aren't you?'

Susannah gave a sombre nod. 'I'm afraid so.'

'But you're a . . .'

'I'm a Jew, you can say it.'

'So what happened between the two of you in the war?'

'You know something, Dennis? I really have difficulty talking about it. All I can say is that I owe your father a big favour. I want to thank him for that and perhaps I can talk to him about things I can't talk to anyone else about.' Then she leaned in close to him and whispered, 'And you never know, perhaps he could do the same.'

Dennis took a few deep breaths, then nodded. 'Okay. It might help him. I'll try anything.'

CHAPTER FORTY-ONE

That evening Susannah sat down in the hotel restaurant and picked up a menu. She was hungry, and the food was of the highest quality, but somehow the process of eating unsettled her, and she felt a little queasy – with that nagging pain in her abdomen again. So she retired to her room and took a painkiller.

She sat in her armchair and wondered whether she was doing the right thing. Would this be upsetting for Teddy? Would it be upsetting for her? Would Teddy thank her for bringing back the memories? And might that, in turn, upset Dennis, who was clearly such a good son?

She shook the thought of so many questions – questions impossible to answer – from her head and switched on the TV.

And as the TV flickered into life, she was no longer in a hotel room, but back at the memorial.

It was just before she'd left the place, while she was in one of those cosy seats in that new-fangled multimedia room, alone apart from that young couple who had just entered the room and had triggered the screen to blink back into life.

And within a few seconds some old guy started talking on the screen.

But, no, it wasn't just *any old guy*; it was that sweet dewy-eyed fool again, this time starting his talk rather than finishing it. But there was more; she was sure there was something familiar about the voice she was hearing.

And then a caption came up, which read: TEDDY COOPER, BRITISH ROYAL ARTILLERY 63RD ANTI-TANK REGIMENT, SPEAKING IN 2007.

Then there was a second caption: ONE OF THE FIRST SOLDIERS TO ENTER BERGEN-BELSEN AFTER LIBERATION.

Susannah started to take more notice.

There were subtitles in German but his words were spoken in English, so Susannah just sat there, barely breathing or blinking, all her attentions focused on watching his blotchy old face and listening to his gravelly old voice:

෴

I got my call-up papers in 1943 when I was eighteen. Like all my pals I was really looking forward to serving my country, seeing a bit of the world and all that. My father fought in the First World War and told me about the horrors of the Somme – I think he was trying to warn me what war was really like – but I was young and geed-up and . . . stupid, I suppose, so I didn't take much notice. As it turned out he was wasting his breath anyway; nothing he had to say could have prepared me for what I witnessed.

First of all I served in France. I didn't see too much fighting, so I was thrilled when I found out I was going to the front. The Allied forces had got the upper hand by then, capturing miles more territory every day, and the idea of being part of that victory excited me. But going to Bergen-Belsen that day brought me down to earth. It didn't seem real – worse than a nightmare. I'd shot a few enemy soldiers and seen dead bodies, but that – what we found at that place – it just wasn't like anything on earth.

But we all did what we had to do, and after the war I got a job back in London and soon got a steady girlfriend. I was fine for a few years. I was just relieved the war was over – of course, we all were.

It was only when I got married and we had children that the flashbacks started to happen. I tried to ignore them, but it got so bad I could hardly bear to look at my own children. I know that sounds callous, but it's the truth. I couldn't control myself, I was in tears every time I saw them, wondering when those images would force their way back into my mind. At first I couldn't talk to my wife, but she knew something was wrong. She was very understanding, I think because her father had served in the First World War, and she understood war could do strange things to you. So we just got on with life, putting the children first, and I've always been a cheerful bloke generally – apart from the bad thoughts.

I never told my wife exactly what happened to me at Bergen-Belsen. She said it was up to me how much I told her, but I thought it might make things worse. The doctor told me just to forget all about my flashbacks, but I told him I couldn't control them, that it wasn't like that. Then he offered me sleeping pills, which I didn't want because I had images coming back to me during the day too. So all I could do was think of my family. I had to be a man and put it all to one side.

It's only now my wife has passed on and our children are grown up and safe that I feel I can talk about it. And also because, well, people don't like me saying this, but also because I haven't got long left myself. Anyway, I think I should. People need to know what it was really like.

You want me to tell you what happened?

Right, well, once we'd advanced to the place, we were just told it was a prison camp – one we'd more or less captured. So we stationed ourselves down the road from it – just for a few days while our bigwigs talked to theirs, negotiating a surrender, like. We weren't exactly cheering and celebrating, but we were victorious, I suppose, talking about our plans for after the war, because it looked like the whole thing would be over in a matter of weeks or months. Anyway, we were all in a good mood.

All that changed the day we went into the camp.

The first sign came as we got close to the fence and saw the prisoners. None of us soldiers were what you'd call overweight, but these people were nothing more than living skeletons. There was nothing to them, just standing there, shivering underneath filthy blankets. One of the lads tossed over a small bar of chocolate, and what I saw next made me scared of going in. They were like a pack of wild dogs, all scrabbling about over a small bit of chocolate, like they were prepared to kill for it. But it was like all this was happening in slow motion, as though they didn't have the energy to move quickly.

After we'd watched that all the bravado stopped, which was just as well because it got even worse when we went inside.

The place looked more like an abattoir. There must have been thousands of dead bodies lying in the mud like they'd been dropped there – every last one of them no more than skin and bone, and lots ripped apart, diseased or just rotting. And the stench was unbearable. It turned out there were thousands of people alive too, and – God's honest truth – there wasn't much difference; the living were only skin and bone too, like skeletons but moving – just about. Some of the ones that were moving were lying down in the mud and didn't want to move. We realized why after a while. The SS guards had turned off the communal water pipes; they were drinking the muddy rainwater from the puddles because it was all they had.

I was in shock. I mean, in shock like I couldn't look but I couldn't close my eyes either. A woman came up to me, she had a baby huddled in her arms. I don't know what language she spoke, but she kept jabbering and pointing to her mouth and the baby's mouth. I could make out her jawbone and the outline of her teeth through her skin clear as daylight. Her eyes looked like they were bulging out, but only because the sockets hardly had any flesh around them. I think I could have coped with that, but what really upset me was that the baby she was clutching to her chest was dead. It was obviously dead – you could tell by the colour of the poor little thing's flesh – and it must have been dead for days.

We all had water, sugar and blankets in our rucksacks. I gave her some sugar and she shared it with her baby. I wanted to say something because she was wasting it – but I just couldn't. I helped her to the makeshift medical quarters we'd set up at the camp, and explained it to the nurses there. I don't know what happened to her after that. It would be nice to know.

Then I left with a few others to search the cabins the prisoners lived in. Most of us were inoculated against typhus but we still tried not to touch any dead bodies we found. We were told to be careful because the typhus was rampant and could easily kill us. What they didn't realize, of course, was that we had to touch bodies to find out if they were dead or alive.

I'll never forget the first cabin I went into. It was a lot worse than outdoors – at least you had fresh air outside. Inside the cabin it really smelt like death itself. It was mildew, it was rotting flesh, it was blood, it was human waste. I had to step outside, and I don't know how I stopped myself from being sick – no, actually I do – we were told not to eat for a few hours before we entered the camp – didn't realize why at the time, of course. Anyway, I knew I had a job to do – I had to go back inside the cabin.

There were bodies everywhere. The problem was telling the dead from the living. I picked my way through, touching bodies here and there – all dead – until I got to the far end, where I saw this figure. I didn't know at the time whether it was male or female, and I nearly turned and left, thinking it was a dead body.

Then I saw some movement. An arm – such a skinny arm

– moved very slightly. I stepped over the mess to get there – over a couple of stinking chamber pots and a pile of filthy clothes – and knelt down there. It was a young girl, a living skeleton like the rest. I touched her shoulder and her eyes opened. I can't forget her eyes; they didn't seem human. It was like a wooden doll – one of those marionettes – a very thin one – moving its arm about in front of me. The arm didn't move much.

Then I turned away and stepped over to the corner, where the other soldiers couldn't see me, and I had a little cry. Then I felt bad because I was thinking more about myself than her.

I took out my fresh water and sugar and offered her some. She didn't have the strength to hold anything, so I dabbed some of each onto her lips – they felt so dry. She started moving about more, like some creature coming alive. I helped her to sit up because she didn't have the energy to do it herself, and gave her some more sugar and water. She wound her fingers around the bag of sugar and started pulling gently – I suppose it must have been all the strength she had. I let her have it and she finished the lot, then started licking the inside of the paper like a dog clearing out its food bowl.

I asked her what her name was, and she tried to talk but she couldn't; only a groan came out. I didn't know whether she could understand English so I pointed to myself and said, 'Teddy,' then pointed to her and raised my eyebrows. Again I think she was trying to speak but she was too weak. I asked her whether she wanted anything else, and she must have understood some English because she nodded to me, then folded her arms and shivered. I took a blanket from my rucksack and wrapped it around her shoulders. She opened her mouth again and tried to speak – I think she just wanted to thank me but couldn't talk. She curled up and I noticed her feet were bare, although covered in dirt and cuts. I felt them and they were like ice.

Well, this was April and it was starting to get warmer, so I took off my boots and then my socks, the usual green woollen jobs – I could do without them for one day. I put the socks on her feet and pulled them up towards her knees but . . . but it really upset me because they wouldn't stay up. There was no calf; the girl didn't have any calf muscle left to speak of. I almost cried again but had to stop myself because I knew there must have been hundreds – if not thousands – like her, and I had to get on with the job. Shedding tears wasn't going to help nobody.

I asked her again what her name was but she just swallowed, so I shook my head and told her it didn't matter. I picked her up – light as a feather, she was – I wasn't a big man but I'll bargain I could have carried ten of her. I took her outside and headed for the medical tent.

We passed one of the SS guards being marched off out of the gates. When he saw us he pointed to the girl I was carrying and shouted out two words – what I assumed was her name. The first word was Dee; I don't know whether it was her name or the initial 'D', but I know it was one or the other because he shouted it out three times. I can't remember the surname after all these years – I wasn't really sure back then.

The two of our chaps escorting the guard told him to shut up. One of them punched him in the face, then the other said to leave off, that he understood how he felt but not to stoop to their level.

Anyhow, I took Dee to the medical quarters, said the guard had told me her name, and left her there.

I worked around the clock for three days in that place, just catnapping here and there to get a bit of sleep. I must have helped hundreds over to the medical tent, and – using what SS guards were left – I must have helped bury thousands; we had to use a bulldozer in the end to push their corpses into a pit. There's no way you can forget the sights and smells – it was so disgusting. But what's stuck with me most – the thing I've never been able to get out of my mind – is that young girl. I always prayed she'd recovered and got her health back. I still wonder what happened to her. Even now after all these years.

❧

The film ended, and for a few minutes Susannah sat with her eyes locked onto the blank screen.

She groaned, which made the young couple who had come in earlier look over to her. Then she shook her head slightly and dropped her face into her hands. Her shoulders started to quiver slightly, and then with greater movement.

After a few moments she sensed a presence next to her, then heard, 'Excuse me, are you all right?'

The shock made her lift her head. It was the woman who had also been watching. Susannah looked directly at her.

'Oh, I'm sorry,' the woman said, backing off half a step. 'I . . . I thought you were crying.'

'"Dee Glucklisher",' Susannah said with a grin, still trying to contain her fit of giggles. 'But . . . *"Dee Glucklisher"*. Can you believe that?'

'I . . . umm . . .' The woman didn't say whether she did or not, but managed to stammer out the words, 'What does that mean?'

'Not much to you, perhaps,' Susannah said, a warm smile replacing her grin. 'But it means the world to me.'

Then Susannah's face lit up and she looked, glassy-eyed, up to the woman. She mumbled the name and regiment of the soldier a few times, then quickly took a pen and notebook from her handbag and scribbled it down.

The young woman slowly withdrew and sat back down next to the man on the opposite side of the room, keeping one nervous eye on Susannah until she got up and headed for the exit, leaving Bergen-Belsen for ever.

CHAPTER FORTY-TWO

I t was the next day. It had been arranged.

Susannah had asked Dennis to tell his father as little as possible about her, that he should describe her only as 'an old friend from the war' who wanted to meet up again, and be careful not to let on she was a woman. Dennis had done this, but at first his father didn't want to go. It took a lot of persuasion, but eventually Dennis told him this old friend was only in the country for one day and desperately wanted to see him, to tell him something important. Only then did he accept the invitation.

Dennis relayed all of this to Susannah and said he would drop his father off at the hotel and tell him which room to go to.

And so Susannah was waiting.

And worrying.

Teddy's possible reaction on seeing her after all this time was something she hadn't thought through when she'd first had the idea of meeting up. If Dennis had told him 'Dee' wanted to see him God only knows what it would have done to him. But, of course, at some stage or other – very soon, in fact – he was going to find out that it was the woman he knew as 'Dee'.

And waiting for him was like waiting to go on a first date.

She tidied her hotel room – which took all of ninety seconds – then tried to settle her nerves by watching TV.

But the knock on the door came early.

She opened it and immediately covered her mouth in shock before regaining some composure. If he'd looked vaguely familiar in the video presentation there was no mistaking him in the flesh. This was her Teddy, her saviour, wearing a neat tie and a smart black blazer with his medals proudly pinned to the chest. Then, just after she'd put on her very best smile and while she was preparing to say how thrilled she was that he'd accepted her invitation, he spoke.

'Oh, I'm sorry,' he said. 'I've got the wrong room.'

That voice again. Just those few words. It hadn't come over quite so clearly in the video presentation, but hearing it live and first hand – even through her poor old ears – was as beautiful as Frank Sinatra performing solo just for her.

'No, you haven't,' she said.

'No, really. My son met an old army chum yesterday and arranged for us to meet here.'

An old chum? She tried to keep her laughter inside but it spilled over the edges.

'You haven't got the wrong room at all, Teddy,' she said. 'Please come in.' She stood aside and waved him to come past.

He looked right and left, straightened his tie and took the opportunity to give his neck a twitch, then stepped forward with a 'Righto' and a puzzled frown.

Once inside the hotel room he became even more fidgety, step-ping from foot to foot. 'But I . . . I don't understand,' he said. 'Do I know you?'

Susannah closed the door and opened her arms wide to display herself. 'Look at me. Who do you see?'

'My eyes aren't too good.'

'I know the feeling. But please, carry on looking.'

He did, but then shrugged.

'Where were you in April 1945?' she said.

'What? But I was . . . I don't get it.'

'My name's Susannah.'

'Susannah?' He shook his head.

'You know me better as Dee Glucklisher.'

He squeezed his eyes to slits as he peered at her face, then they almost blew out of their sockets as his puzzled expression turned to one of shock. He swallowed like someone trying to force down a hard chunk of food. 'Oh, no,' he muttered. 'It can't be.'

Susannah nodded encouragement just the once.

'Dee?' Teddy said, pressing both hands to his chest. 'Oh . . . my . . . giddy aunt.' He bent down to look directly at her face again, then his jittery hands fell onto a nearby armchair and he collapsed onto it.

'Teddy, are you all right?'

He didn't acknowledge the question, and kept his eyes shut.

'I'm sorry. I didn't mean to alarm you. I just . . . had to see you.' She rested a hand on his shoulder and shook it ever so slightly. Then he opened his eyes and looked up at her.

'I have some food laid on for us too. And not just sugar this time. You'll find the room service here a lot better than the last place we met.'

Teddy didn't laugh, but a stern expression cast itself on his face. He swallowed with difficulty once more.

'I'm sorry,' Susannah said.

'Don't apologize. I wish I could laugh it off too.'

'We have so much to talk about, Teddy. And I won't hurt you, so why not wash that fear off your face?'

Teddy sniffed and took a few deep breaths, then stood up. He nodded, and before Susannah had a chance to say she was just joking he tottered towards the bathroom.

He returned with a face that did indeed have some of the shock washed off, by which time room service had brought up a trolley of food and the small desk had been commandeered for dining purposes. They dragged the two armchairs to the desk, and over the next hour of buffet food they talked some more.

Susannah told Teddy about finding and marrying Archie Morgan, about having David and Judy, and about her peppered career as a secretary which never really worked out because she suffered so much from mood swings in those days. And he told her about meeting and marrying Patricia, about their son who was working in the Middle East, their daughter who was a teacher in Bristol, their youngest son who he now lived with, and of his lifetime 'on the boards' as he called it, drafting for an engineering company. He stammered through the description of the twelve blissful years of retirement – half of which was spent at various sunny resorts around Europe – and almost broke down as he described his wife's struggle with the heart complaint that eventually took her away from him.

Susannah talked openly and listened attentively, and by the time they'd had their fill she felt like Teddy was an old friend. He was every bit as kind, honest and down to earth as she'd hoped.

There was a lull in the conversation, and Susannah took the opportunity to reach across and open a drawer. 'I have something for you,' she said, pulling out a small bag and handing it to him.

'Harrods?' he said with a chuckle. 'Never had anything from there before.' Then he pulled out a pair of green woollen socks and all humour dropped from his face. 'Well, I'll be . . .'

'I thought I owed you a pair,' Susannah said. 'I'm sorry I haven't got the ones you gave me.'

And for a few seconds there was silence as Teddy caressed the soft material between thumb and forefinger.

'You want to know something funny?' Susannah said. 'I kept the pair you gave me for about fifteen years.'

'Really?' he said, his forehead doing a passable impression of a ploughed field.

'I don't know why I kept them for so long. I spent those years trying to forget what happened to me, but somehow I found those socks as comforting as the day you gave them to me. But when David was small and Judy was a baby we had to have a major spring clear-out, and somewhere along the way we lost them.' She paused and then said, 'The socks, I mean. Not David and Judy.'

Then Teddy looked up.

He wasn't laughing.

He gulped and gasped and then a couple of tears dripped onto the socks in his lap.

Susannah pulled her chair closer to him and whispered, 'What is it? I'm sorry . . . What did I say?'

Teddy sniffed and checked his watch. 'I need to think about going soon.'

'Oh,' Susannah said in a disappointed tone.

'Dennis is picking me up.'

Susannah bowed her head. 'Of course.'

Teddy pulled a handkerchief out and blew his nose.

'If you're sure you're all right, Teddy.'

'I'll be fine in a bit.'

'I didn't mean to upset you.'

He took a deep, calming breath and exhaled slowly. 'I'll be fine.'

Susannah looked at his face and tried to catch his red, rheumy eye, but he resisted that. 'Could you do me another favour before you leave?' she said.

'What?'

'Could we . . . just . . . stand for a few minutes and hold each other?'

Teddy gave her a suspicious sideways stare.

'Please,' she said. 'Just for me.'

Teddy thought for a second, then nodded uncertainly a few times.

They both stood up and faced each other. They twitched and fumbled for a few seconds like a pair of teenagers, but after a few false starts the side of Susannah's face was resting against Teddy's shoulder.

'I never really thought about it,' Susannah said. 'But I guess you suffered just as much as me.'

'Nonsense,' Teddy said, and Susannah could feel his head shaking.

'Your son says you get flashbacks and bad dreams.'

'They don't exactly upset me,' Teddy said. 'It's not like I cry out or anything, but in my head I'm transported back in time, like I'm there again and I feel I can't escape. It gets me agitated. And it's stopped me sleeping once or twice, but it's no worse than that.'

'Now I know you're lying.'

'What?'

Susannah pulled her body away a little and looked up at him. She lifted a hand to stroke the few strands of white hair remaining on his head. 'I'm sorry, Teddy. That was too blunt. But you can't kid a kidder.' She wrapped her arms back around his torso and squeezed tightly. 'I know what you're talking about, remember. I'm not some counsellor or psycho-quack who's just read every goddam book under the sun about it. I know what it's like when your mind keeps taking you back to that horrible place and you can't control it; it's like all your worst childhood nightmares wrapped into one big dirty heap. It's the nastiest, scariest monster coming out of the blackest lagoon imaginable, and it's coming to get you. You feel the fear of a child, and yet you feel the shame of an adult frightened of something other people don't understand and you're not sure you do either. So you play it down, pretend it's not quite as bad as all that. And when people say you should put it all behind you and move on in life, you agree with them, because that makes perfect sense . . . and . . . and . . .'

And there she stopped, as she felt the whole of Teddy's body quivering and his chest wheezing. He was sobbing like a baby, and she did the only thing she could: she stayed and held him as tightly as he was holding her. She knew that in spite of the infirmity of her age and her condition, she would stay and hold him for as long as it took for his sadness to fly away.

They stood together in the middle of the hotel room, neither saying another word, until Teddy's crying subsided.

He gradually let go.

They sat down again, but didn't speak for some time.

'Better?' Susannah said softly.

Teddy nodded, and a forced smile – but a smile nonetheless – appeared on his face.

'I've noticed something,' Teddy said. 'You . . . you make lots of jokes about it.'

'And?'

'But . . . how can you do that?'

'Oh, I don't know. It helps me to cope, I guess. And believe me, my friend, I've tried absolutely everything else.'

'And does it make the nightmares go away?'

Susannah sighed and gave her head a disconsolate shake. 'We both know you can't undo things like that. But it makes me feel better.'

'Anyway, thank you,' Teddy said. 'It's been . . .'

'Interesting?'

'Good, really good.'

Teddy looked at his watch again, and Susannah clasped her hand over his wrist, covering the watch.

'Teddy,' she said. 'Please stay.'

'What?'

'I . . . I want you to stay with me tonight.'

Teddy shook his head vigorously. 'Oh, no. I've got Dennis coming to pick me up and—'

'Hear me out. Just listen, please.' She turned away from him and looked down at the floor. 'I haven't got much time left.'

'You mean, in the country?'

'Who's joking now?'

'I'm sorry. Dennis told me you were quite ill. I wasn't sure . . .'

'Well, I *am* sure. I can feel the sickness in my bones and I know I won't be here in a few months. So please, grant a dying old woman a last request. Call Dennis and tell him not to pick you up. Stay with me tonight, Teddy.'

'But . . .' Teddy glanced to the bed.

'Oh, I don't mean *that*.' Susannah's eyes searched the ceiling for a moment. 'I'm too old for *that*.'

Teddy let out a sigh of relief. 'Thank God. I think even trying it would kill me.'

For a few seconds Susannah creased up in laughter, and Teddy soon followed.

'I just want you to sleep with me,' Susannah said. 'I want to wake up with your arms around me. I want to feel fifteen again – just once before I die.'

'It's not often I get offers like that,' Teddy said. 'But are you sure you want to? I mean, you don't really know me that well.'

'Oh, Teddy. I know the sort of man you are.'

He let out a short laugh, then his jaw bobbed up and down, searching for words.

'Ah, come on. It's not like I don't trust you. How can I not trust you?'

Teddy thought for a moment, then looked at his watch, fidgeted with his hands, and thought for another moment.

'I'll do you a deal,' Susannah said. 'I promise not to get upset if you think of me as your Patricia, so long as I can think of you as my Archie.'

'Well . . .'

'One last night in the arms of a woman, Teddy. Whaddya say? If you could ask Patricia do you really, really think she'd mind?'

'She was a very understanding woman, was my Patricia.'

'I know *exactly* what you mean.'

Teddy leaned back and ran his hands up and down the arms of the armchair. 'It was difficult . . . I mean, *I* was difficult. She was strong for both of us – mentally strong. And I tried – God I tried – but I was never a perfect husband. I was too . . .'

As he paused for breath Susannah put a finger to his lips. 'Oh, Teddy, we have such a lot in common. So what do you say to a night of talking about our loves, our lives and our demons?'

He nodded.

'So go call your son,' she said. 'Tell him you're staying with me, or tell him you've rented another room. Do whatever you need to, but come back here, and let's go to bed and spend the night talking, and fall asleep in one another's arms.'

'You know,' Teddy said, with the first genuine smile Susannah had seen on his face, 'I think I might do that.'

PART SIX
Settling Dust

CHAPTER FORTY-THREE

David and Judy glanced at each other across the bed, then both turned to their mother. Susannah's voice had begun to weaken some time ago – when she'd started speaking about Teddy. Also Judy noticed her eyes by now had half closed, and her breathing was starting to get laboured.

'So what happened after that?' David asked, leaning forward.

'Can't you see she's tired?' Judy said.

'I'm sorry. I just wanted to know whether she—'

'Hey,' Susannah said, her voice suddenly regaining its full strength. 'Haven't I told you two schmucks off before for talking about me as if I'm . . . ?' Then her words trailed off as her chest sank a little deeper. 'Jeez,' she muttered. 'All that talking sure has taken it out of me.'

This time both David and Judy apologized.

'Some things are best kept private,' Susannah said, words that clearly raised David's interest rather than dampened it.

'Well, I don't think it's an unreasonable question for a son to ask,' he said to her. 'This Teddy guy, did he do anything at the hotel?'

'Yes. He ate a free breakfast. You want to know what he ordered?'

'No. I mean, *in bed.*'

'No. We didn't have breakfast in bed.'

David groaned. Susannah snorted a laugh.

The reality was that Judy and David both knew what had happened next – well, later the next day anyhow.

Susannah had called her daughter from Heathrow airport to tell her she was leaving, and that she would call again when she got to Wilmington airport.

A few hours later, however, Judy got a call from a man with such practised calmness she knew something was wrong. He was from the first-aid facility at Charlotte airport. Judy's mother had felt unwell on the plane from Heathrow to Charlotte, and had needed assistance to get off when it landed for the connecting flight to Wilmington. The first-aider wanted to take her into a local hospital for observation, but she was having none of it and insisted on getting onto the Wilmington flight because she reckoned that whatever was wrong with her, the stink of disinfectant and the sight of so many white coats would finish her off for good.

And when Judy insisted she or David would drive the couple of hundred miles to Charlotte rather than have her get the connecting flight, she was similarly stubborn, insisting that they wouldn't. It was a close call but eventually the first-aiders let her onto the connecting flight, and by the time she landed at Wilmington she was as weak as a newborn lamb. However, she still didn't want to go to hospital, preferring to come home and get 'old penguin face out to check her oil', so that was exactly what Judy arranged. And when 'old penguin face' told Judy her mother only had weeks left to live she felt an anger rising up inside her that she struggled hard to keep to herself. *How dare her mother go swanning around Europe and denying her children those precious extra few days.*

Now, however, having heard about what happened on her mother's trip, Judy just felt emotionally numb. It happened gradually, as those childhood memories she'd filed under 'forget' suddenly took on a new significance. There was the long conversation through the bathroom door when she'd thought her mother was physically ill and kept asking her whether she could get her anything for indigestion, and her mother said nothing except that she'd be out soon. There was that time they were walking down the street together and Mother suddenly grabbed her and held her so tightly it hurt her little body – and the only thing she could connect it with was the dog's bark that had just gone in one of her little ears and out of the other. There was that week Father was working away and Mother insisted on all three of them sleeping in the same room and double-checking that every door and window was locked – she obviously feared those shiny jackboots might catch up with her even in the 1960s. There was Mr Carlton's comment about Mother's drinking habits at one of their house parties, which forced a twisted but good-humoured smile from her – they must have eventually made up after the car accident because Father even read the eulogy at Mr Carlton's funeral in '98. And throughout it all were the jokes she and David had to put up with from their visiting school friends, astonished at the food stocks they kept.

That made more sense now, but one thing mattered above everything else. In fact, it was the blunt instrument that was crashing through it all: Mother was dying. Judy's thoughts tangled themselves up, her head turned to an unbearable shaking, quaking fuzz. She did the one thing she swore to herself – for Mother's sake – she wouldn't do now.

She burst out crying.

The tears leached out of her and, try as she might, she couldn't push the damned things back in or stop more forcing their way out.

She caught the slow blur of her mother pulling back the bed sheets and felt even worse; this wasn't at all how she'd planned it.

Frail as Susannah was, she slowly but surely shuffled her legs to the side so her feet dangled over the edge. Then Judy collapsed into her arms and her mother started rocking her back and forth, and for the next few minutes Judy was her mother's little girl again.

After those few minutes, as Judy sat there drying her face, she found her sight returning to a stinging version of its normal self. She looked straight ahead and saw David wiping his face too, which was most unlikely his usual hard-nosed self, and she wondered whether he'd had the same thoughts as her about their mother's behaviour when they'd been kids.

Above all else, however, she wondered why the one person who should have been crying wasn't.

'I just don't get it,' David said, sniffling. 'Why haven't you told us all that before? About what happened to you in Germany and the Netherlands?'

Susannah gave a tired shrug. 'It was all such a long, long time ago, and I've spent most of my lifetime trying to forget it. There was no way I wanted to burden anyone else with it – especially not my own family.' She looked at both of her children in turn, both still drying their eyes. 'All right, all right,' she said with a smirk. 'If you're gonna get all upset on me I'll tell you what happened between me and Teddy.'

She waited for their sniffles to completely finish – a mother always knows a little laughter helps with that one – then brushed a wayward lock of silver hair out of her face with her hand. 'Right,' she said. 'No more teasing. Anyhow, I don't feel well enough for more of that.' She let out a sigh that was short in length but high on exhaustion, then her eyes glazed over as if the energy to focus wasn't within her grasp. 'Nothing happened,' she said. 'Well, nothing like that – nothing like *you* mean, David.' She tightened up her already small eyes. 'I'd taken the liberty of buying him some cotton pyjamas from Harrods too – not that I'd planned the thing, you understand.' She smirked again and waited for her children to catch on. 'Then we went to bed. We spent a few hours talking some more about our lives, loves and fears. But most of all he held me all night – or, at least, he was still holding me when the daylight woke us up in the morning.'

She brought her gaze back from the distance to look at David. 'And after we'd had breakfast together we talked some more, exchanged phone numbers and said our goodbyes. And then I checked out of the hotel and made my way to the airport.'

'And that was it?' David asked.

Susannah nodded.

'And are you going to call him?'

'I expect so.' Susannah closed her eyes and her head nestled a little more deeply down into the pillow. 'But first I need some rest.'

She began to breathe deeply. Judy looked to David, then nodded to the door. They quietly closed the drapes and went downstairs.

There, Judy started making herself a drink of sweet chocolate and they talked.

'How about,' Judy said, thinking it through as she spoke, 'how about I wait here with Mom while you go home and get a few clothes and stuff, then when you get back you can do the same for me.'

'What?' David said, screwing up his face.

But he was her brother, so she knew when he was playing for time.

'So you're not going home now?' she asked.

'I need to stop off at the office and see how Gary's coping alone, then get home, sure.'

She stopped pouring the milk out for a second and turned to him face on.

He got the message.

'Why are you being like this?' he said. 'You know I can't stay here when—'

'Fine,' she said, now getting on with making her drink but fully aware her face was telling a story.

David shook his head and thrust his arms into a fold. 'Oh, don't be like that.'

'Like what? Putting Mom first?'

'It's not like that,' he said. 'This is my livelihood we're talking about. It doesn't mean I don't care about—'

'David, really.' She snapped those two words out, then took a moment to get her voice under control. 'Just leave it and go home. I'll be fine on my own with Mom. You can decide what to do later.'

He huffed and puffed and grabbed his head with his hands.

Judy laughed.

'What?' he said. 'What's so funny?' Then he started laughing too.

'You used to do that thing as a kid. Mom always said it looked like you were trying to pull your own head off.'

Then the light that had briefly shone in his face suddenly went out. He looked over to her and beneath his wrinkles she saw the fifteen-year-old in him. 'Did you ever think,' he said, 'I mean, when we were kids . . . the way we were brought up . . . ?'

And there he left the question hanging. Judy stayed still and quiet for a moment to give him the floor, but he didn't take it.

'We can talk again,' she eventually said. She gave him a kiss on the cheek and he gave her a hug – again that was unlike him but these were strange times without precedent for them both.

Then David left, and Judy took the drink to her mother's bedroom. She crept over to the armchair, placed the drink next to it, and sat looking at her mother's peaceful face for a few seconds. Then she grabbed a nearby blanket, covered her legs and torso, and closed her eyes.

CHAPTER FORTY-FOUR

When Judy opened her eyes again her chocolate drink was cold with a dirty skin on top, and the sun was lighting up the drapes. But her mother seemed to be in the same position and for a moment Judy could feel her nerve endings sparking.

'Mom?' she said, then, more stridently, 'Mom? Are you okay?'

Then Susannah let out a groan, and Judy's nerves settled down. Susannah stirred, gave a little stretch, and between yawns said that she'd slept well and was now hungry.

Judy smiled inside; her mother had been granted some more precious time to spend with Judy, David and their families.

As it turned out, for most of that time it was just the three of them, and Judy, at least, quickly started to see her mother in a new light. It was almost as if she had to get to know her all over again. She got time off work – she simply told them to stop her paycheck for the time being and that she would come back when she was ready – and David gave up just as much time too. In fact, his whole attitude noticeably changed – not immediately, but more like a slow burn so far as Judy could discern. At first he said he couldn't spend too much time with Judy and their mother, but that it would be as much time as he could afford. Within a couple of weeks, however, he'd left the company at arm's length to get on with itself for better or worse.

At first, when Judy asked him how the business was going, he was very quiet and non-committal – almost sullen. It was only when his mother asked that the truth came out.

'Haven't you got to get back to work?' she asked him as the three of them started eating in her favourite Italian restaurant a week later.

He shook his head.

She put her fork down and placed one of her frail hands on his shoulder. 'I know that business means a lot to you. Have you left that old school friend of yours to run it on his own?'

'Name's Gary,' David replied. 'And actually . . .'

Susannah fixed her gaze on him, then Judy swallowed and did the same.

David didn't look at either of them, but cut off a piece of chicken and put it in his mouth.

'David?' Judy said.

He took a breath before saying, 'There is no business. Not anymore.' Then he carried on eating.

Judy and Susannah glanced at one another.

'Oh, my God,' Susannah said slowly. 'What happened?'

'It's all to do with market segmentation, Mom. It just . . . It's not important . . . It wasn't viable anymore.'

'That's terrible,' Susannah said.

Then David stopped eating, rested his hands on the table, and spoke in almost light-hearted tones. 'You know something? It isn't. It really isn't. It's not good, but *terrible*?' He shook his head. 'Uh-uh.'

'What'll you do?' Judy asked.

'Same as you.'

Judy knew what meant: relying on his wife just as she was relying on her husband.

'I'll find something, don't worry.' He picked up his knife and prodded it towards the other two plates. 'Now eat up, won't you – especially you, Mom. The chicken's delicious.'

Judy almost started crying there and then in the restaurant. For the first time since his teenage years David had clearly fallen out of love with business and making money, and seemed almost relieved his own venture had folded – as if he'd been released for a new love.

So from then on the three of them spent almost every minute of every valuable day together. They hardly left Wilmington – partly because Susannah had become increasingly frail, and partly because that wasn't what it was about. It wasn't about her making the most of her time left by cramming as much 'life' as possible into it; it was about the three of them and what they meant to one another.

It was a time for reminiscing about childhood holidays, about the goofy things David and Judy did as kids, and about their father and what he'd done for all three of them. It was a time of joyous and uninhibited self-indulgence – or, at least, indulgence in their memories.

They stuck together for four unremarkable but priceless weeks. Every day they went to one or other of their homes or to a park or zoo, or the shopping mall. They ate at fine restaurants and on a couple of days a week they saw a show or a movie.

Judy could have been forgiven for thinking it would go on for ever, but by the end of that fourth week Susannah didn't feel like leaving her house. So they all stayed there and spent time doing the kind of things they'd done forty or so years earlier – playing board games, watching TV together and eating together. And Susannah occasionally poked fun at David, and he always laughed.

There were no more tears because it was a time of celebration for all those years Susannah very nearly didn't have, and for the husband and children she nearly wasn't around to have. She said once or twice that, for her, all of those years were a bonus in the lottery of life.

And as she stopped feeling like going out, David and Judy became, in effect, lodgers. Judy's husband, David's wife, their children, and a few close friends and neighbours formed a steady stream of visitors that helped take Susannah's mind off the pain that inexorably worsened every day. She was particularly touched when Reuben turned up; he was her final connection with her birthplace, and his visit seemed to close the circle of her life.

The doctor, of course, was a regular visitor too. He and Susannah had a long history together, and on one occasion when she called him 'old penguin face' Judy thought she saw a tear drip from the corner of his eye. Again her mother declined chemotherapy, which would have prolonged her life at the cost of making her feel constantly sick, because she said she'd suffered enough for one lifetime. She did, however, accept increasing amounts of pain-relief medication – presumably for exactly the same reason.

And then, one afternoon, when the cool breeze through the window was fluttering the drapes – as if it was trying to say summer was over – she said she was feeling particularly tired and wanted to go to bed, but didn't want to be alone. David said she hadn't been alone for weeks and that wasn't about to change now.

Judy knew what was happening and got the doctor out to check her mother over again and give her some more pain-relief medication, and while they were all gathered around the bed David asked him whether he could do anything else for her besides pain relief.

The doctor gave the answer directly to Susannah. 'Well, it's a little late, but there are certain palliative drugs available that would extend . . .' And there his words tailed off because Susannah was slowly shaking her head.

'Just ignore my son,' she said, letting out a wry chuckle. 'I've spent too many years feeling guilty about living to feel guilty about dying now.'

David apologized for bringing the question up, then Susannah told him not to apologize.

Soon after that Judy had to make the most difficult phone call of her life – to call in the hospice team. They put Susannah on a morphine drip that she could control the dosage of herself, and visited every day to check on her condition. On some days she was drifting in and out of consciousness; on others it was as if there was nothing more than tiredness wrong with her.

On one of her less good days the doctor visited again, and while she was having a nap he asked Judy and David to follow him outside into the hallway. And there, surrounded by a sixty-year chronicle of the family in photographic form, he told them what they didn't want to know. He put on his most leaden face and said that now it was most definitely days and not weeks – and possibly not even days. Neither Judy nor David could muster much more than a thank you, and even though their mother was asleep they couldn't wait for him to leave so they could creep back into the bedroom.

Soon Susannah woke up again, and in spite of her weakness was able to talk just as much as ever. Judy knew there wasn't much to talk about – they had gone over every inch of their shared history in those previous few weeks. Almost.

It was then that David said, 'Have you spoken to your friend, Teddy, recently?'

Although he said it as gently as the breeze through the open window, at first Judy could feel a little anger rising, wondering whether he was implying, again, some ulterior motive of this poor old British soldier.

But he followed it up by reaching for the phone and saying, 'Would you like me to call him for you? We can leave you alone if you want.'

Yes, Judy was wrong. Even at his age, it seemed the experience of the last few weeks had softened a few of his edges.

'I've already talked to him today,' she said.

David's eyes widened. 'Oh?'

'I talk to him almost every day.'

And that was probably true. Judy and David hadn't spent *absolutely* every waking second with her, and somehow she'd obviously found some time alone to call him.

'So, how is he?' Judy asked.

'Old, like me.'

'No,' David said. 'I think she means, *Does he still get the nightmares?*'

Susannah wet her lips while she gave it a moment's thought. 'I think he's glad we got together.'

'Does he sleep better?'

'He doesn't give me a night-by-night account, but . . . mmm . . . I'm pretty sure he does. He keeps thanking me, which is nice. And I know *I've* been sleeping better. That could be me just getting more tired, of course.'

'Do you want us to leave?' David said. 'So you can rest.'

'Stop fussing,' Susannah said, giggling. 'You'll know when I want you to leave – I'll be snoring.' She sat up in bed a little more. 'No, I just want you here. I just want to talk with you while I still can.'

David rubbed his chin, rasping the stubble. 'I think we've pretty much talked all the talk there is over the past few weeks.'

That was when it hit Judy. There was one question she'd always wanted to ask her mother but never dared even to skirt around. But she now realized that as *now-or-never* situations went, this was up there with the best. Why shouldn't she ask the question that was now itching the back of her throat?

Her mother had never tried to hide the fact that she was Jewish, but didn't follow the faith herself, and so hadn't made any attempt whatsoever to encourage her children to find out about it, never mind follow it. Sure, she'd always given them the spiel about being half Jewish, half Scottish, whole American, but there were no visits to synagogues, no bar mitzvahs, no sacred days, no worshipping at all. In fact, the only obvious vestige of the religion she followed as a child was a penchant for bagels.

There had been a few Jewish visitors over the years – but never people who were visiting *because* they were Jewish. They regularly met up with the people they knew as Uncle Paul, Aunt Helena and Uncle Reuben (and, yes, they called them that even though it confused the heck out of Reuben at first), and in spite of them all being devout Jews and the Morgans not, it was never mentioned and no concerns or friction seemed apparent either way to the young Judy.

In Judy's college days of 'finding herself' she'd gone through a short phase of discovering her Jewish roots. In hindsight it was clear she'd been egged on by David, who had probably had the same feelings a couple of years before, but for Judy it ultimately amounted to little more than reading up on Jewish history and culture, after which she largely forgot all about it and carried on with life.

It only became apparent to her when she thought about it at that moment, but there had always been a part of her that resented the fact that her generation – hers and David's – had been the one that had broken the link with Judaism – or, at least, Jewish practices. It felt as if Hitler had lost his battle but subsequently won on appeal.

And so she asked. She knew if she tried to engineer the conversation around to it in some subtle or clever way she would only chicken out, so she just said it. She spoke the words slowly and clearly so there could be no misunderstanding – and so her mother couldn't pretend she hadn't heard it.

'Mom, why weren't David and I brought up as Jews?'

Both David and Susannah stared at her, and for a few moments looked like they'd stopped breathing.

Then David gulped loudly, flicked his face between his sister and his mother and said, 'Let's not go there, huh?'

'I'm sorry,' Judy said. 'David's right. Ignore me.'

But Judy knew from her own first-hand experience how a mother can read her child's facial expression better than any fairground con artist could ever pretend to.

'No,' Susannah said, her voice getting stronger instead of weaker as Judy expected it to. 'That's a very good question – and a fair question.'

David and Judy stayed silent. The trouble was, so did their mother. It was clearly a subject area she had to give some serious thought to. But slowly, and with a few false starts, she started to speak.

'If I'm completely honest,' she said, measuring her words with an almost scientific accuracy, 'it's a big regret in my life.'

And then, once she got started, she really got started, speaking softly but with conviction.

'You know I have the utmost respect for people of all faiths,' she said. 'But especially for practising Jews. Partly out of jealousy, partly because they remind me of my parents, but mostly because I admire the mentality; it's saying to the whole world that the Nazis weren't going to beat them, as if every time they celebrated Yom Kippur or observed the Sabbath it would be like poking Hitler in the eye.

'I'd love to say I'd thought it through and come to a decision about what I did and didn't believe in, but in all honesty I just couldn't face that sort of question head on. After the war we all moved to America because those awful years destroyed our faith in our own country, but for me I reckon they also destroyed my faith in . . . well . . . in my faith. It wasn't a *choice*, you understand, it was just my way of running away from the whole thing. Of course, I didn't see it like that at the time, but apart from anything else I got panic attacks at the mere thought of being in a building full of Jews. And you have no idea how ashamed I am to say that, but it's the truth.'

'Mom,' Judy said. 'You have nothing to be ashamed of.' She looked to David and he nodded vigorously.

'Distancing yourself from your faith must have helped you get over things,' he said. 'Anyone can see that.'

They waited and their mother started to speak once or twice before she got back into gear. 'I guess it probably did. But what I'm certain of is that I got sick of all the bitterness and hate – from the Nazis to the Jews, from the rest of the world to the Germans. I just wanted to step off of that particular carousel. I know I saw things so horrific that no young girl – nobody at all, in fact – should ever see. But I also know that however bad some people were, there were good people too. And you know something? Before I went back to Europe I'd forgotten just who those people were.'

'Yes,' David said. 'That . . . that makes perfect sense.'

Judy simply nodded, leaving her mother to continue.

'And, of course, when I met your father – a Gentile – that was the end of the matter as far as I was concerned. I just had so much more to worry about. These days they'd say I had a mental illness – post-traumatic stress or whatever – but whatever you call it I wasn't thinking straight, and on the few occasions I did consider returning to my faith, the big worry was how Archie might take it. My thinking was that I couldn't risk losing him – not after I'd lost so many others. The reality I know now is that he would have accepted me whatever my faith. And I think a little of me wasn't so much afraid he'd leave me – more that he'd get taken away from me.'

She stopped and let out a long sigh.

'That's enough,' David said. 'You're getting tired.'

Judy tried to agree but the words just wouldn't come.

However, with a cough and a deep breath Susannah continued. 'It's all right, I'm fine. I was just thinking about your father.'

'Thinking what?' David asked.

'Thinking how his shock of reddish blond hair had a life all of its own, thinking how he used to hold my head so gently in his hand whenever he kissed me.' She closed her eyes and her voice weakened. 'And thinking how my Archie did, in fact, get taken away from me.'

'You don't have to carry on talking, Mom.'

'But I want to, David. I have more to say. You see, once your father and I started to try for a family, it got more complicated. I was obsessed with blanking out those memories even more but they just wouldn't go away, there were reminders everywhere I looked and in everything I tried to do. And the thing was, well . . . I'd . . . how can I put it . . . I'd stopped being a woman for about a year when I was a teenager because I hardly ate at all for that time, and I wondered whether motherhood would ever happen – whether I was even capable. And also I wondered whether your father would still want me if he couldn't have a family with me – *so, so* stupid of me, I know. That was about the only time I talked to him about specific things that had happened to me and how it worried me so much. And, God bless the man, he told me he'd married me for the woman I was and not for my baby production skills, so I wasn't to worry.

'We had a long wait, but when those dreams came true and it finally did happen – when I became pregnant with you, David – there were more bad thoughts I had to try to blot out. I didn't manage to do that, of course. I thought back to those poor women who'd had miscarriages and stillbirths and deformed children because of the disease and starvation, and wondered whether the same thing would happen to me, that I'd be carrying for a few weeks, then I'd lose it. I tried so hard not to think like that, of course, but the images just kept flashing in my mind. They still do; I came to accept about fifty years ago that it just goes with the territory. My bad memories have always been a part of who I am, but when you two came along I sure as anything didn't want them to be part of you as well.'

Then Susannah slowly moved her hand to her face and rested her fingertips on her forehead.

'That's enough talking,' David said. 'You need rest.'

Susannah didn't say anything for a moment. Judy asked her whether she was okay.

'Your brother's right,' Susannah said eventually, almost slurring the words out. 'I think I've said all I wanted to say. Does that answer your question?'

'Forget the question, Mom. Just rest.'

But Judy's mother had pretty much said it all, and Judy spent a few minutes thinking the words through while David made their mother more comfortable.

Susannah fell asleep, so Judy picked up the tray and headed for the door. 'You coming?' she whispered to David.

He shook his head. 'I don't want her left on her own.'

The next morning it took Susannah almost half an hour to fully wake up. She seemed delirious and Judy and David feared the worst. However, she perked up in the afternoon, talking more about years gone by, and especially about how much she missed 'my Archie'. She even talked on the phone to Reuben and then Teddy, and in each case Judy heard a tremble in her voice as she said goodbye.

It was later that day that she laid the palm of her hand on the top of her chest and looked up to Judy with eyes that were now just that bit more weary and sunken.

'What is it, Mom?'

Susannah said nothing.

David pointed to the phone. 'You want the doctor?'

'No,' Susannah said.

David and Judy looked at each other, neither knowing what to say.

'Just . . . just let me rest,' Susannah said, almost gasping the words out.

David shrugged, and when Judy sat down so did he.

They followed their mother's instructions, making sure she was never alone, and later on that night they both settled down in the armchairs either side of the bed.

It was in the dark, early hours of the morning when Susannah woke again, this time talking incoherently, breathing in fits and starts, and lacking the energy to move her arms much.

This time David didn't just point to the phone, he picked it up. 'I'm calling the doctor.'

Susannah's eyes were now about three-quarters closed. She managed a frown as if David's words were taking time to register.

'We're calling the doctor,' Judy said, holding her hand. 'You'll be okay.'

Now Judy saw no reaction in her mother, her eyes were now closed fully. She told David to hurry up, just as their mother breathed quickly but shallowly a couple of times. But David was frozen – all his concentration on his mother.

Susannah opened her eyes slightly and smiled at both of her children. In truth it was little more than a hint of a smile, but it was clearly as much as she could manage and there was no mistaking the feeling. Then she spoke between gasps of air. 'No doctor . . . got my girl . . . my boy.'

Judy and David knelt down either side of the bed and each held one of their mother's hands.

'Mom,' Judy said, her voice crackling. 'Please don't. *Please!*'

They waited for what seemed like a season, until Susannah's head seemed to sink into the pillow a little more and fell slightly to one side. She took a few more short gasps, then a long slow breath.

Then she breathed no more.

CHAPTER FORTY-FIVE

This time it is different – another sense is present.

The light is bright yet soothing rather than harsh. The sound is of a multitude of choirs singing in harmony. The smell is sweet and fresh and of every known pleasure captured in a fragrance. The very air feels and tastes of a long journey's end. And rest.

And yet there is another sense.

The light disperses itself, shooting around in dazzling formations, then the beams unite to form three figures in the ether – all perfect, all flawless yet individual. The figures glow and radiate love as they approach her.

They are the figures bonded by family. They approach her, and now there is no fear, only a love that engulfs and transcends every other emotion. They reach out with arms healthy of flesh and clear of skin, and touch her with hands that are soft and comforting.

And as they touch her she is home. She is now content, and is everything she has ever wanted to be. The three figures embrace her one by one, with the warmth of a lifetime's yearning.

But there are more ghostly shapes. A small girl with large, happy eyes appears, who skips towards her. Then there is a tall man with unkempt blond hair – the man she never forgot.

Yet more figures emerge from the white fog, first the two guardian angels who ensured she could live that other, better life; then a hundred friends she has missed.

She feels the embrace of every one of them in the heady mix of senses, and then they all step to one side. In the distance is another saintly figure, one with hair that is light yet has hints of red, and a crooked smile that makes her heart pump harder. He slowly comes closer, then as she stands there powerless he cradles the back of her neck and kisses her full and sweet and tenderly on the lips.

He says he's missed her as much as she has missed him, then takes her hand. They turn together and she sees that now there are thousands of figures, all reflecting light and love as if it were the same thing.

And they all move as one into the bright, dazzling light that warms.

෨෧

For Judy it felt like the planet had stopped still for some length of time. If somebody were later to tell her that she and David had stood over their mother for an hour she would have believed them. But eventually her senses returned and again she told David to call the doctor. He ignored her and just stared at their mother's lifeless form, his lower jaw hanging in mid-air. Then Judy told him again to call the doctor, this time shouting the words as she cried. That made him look in her direction, although he appeared to have little focus. And he still didn't speak, but Judy saw his pained expression move slowly from side to side and it took her a few seconds to work out that he was shaking his head.

With her eyes now blurring she looked at their mother again, and a few seconds later felt David's arms around her. He held her as only a big brother can, and they both wept at the passing of a generation.

CHAPTER FORTY-SIX

Susannah's funeral took place on a warm September morning in 2009 at the Greenview Cemetery in Wilmington; the place she always maintained was her home town.

Judy was surprised at the number of people that turned up at the small multi-faith chapel in the centre of the cemetery grounds, many of whom she didn't recognize. It was another sign, she now realized, that there were elements of her mother's life she knew little about.

The ceremony went as well as any funeral could have done, with eulogies from Reuben, from the oldest neighbour in the street, and lastly from David. This final one was especially touching because Alex, David's eleven-year-old son, also went up to the lectern, and David went into detail about how his mother had doted on her grandson, reading him stories as a toddler, helping teach him to read, and even feigning an interest in soccer for his benefit. Judy listened to every word with a pride that made her feel four inches taller, because it showed the congregation that their mother had been so much more than just a survivor. The congregation was largely unaware of her mother's past and that was the way she would have wanted it. Alex was too young to have any comprehension of that – to understand what had happened to his grandmother in the years following her own eleventh birthday. But the very fact that he was there only validated her opinion that you could overcome the worst of any ordeal given enough time, love from those around you, and inner strength.

In spite of the warmth, there had been a strong coastal breeze when they'd entered the chapel. Now, as they filtered out and followed the pallbearers along the gravel path, even that breeze held off, so the longleaf pines standing guard over the cemetery kept still, as though showing their respects.

The colours, too, were discreet, the rusty orange and yellow lichens clinging to headstones long after the azaleas and sweetbay magnolias had shed their bright flowers.

Soon the gentle scrunch of shoes on gravel ceased and the assortment of Susannah's friends, relations and old acquaintances gathered around the graveside. At the front of these people were David and Judy, with their own families close at hand.

The rabbi spoke a few final words in honour of Susannah as they lowered her coffin – a deliberately plain wooden affair – into the space next to her husband's grave, and David and Judy each pushed earth on top using the back of the shovel while the rabbi recited a Kaddish. Then one of the pallbearers took the shovel from Judy and rested it against a tree trunk a few yards away. As he returned Judy caught a glimpse of a bird fluttering along and taking a second to perch on the handle of the shovel before moving on. She couldn't have been sure but it might even have been a wagtail.

David and Judy and their families stayed on as the others started drifting away, each giving them a solemn nod or a touch on the arm. The last of those to go was Mr Brown, a middle-aged neighbour of their mother's who had helped her out in her closing years by doing the odd job around the house – replacing light bulbs, fixing the occasional door, the kind of thing she wouldn't employ a tradesman to do. Mr Brown placed a hand behind David's back and gripped his far shoulder, pulling in tightly.

'Your mother was a fine gal,' he said. 'Quite a woman.'

David nodded but kept his gaze low and in front of him, then said, 'More than we'll ever know.'

The man turned as if to go, but waited a few seconds before turning back to David. 'If there's anything I can do . . . ?'

'Thank you.'

'I mean, for you or Judy.' The man nodded in her direction. She stopped dabbing her nose with a tissue for a second to smile a thank you back to him.

'That's good of you,' David said. 'Thanks again.'

Then the man took another look around and rolled on his feet a little before saying, 'Must have been a hell of a year for you – your mother, your business problems.'

David shot a glare at the man and for a horrible moment Judy thought he was going to forget the occasion and say something rude. Perhaps a few months ago he would have done. But he didn't, he simply softened his glare a little and said, 'You know something, Mr Brown, I don't think any of us here has the slightest notion of what hell is really like.'

And, as David's expression stayed rigid and unforgiving, so the man's face started to droop. He pulled it back and shaped his mouth to speak, but stayed silent and simply looked to the ground beneath him.

'I'm . . . I'm sorry,' David said after a moment. 'You're right. It's been a difficult few weeks. I appreciate your concern.'

Mr Brown smiled a crooked, uncertain smile, then turned and walked away.

David's wife, a slight woman some fifteen years younger than him who'd been keeping one pace behind him, stepped forward and gently laid a palm on the sleeve of his suit.

She gave him that look that asked if everything was okay, and he answered by holding her hand and giving it a squeeze.

Her other hand was holding Alex's hand. David leaned across in front of his wife and said with as much cheer as he could, 'You bearing up, old buddy?'

The boy gave a wide upturned smile but held onto his sad eyes, then nodded.

'Excellent,' David said. 'Oh, and . . . cool suit, by the way.' He gave a subtle wink to the boy, whose eyes briefly showed a little sparkle. Then he stood back up straight, gave his wife's hand another squeeze and looked up towards the sky.

David might have been holding onto his tears, but there was no such stoicism on Judy's part. She pinched her eyes shut and wiped them once more. A hand came to rest on her shoulder, and she was relieved to have the opportunity of laying her fingers on it for a few seconds. She turned and looked up at her husband.

'Hang on in there,' he said to her in a deep, rough whisper.

All she could do was gulp and nod back at him.

೧೨

After the funeral Judy didn't see her brother again for another month. They'd been together almost constantly during their mother's illness and needed a break – she to get back to work and make up for time off, and he to do whatever it was he'd been doing.

So when he came to collect her she thought there might have been a lot to talk about. She already had her coat on when the doorbell went, and when the door opened the first thing she did was give him a hug and tell him she'd missed him.

'Same here,' he said. 'I was thinking, we need to meet up for dinner once a month.'

'At least,' Judy said, shutting the door behind her and shivering.

Winter was coming early to Wilmington this year, so she pulled her coat tighter and hurried to the car. 'You been up to much?'

'Got a job.'

'Really? That's great. Enjoy it?'

He shrugged. 'Pay's not so bad. We'll see how it goes. No pressure.'

Judy stopped for a moment at the car and looked at her brother's face; it seemed brighter, younger even. It was clear what 'no pressure' was doing to him. She opened the car door and jumped inside.

'Hi, Aunt Judy,' came a voice from the back seat.

She turned and smiled. 'Oh, Alex. Good to see you.' Then she turned to David. 'I thought it would be just the two of us?'

'He insisted on coming along,' David said, driving off. He flicked his head to the back and winked. 'Didn't you, buddy?'

'I miss Grandma,' Alex said.

'Oh, sweetheart,' Judy said, creasing her face up in sympathy. 'We all do.'

Ten minutes later they pulled into Greenview Cemetery and started walking along the same path they'd been down a month before.

By now many of the trees and ornamental bushes had started to drop their leaves, and although the air had turned colder it was also still and every bit as peaceful as the day Susannah had been buried. And with only the three pairs of footsteps on the gravel the sound seemed to hang in the dampness.

'You haven't seen it yet?' Judy said.

David shook his head. 'Uh-uh.'

Nobody spoke until they were standing next to it – the shiny black granite headstone that was now erected next to Susannah's grave.

'That looks pretty,' Alex said, both of his little hands holding onto his father's wrist as if they were clinging to a rope.

David and Judy said nothing except a silent prayer, and the three of them stood there for more time than anyone cared to consider.

'Dad?' Alex whispered eventually.

'What is it, buddy?'

'Was Grandma in a war?'

'Yes, she was, buddy. Quite a big one.'

'Will you tell me about it?'

'Definitely,' David said. 'When you're older.'

Alex looked at his father for a few seconds, then said, 'Will you tell me about it now?'

David looked to Judy and they smiled at each other.

Then David looked at his son. 'How 'bout you start by reading the headstone?'

And then Alex read aloud the words engraved on the shiny granite:

Susannah Lisbet Morgan née Zuckerman
Born 2nd May 1929
Deceased 9th Sept 2009
As the dust settled, I found my home.
As the sun set, I found my truth.
I was one of The Lucky Ones.

'Good boy,' David said, wiping away a tear.

'Those are really nice words,' Alex said.

David gripped his son's hand tightly. 'They are, buddy. And you shouldn't ever forget them.'

Judy nodded. She was sure the Sugar Men would agree with that sentiment.

ACKNOWLEDGEMENTS

I would like to take the opportunity to thank Delphine Cull for her content editing and unstinting encouragement throughout the development of this piece of work, and also Jill Worth for her copy-editing advice and occasional storyline suggestions.

ABOUT THE AUTHOR

Ray Kingfisher was born and bred in the Black Country in the UK. He wrote a singularly awful novel in the early 1990s, and so concentrated on his IT/engineering career (and renovating a house) for the next fifteen years. In 2009, the urge to write broke through again, and this time he decided to learn how to do it properly. Ray now writes in a few different genres, through indecision and belligerence as much as through choice. To find out more about Ray and his stories, please visit his website at www.raykingfisher.com.